The

C000075683

Sarah Ward is a critically acclaimed crime and gothic thriller writer. Her book, *A Patient Fury*, was an Observer book of the month and *The Quickening*, written as Rhiannon Ward, was a Radio Times book of the year. Sarah is on the Board of the Crime Writers Association, Derby Book Festival and Friends of Buxton International Festival. She is an RLF Fellow at Sheffield University.

Also by Sarah Ward

A Mallory Dawson Crime Thriller

The Birthday Girl
The Sixth Lie

THE
SIXTH
LIE

SARAH WARD

CANELO CRIME

First published in the United Kingdom in 2023 by

Canelo
Unit 9, 5th Floor
Cargo Works, 1-2 Hatfields
London SE1 9PG
United Kingdom

A CIP catalogue record for this book is available from the British Library.

Print ISBN 978 1 80436 318 8
Ebook ISBN 978 1 80436 317 1

Cover design by Andrew Davis

Cover images © Trevillion, Shutterstock

Look for more great books at www.canelo.co

Printed and bound in Great Britain by Clays Ltd, Elcograf S.p.A.

1

For Pete Westlake

1

'It's New Year's Eve, for God's sake. Come on, Heledd, we agreed on our plan.'

Heledd looked down at her grubby T-shirt, still damp from doing the dishes. Huw liked to wash up alongside her and she put in extra detergent so he could flick soapy suds at her, his chubby arms flailing in the water. It was their post-lunch treat but it irritated Jack, who kept measuring up to see if he could fit a dishwasher into the tiny galley kitchen. The activity had tired Huw out and he'd gone to bed for his afternoon sleep. Heledd had read somewhere that, at three, Huw was likely to be stopping these naps soon but she was in no hurry to break the habit. She liked the time to herself to tidy up and, if she was lucky, do a bit of knitting in front of the TV.

'I can't go out like this,' she said, knowing Jack liked her smart. He often told her that her dark Catherine Zeta-Jones looks had been what first attracted him to her. Well, there was nothing like motherhood to remove the last vestiges of glamour.

Jack was itching to go to the party, a hop and a skip up the road. They'd agreed they'd go in shifts – first her and Huw, at four o'clock, when there'd be other children for Huw to play with. Then, when things were getting going, she'd bring Huw home and Jack would get his turn to join his pals. His five infuriating friends who, despite her best efforts, had never taken to her. Eleri, leader of the local council, who made no effort to hide the fact she found Heledd dull; Gruffydd, the curate in a rural parish, who was kind to her, although his girlfriend, Bethan, wasn't; Duncan, who was working for his father's tour company and dead set on expanding the business; and Gemma, a doctor, who constantly looked tired. None of them had children and, if she was to be honest, Jack sometimes behaved as if he was footloose and fancy-free too.

They'd all be there at the party hosted by Eleri. Although Jack had made plenty of other friends when he went to university in Cardiff, it was this close circle from school that demanded his attention. They all had high-flying jobs and Heledd could see speculation in their eyes when she managed to catch their notice. Why on earth had Jack married a shopgirl with few prospects and fading looks?

Heledd ran her hands through her hair. Despite her promise to bring over Huw to play with the other children, she wasn't going to wake him up from his nap. He was always furious when woken up before he was ready and she wasn't going to inflict him on other youngsters when he was in that mood. She'd half hoped this would be her excuse for not going to the party but it seemed Jack was keen for her to make an appearance. The solicitor's wife. Good for business, because you never knew when someone would be needing legal advice.

'I'll have a wash and get over there. You can bring Huw if he wakes up, otherwise wait for me to get back.'

'Attagirl.'

Heledd spent a long time in the shower and put on the only smart item of clothing that fitted her from her pre-pregnancy days, a blue velvet A-line dress that she teamed with sparkly grey tights picked up in last year's winter sale. She only applied makeup because she was sure that the other women at the party would be looking and judging. When she came out of the bedroom, she saw a gleam in Jack's eyes which meant only one thing. She'd need to remember to take her contraceptive pill before going out. She was only just beginning to get her old sparkle back after Huw's difficult twos. The last thing she wanted was another baby on the way. As she walked past Huw's room, she glanced in and saw him lying on his back, his mouth open. He'd be waking up soon and Jack could decide whether to bring him to the party. She had a strong hunch he'd wait for her to come home. For Jack, parties didn't mean the child-friendly kind.

She shut the front door behind her and opened the iron gate that no longer squealed on its hinges, although Huw still called it 'creaky gate'. The streets were quiet. People were probably getting ready for a late night or just having some downtime before partying. In the distance she heard the cathedral clock strike four, its chimes overlaid by the racket coming from the house in her sights. Eleri Tew's detached house was neater and newer than the tall terrace she and Jack had bought three years earlier. Eleri had told Jack that she needed to keep up appearances as leader of the council and she employed a gardener to clip the box hedge which surrounded the garden. She'd strung up fairy lights over the front door and they pulsated with a neon blue light that gave Heledd an instant headache. She wished her sister Becca was here. She'd had an invite but had rung that afternoon to say she was coming down with the flu and wanted to stay away.

Heledd pushed against the front door and was plunged into a riot of noise and laughter. The hall and living room were packed with people – mostly sober, although God knows what they'd be like later.

'Heledd? Have you come on your own?' It was Duncan, Jack's best friend, whose appearance so early in the party, she was sure, wasn't due to the fact he wanted to see the kids. It was to get an early start on the alcohol.

'Jack is looking after Huw. He'll be over when I get back.'

She saw a flash of displeasure on Duncan's face. Jesus. She was hardly keeping Jack from the party. She was making a brief appearance and then Jack and his friends could enjoy the evening, well into the early hours if that's what they wanted.

'Heledd? You made it, can I get you something to drink?' Bethan Rees waved at her from behind Duncan, who had already turned his back. She pushed her way past a crying baby towards Bethan, who was holding a glass of red wine. That's not what I want, thought Heledd, suddenly thirsty. I want tea, not wine.

'Not brought Huw?' asked Bethan.

First Duncan and now Bethan. Was no one actually glad that she had made it over to the party?

'He's asleep and I didn't want to wake him. He's been a horror all day.'

Bethan made a sympathetic face but her eyes strayed over Heledd's shoulder, looking for someone more interesting to talk to. Her boyfriend Gruffydd must be here somewhere, although he too would be itching for Jack to arrive. Heledd moved on, the crush of people making her nervous. She'd been a fool to come. Her makeup felt plastered to her face and her velvet dress clung to the folds in her stomach which hadn't been there when she had first bought the garment. Despite the cold, someone had left the patio door open, and sharp icy air was blasting into the steamy living room. A group of smokers huddled outside, probably a nod to the clutch of children inside the house. Heledd took a glass of wine from the table and stepped outside. Gemma and Gruffydd were talking, and Heledd wasn't sure who she was more surprised to see smoking – a medic or a clergyman. Only Gemma looked abashed when she caught Heledd looking at the cigarette. She probably lectured her patients on the harmful effects of smoking.

'Nice dress, Heledd.'

Heledd forced a smile. At least they hadn't yet mentioned Jack or Huw. 'It's good to get out of jeans. Have you seen Eleri? I ought to say hello.'

'She's probably speaking to someone important. The mayor's here, did you see him?'

'God, no. I'll leave it then. I don't want to interrupt them.' She noticed that Gemma was looking at her sparkly tights, a frown on her face. Duncan came out into the garden and lit a cigarette, an unopened bottle of wine under his arm. Gruffydd moved towards him, speaking urgently into his friend's ear. Duncan shook his head but she saw them glance towards her before moving off.

'Was it something I said?'

Gemma laughed. 'I don't think your husband will be on his own for long. I think plans are afoot.'

Heledd watched the two men squeeze their way back through the living room, and Duncan grabbed another bottle of red wine from the table. There was an air of intrigue about the night and she guessed it was because of those two sneaking over the road. Realising Gemma was observing her reaction, she kept her face neutral. She didn't suppose it mattered. She'd be home before long to kick them out.

Eleri must have finished with the mayor, as she stepped out into the night, bringing along with her a waft of citrus perfume. Heledd was struck again by how much older Eleri looked than the rest of her group of friends.

She kissed Heledd on the cheek. 'Did I just see Duncan filch a bottle of wine from my table?'

'Going to keep Jack company, I think.'

'Are they?' Eleri looked in the direction of Heledd's house and smiled. 'Well, don't worry about them. Just enjoy the party.'

But there was no one to talk to. Gemma had taken the opportunity to move away while Eleri was speaking to Heledd, and soon her host disappeared too. At a loss what to do next, Heledd went into the kitchen and found the kettle. Through the doorway, she could see Bethan looking furious at being abandoned by her boyfriend, her eyes straying towards the front door as if it exuded a magnetic force.

Heledd caught the eye of a young mother sitting on the floor and playing with some Lego with her son. Her daughter was shoving a book in front of her face in a desperate attempt to get Heledd to read it to her. Tea forgotten, she went over and knelt down beside the girl.

'I'll read you the story.'

–

When Heledd lifted her head, she saw that over an hour had passed. The party had thinned out a little – two

6

families had taken their little ones home – and she couldn't see Gemma or Bethan in the room. Two teenage girls were giggling in the corner, their hysteria suggesting they'd drunk some of the cider from the bottle sitting suspiciously close by on the windowsill. I've had enough of this, she thought and stood, shaking her dead leg. She left the hubbub of the party and walked into the cool night. A group of revellers was arriving at the house carrying packs of lagers. The party was about to start in earnest and it was time for her to go back to the peace of Y Bwthyn, her home. She hadn't disgraced herself and, given it was half-five, she surely couldn't be chastised by Jack for arriving home too early. More time for him to enjoy himself with his friends. As she put her key in the lock, she heard the tinkle of Eleri's laugh. She'd left her own party to join the others. Glancing into the living room before unlocking the door, she saw Gruffydd in a chair, with Bethan draped over him, as Gemma poured wine into his glass. Jack was out of sight, although she could see Duncan's legs sticking out from where he was sitting on the floor.

Irritated, she opened the door and climbed the stairs to check that Huw was all right. She was surprised he hadn't been woken by the chatter, which meant that bedtime would be a nightmare later. They'd removed the child monitor last year, when Huw's lungs had made it possible to hear his cries anywhere in the house. As she approached his room, she felt the emptiness of absence. Frowning, she pushed open the door and saw the rumpled bed without her child in it. She hurried to her own bedroom but saw it was empty too.

'Huw, *cariad*, where are you?'

She flung open every door but could only sense silence. In a panic, she stumbled down the stairs and flung herself into the living room, ignoring the startled group of six, to look for her son.

'Have you seen Huw?' Her gaze met Jack's. He was already flushed from the alcohol but he picked up on her panic, clambering to his feet from the sofa.

'He's upstairs.'

'Upstairs? When did you last check on him?' She saw him wince at her shrillness.

She snapped off the music from the stereo.

'Where's Huw?' she asked the six, each looking at her in horror and confusion. 'What the bloody hell have you done with my son?'

2

Mallory Dawson looked at her watch and saw it was only ten minutes until the cathedral closed its doors. The shop had shut twenty minutes earlier and the final half hour of her shift involved helping the sole volunteer with any stragglers who might be inclined to linger when the staff wanted to return to the warmth of their homes. Visitors, though, had been sparse because of the bitter temperatures, with only a school party relieving the boredom. A gaggle of children from Neath had sped around the building, caring nothing for the hushed atmosphere, until exhausted teachers had gathered them up and marshalled them to the waiting coach. Now there was just herself and Janey, who was stationed at the door to stop any new visitors entering.

'Got any plans this evening, Mallory?' Janey shouted across to her.

Mallory restacked the leaflets on the desk and shook her head. 'Nothing except to get warm. You?'

'Gotta cook for Alan when I get home. He'd never think of actually boiling the saucepan of potatoes I peeled this morning, so they'd be ready when I got in.'

Janey was a volunteer, originally from St Albans, who'd retired to the miniature city of St Davids. She was spending her free time at the cathedral, answering visitors' questions and checking everyone had a positive experience in the ancient building. Mallory had soon realised that the cathedral relied on a rota of people like Janey, who were prepared to give a few hours on an icy February day to keep the building open.

'Why don't you head off now?' called Mallory. 'It's nearly closing. The visitors have gone – just a member of the clergy hanging around near the refectory, I think.'

'It's Canon Stack. I saw him come in about ten minutes ago but I'm not sure what he's doing here. He'd normally be in front of the fire at Rosewood Lodge.'

'He's retired?'

'Exactly. Although, he helps out at services when we're short-staffed. I wouldn't expect him to be here on a day like this, though. You'll make sure he's left, won't you, before closing up?'

Mallory smiled to hide her unease. It was one of her nightmares that one day she might accidentally lock someone in the building. 'I promise this place will be empty when I turn the key.'

Janey relaxed. 'I think I will go, given the weather – I've been jittery for the last hour, to be honest. I'll retrieve my handbag from the office. Will you stand by the door in case anyone tries to have a late look around the place?'

Mallory moved towards the entrance and grasped the handle of one of the inner doors. It was unlikely that anyone would try to visit so late in the day, although she suspected it would be a completely different story in the summer. The cathedral felt chilled near the entrance and she'd be glad to get away too. Janey reappeared, wrapped up as though for an arctic expedition, and slipped out into the night.

'Mind you don't forget the Canon! And give those outside doors a big rattle to make sure they're shut.'

Mallory rolled her eyes when Janey turned away. Being treated like she was a five-year-old was a new one on her, but she suspected Janey wasn't aware of her police background, which might be a good thing. Janey was a chatterer and she didn't want to be pressed on 'her career's worst cases', as someone had once quizzed her about. She stood by the door, counting down the minutes to closing, when she saw a figure peering through the glass. She opened the door, ready to do her spiel about opening hours, when she realised it was a member of the clergy, his clerical collar showing beneath his black overcoat.

'Evening, Mallory. All OK?'

Mallory frowned, not recognising the figure. Still new to the post, she was embarrassed to admit that once in a clerical collar, all the men looked the same to her. Ditto the women.

He noticed her confusion. 'It's Gruffydd Ellis from St Madoc's. We met at the Epiphany service.'

He was accompanied by a woman, her hood pulled over her head so only the tip of her nose and mouth were visible.

'We're closing at four and there's no evensong this evening. I didn't realise there was anything else going on.' She wasn't expecting to hang around at night. The vergers took over when there were services involved, allowing her to slip off home, but she hadn't got used to the sometimes unexpectedness of cathedral life. Perhaps she was meant to stay when ad hoc meetings took place.

'We're here to see Canon Stack,' said Gruffydd. 'He said he'd get here around quarter to.'

'He's in the refectory, I believe. I was going to check he'd left before I locked up.'

'You can leave it to us. Bethan here has a key.'

The woman pulled down her hood, her expression wary. 'It's Mallory, isn't it? You might remember me from your interview. I'm Bethan Rees, one of the lay helpers.'

'Of course.' Mallory remembered Bethan from the interview panel for the job. The discussion hadn't gone particularly well and she'd fully expected to be rejected, so it had come as a surprise when the email offering her the post arrived.

'It's OK, Mallory,' said Gruffydd, noticing her confusion. 'I'll take responsibility for locking up after us. Just close the main door when you leave.'

'You don't want me to wait for your meeting to finish?' asked Mallory, watching Bethan glance up at Gruffydd as he shook his head. They had an air of conspiracy about them.

'Well, OK. Fine by me.'

Mallory hurried to the small room where her rucksack was stashed and pulled it out. From this angle, she could see a light glimmering from the upper refectory window. Funny, as she had never seen the space used for a meeting so late in the day. There must surely have been somewhere more comfortable to conduct whatever business was necessary. She left that part of the building and stepped into the darkness, using her torch to navigate her way along the stone passage to the front door. The light bounced off a marble effigy wearing a bishop's hat, its face eaten away by the ravages of time, and she turned away, not yet at home amongst the dead in the imposing cathedral. The air smelt reassuringly clean, the frosty draught from outside seeping into cracks in the stones.

Her bones ached from the cold and she stepped out into the night air, pulling the door to and twisting the key in the lock. Thinking of Janey, she gave it a good rattle and set off up the hill. At four o'clock, it was already dark, and icy underfoot. The afternoon's snowfall had settled and frozen into a crisp layer; the temperature hadn't lifted much above zero all day but Mallory had been working and she'd put the cold to the back of her mind. Only now, as she stepped away from the building, did she become aware of the plummeting temperature and the treacherous passage up the slope to her lodgings on the edge of the city.

She pulled up the hood of her coat and shoved her hands into her pockets. Above her, she could see the lights of St Davids glimmering down the hill. The shops were still open, although they had precious few visitors at this time of year and it had been a difficult winter because of the weather. Many were biding their time for the season to open up.

Mallory followed the path around the cathedral, breathing in the iciness of the air. Her boots slipped on the treacherous surface and, suddenly weary, she felt like dropping to the floor with exhaustion. She plunged on – the mediaeval gatehouse her goal – and, once there, she stopped for a moment to catch her breath. Her leg, which had suffered first at the hands of an assailant when she'd been in the Met Police and then had been poisoned in her last job, was finally beginning to heal. However, it was still temperamental and even now she could feel the dull ache of the old injury. She carried on, passing the ice-cream shop, unfathomably open at this time of year, and turned to look through the lightened entrance. She spotted her upstairs neighbour Ffion talking to the woman at the till. They didn't look in her direction, immersed in their conversation.

Mallory turned right into the narrow street at the top of the hill, and walked away from the shops, passing darkened Airbnb properties, shut galleries and houses where lights glimmered through cracks in the closed curtains. It was obvious which places belonged to the locals. They were more homely: less a tourist's idea of what a Welsh cottage might look like, more practical and lived-in. Mallory's flat was on the ground floor of one of the last buildings. From here, the land flattened out and, in the distance, she could hear the draw of the sea as the tide pulled away from the beach. She was exhausted and, not for the first time, she thanked God she didn't have any stairs to climb. She'd been lucky to secure the flat last November but, come the high season, she'd probably be looking for another place to stay. Perhaps, though, by summer she might also want to move on from what was essentially a dull, repetitive job.

As Mallory put the key in the door, she felt a shadow behind her. She spun around, her defences down in this safe community.

'You're a hard person to get hold of, Mallory Dawson.'

She recognised the voice but couldn't immediately place it. Her instincts told her that despite the Welsh accent, it wasn't someone from her new place of work. A man stepped into the lamplight, his grey raincoat stirring uneasy memories for Mallory.

'Detective Inspector.'

Harri Evans smiled, pleased that she'd remembered him. Mallory hesitated, wondering whether to invite him in. She could hardly keep him on the doorstep on a night like this, but she'd found a sanctuary of sorts in this small flat infused with the sound of the sea as she slept. Harri represented officialdom and, she suspected, had a case he wanted help with. Why else would he be here? She inclined her head back down the road she'd just passed along.

'Want to go to the pub? It won't be busy.'

He shook his head. 'We need to be private. I'm sorry, Mallory.'

Mallory shrugged and opened the door. The communal hallway smelt of the sea. Ffion upstairs liked to swim whatever the weather and she must have braved the icy waters this afternoon, leaving the aroma of salt and brine in her wake. Mallory took him into her flat and dumped her things on the pine table tucked into the corner of her living room.

'Do you want a drink anyway? You look like you need a snifter after standing in the cold waiting for me.'

Harri grimaced. 'I'd love one but I'm still working.'

'Coffee?'

'Nothing. I've a long drive back to Carmarthen and I don't want to be stopping four times, looking for somewhere to take a piss.'

'Four times? You need to see a doctor.' She said it in jest but saw his face cloud over.

'I'll make a cuppa for myself, if you don't mind.' Mallory disappeared into the kitchen. The fact he'd driven out to see her suggested there was a story to tell, and Mallory wanted a clear head. He followed her and watched while she put a heap of coffee into the pot.

'I thought you had my mobile number. I'm perfectly capable of talking over the phone,' she told him, a little miffed her plans for the evening were in disarray.

'You haven't changed it?'

'No.' Mallory pulled out her iPhone and looked at the display, noting she hadn't missed any calls.

'I've got the wrong number, then. I tried your old place of employment but no one could give me your whereabouts, so I went about it the old-fashioned way. The DVLA is still good for something.'

Irritated, Mallory bristled. 'Harri. What's this all about?'

'Make your coffee and I'll tell you.'

He took off his coat and draped it over the door, reinforcing Mallory's impression he was settling in for the evening. She watched as the snow slid off the fabric into pools on the floor. She poured coffee into a mug, as well as a glass of water for each of them. 'We might as well be comfortable.'

In the living room, Mallory removed her boots and massaged her aching feet. Her socks were damp to the touch and she resisted the temptation to peel them off. The room felt too warm and cosy for the conversation they were about to have. She'd programmed the heating to come on at four but she'd have preferred to sit in the cold with this man, so she could concentrate. The heat was already making her drowsy.

'How long have you been in St Davids?' Harri sat back on the sofa. He was wearing a navy jacket and a pair of trousers that almost matched. Not quite a suit, but then not exactly co-ordinated separates. In fact, he looked like he'd got dressed in the dark. There was a shadow across his chin, suggesting either he hadn't shaved or had done so badly.

'I started my new job in November. I wanted a fresh start.' Mallory made a face. 'Another one. I looked around and the cathedral was advertising for an assistant retail manager. They were struggling to recruit, which I suspect is why they offered it to me.'

'Perhaps it's the pay,' said Harri.

Mallory laughed. 'Probably. It's only eighteen hours a week but I have my police pension on top so I can afford the low wages.'

'It's not quite how I imagined you living. It's a long way from Eldey here.'

Mallory's previous job had been at the luxury Cloister Hotel on the island of Eldey. She'd planned on going back after the winter season but Alex, its owner, had sold the place on to a hotel chain specialising in luxury resorts. News of the sale had prompted Mallory to look around for something else and the cathedral job was as good as anything.

'I like it here. I like my flat and the job's fine. No errant guests to be looking after. No killings, too, so I really hope you're not trying to drag me into one of yours.'

He kept his eyes on her. 'There's been a death on a farm out near Middle Mill. It's a remote place, a smallholding barely subsisting.'

'One of the family died?' Mallory took a sip of the scalding coffee.

'Not the family, no. It's owned by Thomas and Catrin Cross. She's local, although I don't know the family, and they've been living there a couple of years. Anyway, this morning, Catrin found the body of a woman, a near neighbour, at the top of her field, partially covered by snow. Catrin recognised the deceased, whose identity was confirmed by one of the attending officers. The woman was called Heledd Jones.'

'She was murdered.' The woman's name meant nothing to her.

'We're still in the early stages of the investigation. The death is being treated as suspicious, pending the autopsy, which I've asked to be given top priority. At this stage, we're keeping our minds open as to the cause of death.'

'It doesn't sound particularly complicated. Well within your resources, I'd say.'

That made him laugh. 'Don't know what you think our resources are but they're a damn sight less than you had in London. I dare say you're right, but remember I said we're always up for a bit of consultancy work.'

'No.'

'Mallory, listen to me.'

'I'm not in the slightest bit interested in getting involved in an unexplained death, especially if it turns out to be a murder case. I'm sick to the teeth of death.'

'That's OK, as I don't want you involved in the current investigation.'

'You don't? What the hell are you doing sitting on my sofa, then? I could do with that hot bath you're preventing me from enjoying.'

Harri ran his eyes over her, his gaze professional rather than sexual. 'How *are* you doing, Mallory?'

'I'm OK. Better than when you last saw me, and trying to avoid any unnecessary stresses.'

'The reason I'm here is, whatever the results of the autopsy are, Heledd Jones shouldn't be lying dead in a Pembrokeshire field. Something odd's going on and I need help unpicking it. I want you to look at a death that took place over a decade ago, which might be connected to today's events. You're perfect – someone from outside who can see beyond the suspects. You could do it part-time, say, four days a week.'

'Oh, right. Three days at the cathedral and four days working for you. Got any suggestions for when I have some downtime for myself?'

Harri glanced around the flat. 'Planning some days at the beach? This is an old, cold case, Mallory, and people around here are still a bit prickly. When the identity of the victim is revealed, there's going to be a lot of chat and raking over of the past. I want you to help me sift through that.'

Mallory stared at him. 'What are you talking about?'

'I'm talking about the death of Heledd's son, Huw Jones.'

3

Mallory frowned, watching Harri scrutinise her face. He was expecting some kind of reaction but the name meant nothing to her.

'Huw Jones?'

Harri sighed. 'I guess you had your own unexplained deaths in London to deal with in 2011. I forget that our tragedies often don't extend beyond the Welsh borders.'

Stung, Mallory got to her feet. 'That's a little unfair. I was still in uniform back then. Remember those days? Ten-hour shifts, most of it spent dealing with the criminal underclass.' She unbuttoned her cardigan and threw it on the couch, suddenly too hot. 'Are you going to tell me what happened or do I have to play ten questions?'

'Sit down, Mallory. I'm sorry.' Harri leant back in his chair, his eyes fixed to the clock on the wall. 'I'll be brief. On New Year's Eve 2011, three-year-old Huw Jones went missing from a house here in St Davids. Y Bwthyn, it was called. His mother, Heledd, was at a party across the road and his father, Jack Jones, was looking after the boy while he finished his afternoon nap. Five of Jack's friends came over to keep him company, something that Heledd said she had no idea was planned. When she came back from the party, after an hour and a half, Huw had gone.'

'Christ.'

Mallory hadn't heard of the case at all but it sounded like every mother's worst nightmare. When her son Toby had been small, she and Joe had often taken him along to a party and left him sleeping in a buggy in the spare room. She'd usually been the one to keep an eye on who was hovering near the doorway, but it had been a relaxed watch. She'd never actually thought Toby would come to harm in a place where everyone was someone she knew or a friend of a friend. What Heledd Jones must have felt when she realised her son was missing didn't bear thinking about although, she suspected, that was exactly what Harri wanted her to do. She felt the prickle of interest, cursing her curiosity that had got her into all kinds of trouble in the past.

'So, what happened next?' she asked. 'You said Huw Jones died.'

'Police were called after an initial search of the house, garden and street by Heledd and Jack and their friends. News of the missing boy passed through the community quickly and by the time we arrived on the scene, everyone was out looking for him. It was a clear night, not like now, so there was hope he'd be found wandering the lanes somewhere. It seems he'd walked further than we'd anticipated, and his body was found on the cliffs near St Non's Chapel. It's about a mile from here.'

'Oh no.' The tragedy of a decade earlier still pulled at her, and her thoughts turned to Toby. If she had been the boy's mother, she doubted she'd ever have recovered. She looked at Harri, who was also pale. When they'd last met, he'd given her the impression of sharpness and confidence. That hadn't changed but he also looked tired: the fatigue of when you were at the end of a case, not the beginning.

There was going to be plenty of story left and they needed sustenance.

'Right, I'm starving. How long do you have to spare me?'

Harri looked at his watch. 'I want to catch up with the team back at HQ but I could stay another twenty minutes or so. What do you have in mind?'

'I have some seafood in the fridge that I picked up yesterday. Shrimps and whelks. We can share.'

Mallory rose from the sofa, her joints stiff after a day on her feet. Harri also got to his feet, swaying slightly. A long day, Mallory guessed. She opened the fridge, pulled out a lettuce and made a vinaigrette as Harri watched.

'Who found him on the cliffs?'

'A tourist who was helping with the search. He was a hiker so had plenty of equipment, including a powerful torch.' Harri loosened his tie. 'It was Heledd who suggested looking at St Non's. She was a weaver of stories, Heledd. Mother and son would go down to St Non's and she'd say you could hear the mermaids singing if you were quiet enough. If you were ever lost or sad, talk to the *morforynion*, the mermaids. It was his favourite place.'

'I can see how a child would have loved that.'

'Huw's body was found on rocks just below the cliff's edge. He hadn't fallen far, but far enough. The consensus was that he'd walked out of the house towards the chapel. It was a clear night and he knew the path well. Why he'd decided to go there, no one was sure, but he evidently reached the chapel. Once there, he'd have been stumbling around in the dark and it was icy underfoot. A winter's night. It doesn't take much to slide over the cliffs.'

'The consensus?' Mallory stopped whisking the dressing and looked up at him. 'Surely there was an investigation into how Huw got to St Non's? There could have been another party involved.'

'The post-mortem found no evidence of violence on the boy, except what was consistent with falling from a height. It was deemed an accident.'

'But...'

Harri grimaced. 'I was also otherwise busy that night. Remember the riots of 2011? We were worried things might kick off in the cities during the New Year celebrations so I was in Swansea, keeping an eye on an estate where we'd had trouble. They wanted CID on standby in case of any serious criminality.'

'And was there?'

'Quiet as a mouse. All the action was happening here and I was miles away from it.'

'You don't agree with the verdict that Huw's death was an accident?'

'I think things were glossed over a little quickly in 2011, but I wasn't in a position to do anything about it then.'

'And are you now?'

'If I can find a link to the fact Heledd was found dead in a field this morning then I'm very interested in what happened in 2011.'

Mallory grimaced. 'It's every parent's nightmare. Do you have kids?'

Harri looked surprised at the question. 'Two. Why do you ask?'

'I don't know. I was wondering if you remember the days when they're three. They're impossible to keep hold of – a little dynamo of energy.'

Harri looked like he was going to say something and then stopped. 'I remember it well. God knows what the group of them were doing back at Heledd's house. Jack was supposed to be looking after Huw, not having a mini party of his own.'

'Can you tell me something about those six?'

'A little, for the moment. There was Eleri Tew, who was hosting the party that Heledd attended, Duncan Lyall, Bethan Rees, Gruffydd Ellis and Gemma Bowen. Plus, Jack Jones, of course. Eleri Tew is ultra-high profile now, and the other five are all respectable members of society.'

'Two are connected to the cathedral: Gruffydd Ellis and Bethan Rees. I saw them this afternoon. They were having a meeting with a retired canon and no one had warned me there was a gathering taking place.'

'It's probably not a coincidence. There will be lots of these get-togethers as news of Heledd's death leaks out. And not just in St Davids. Jack, the boy's father, is a high-profile Cardiff solicitor. I know it's going to be frustrating for you but I don't want you to contact them for the moment.'

'Not until I've been officially co-opted onto the team?'

Mallory turned in time to see Harri repress a smile. She'd given her tacit agreement, without actually agreeing to work for him. What would her son, Toby, have said? 'Say you're interested without saying you're interested.'

'Exactly. What I want, until the contract is signed, is for you to keep your ear to the ground so I know what people are saying about Heledd and anything that might be relevant to what happened on that New Year's Eve.'

'Six of them…' Mallory put the seafood on a tray and added the plate of salad. 'Let's eat at the table, shall we? Do you want to fill that jug over there with water?'

'Sure.'

As Mallory carried the tray into the living room, she tried to remember where she'd heard of Eleri Tew before. She grabbed a notepad from a drawer and jotted down the names.

'Doesn't Dyfed Powys have a cold-case team? Can't you get them involved in this?'

'Huw's death was ruled an accident and no one has ever come forward to suggest any other scenario. This is where I need you, Mallory. If I discover a link between Huw's death and what happened to Heledd last night then things will be looking very different.'

'You'll be pursuing that angle as part of any potential investigation, surely?'

'That's where we come down to resources. If it's a murder investigation, I'll have more resourcing leeway, but none of us could see any obvious marks of violence on Heledd's body. We're setting up an incident room and I'm the senior investigating officer but it's low-key at the moment. It wouldn't be the first time someone has lain down drunk in a field and not woken up.'

'You think the autopsy will be inconclusive?'

'I do. Which will mean waiting for histology and toxicology results. Given Heledd's history of psychiatric problems, I don't want this automatically to be assumed a suicide until I know that's definitely what happened.'

'Any evidence she might have taken her own life?'

'Not at the moment. The Jones's marriage didn't survive Huw's disappearance but our records still have Jack as her next of kin, even though he's since remarried. So, he was the first to be informed.'

'How did he like getting the call?'

'He was surprised and exasperated, I'd say. He's kept the same mobile number so we got hold of him quickly enough, but he's in France, where he's skiing and staying at his chalet there, with his wife. He's definitely *in situ* – I contacted the gendarmerie and asked them to pay a visit – so I can rule him out of this death. They hosted a dinner party for friends yesterday evening, so he's completely alibied.'

'What about in relation to the death of his son?'

'I gather at the beginning, when we arrived at the scene, he was questioned closely about his movements. It makes sense. We've only got his word that, as far as he was concerned, Huw was in the bedroom the whole time Heledd was out of the house. There was a period, before his friends arrived, when he was alone with his son. So, of course, he was interviewed on numerous occasions, but he always stuck to the same story – he left Huw in the bed and, although delighted his friends had come to see him, he'd asked them to keep their voices down so his son could sleep.'

Mallory pulled a whelk from its shell and put it in her mouth, enjoying the saltiness of its flavour. 'There must have been some sightings. I don't know this place well but surely a child can't walk down to the cliffs without someone seeing them.'

'No sightings at all, which understandably raised suspicions, but you take a walk down to St Non's sometime. It's entirely possible to get there, once you've left the town, without anyone spotting you.'

'And the timeline for the six in the house didn't throw up anything?'

'The chain of events wasn't complicated to construct. Duncan and Gruffydd were the first to arrive, at about ten past four. The three of them were alone, drinking, until Gemma popped in to say hello at about twenty to five. Five minutes later Bethan went to see what Gruffydd was up to. Duncan and Gruffydd nipped out to the off-licence when stocks were getting low and while they were out, Eleri turned up.'

'What about Heledd?'

Harri sighed and leant back in his chair. 'If Jack's a suspect, then logically Heledd must be one too. We only have her word that Huw was in bed when she left the house. She says she passed his bedroom and he was asleep, in his bed. Jack didn't see her leave so it's possible she took Huw with her. The problem is that it was a matter of minutes, because we know Heledd left her house at about four p.m. and she was seen not long after at the party.'

'So, if Heledd had kidnapped her own son, she would have needed an accomplice to give him to. It's still a possibility.'

Harri made a face. 'There was never any evidence of an accomplice, although of course it's possible. As I said, Heledd took a lot of flak from the local community after Huw went missing. I don't know if it was sexism – blame the mother rather than the father – or whether it was due to the fact she stayed around to carry the can after Jack left, but Heledd's life was blighted by those events.'

'She never remarried?'

'She's spent the last ten years under the management of the mental health team. She's been sectioned three times, the last about three years ago. The sad thing is that she'd been getting better. She'd been seen around the local pubs and was talking about finally moving away from St Davids. It was something she'd always wanted to do.'

Mallory frowned. 'What caused this change?'

Harri passed his empty plate to her. 'That's what I need to find out.'

There was more Mallory wanted to ask Harri but he was in a hurry to go, his eyes constantly straying to the clock.

'When's your next day off?' he asked her.

'Monday, but there's plenty of time for me to look into this. Can I see the crime scene?'

'Where Heledd died? I told you…'

'I know, you want me to focus on 2011. But Heledd's death is important and I'd like to see the potential crime scene. I assume the body is still *in situ* – or have you moved it already?'

He gave her an admiring glance. 'We're still processing the scene but the body's been removed. We got the pathologist there by midday and Heledd was taken to the mortuary at three. That was when I left to find you.'

'So, can I visit the farm?'

Harri sighed. 'I'll have to ask the boss. I'm going to push your contract through as soon as I can, but you know how procedure works. I'll say this about the Superintendent, she makes quick decisions. I'll call you after I've spoken to her. What I can do is send through the six statements from 2011, plus Heledd's. That'll speed things up and save you asking a lot of questions.'

Mallory scribbled a note on a piece of scrap paper. 'This is my mobile number. What do you want me to do in the meantime?'

'Speak to people. Read the news reports if you have to, but keep to the facts. It's more important you listen to what people are saying. News of Heledd's death will already have leaked out into this community, that much I can guarantee.'

'You sure?'

'Dispatcher, police personnel, paramedics, forensics. They're all local, Mallory. Believe me, it'll be out there.'

4

Harri retrieved his car from the side street. He'd parked on double yellow lines but didn't think traffic enforcement would be out in this weather. After a brief respite, it had started to snow again: not the thick flakes of the previous evening, but icy sleet that bounced off his windscreen, like being in hyperspace inside a 1980s computer game. Harri tensed as his tyres slid while he inched forward. He'd brought his own car; after the early-morning call, he hadn't had time to pick up a fleet vehicle. Freezing sleet made for treacherous conditions and who knew what idiots were out on the roads. He used his Bluetooth to make a call to his boss, DS Steph Morris, and update her on how the meeting had gone.

She hadn't needed much persuading to bring in Mallory. His boss was all about consultants and contracting out, where possible, to make the strained budgets stretch a little further. Her eyes had lit up when she realised Mallory had Met murder experience too. Mallory, though, he had thought, would be a little harder to persuade but she had seemed genuinely interested in what had happened to Huw Jones. It was good news. Harri preferred his colleagues to get the bit between their teeth rather than be steamrolled into joining an investigation.

'Are there any links to the 2011 accident?' Steph was almost hyperventilating. She didn't want a connection to a decade-old tragedy and Harri couldn't blame her. Cold cases were called that for a reason. The chances of finding killers were stone cold but Harri couldn't give her the reassurance she needed.

'I don't like coincidences. What was Heledd Jones doing in that field in the first place?'

'It's only a mile or two from where she lives. Have you been able to pin down her movements the evening before she was found? She was smartly dressed, wasn't she?'

The image of Heledd's red coat against the dirty white snow flashed in front of Harri.

'She hadn't dressed up for a walk in the snow. We're looking into her movements now. I'm heading into the office for an update. I'm going to send Mallory the statements from 2011, if you're OK with it. She needs to get started as soon as possible.' Harri paused. 'She also wants to visit the crime scene.'

'What, now?'

Harri rolled his eyes. 'No, boss. In the morning, I assume. I said I'd ask you.'

There was a short silence. 'She can go when recovery of physical evidence is complete.'

'That might be a few days. I get the impression she just wants to see the lay of the land. She's no terms of reference. She doesn't remember the Huw Jones case and she doesn't really know this area. She could at least visit the farm.'

'Is she discreet, this Mallory? There's still a lot of bad blood about what happened in 2011.'

'I'd say so. She's a bit of a loner but an experienced detective. She'll get up to speed quickly and once she's signed a contract, she can come down to Carmarthen for meetings.'

'Then push through the paperwork, and by all means pass on the statements from 2011. She can visit the farm only in an unofficial capacity, though. Get one of your team to meet her there, but she leaves the forensics to the experts.'

'I think she'll be happy with that.'

'Good. I want this cleared up as soon as possible. Thanks, Harri.'

The line went dead, leaving Harri with the swish of the windscreen wipers as the only background noise. He'd lost the lights of Solva and it would be darkened roads for the rest of the way. Funny Mallory asking him if he had kids. He knew she had a son, Toby, whom he'd met on Eldey, but she didn't seem the type to ask him about family. Harri did indeed remember those days when his children could take themselves off, unheeding of the dangers a road represented. His wife Paula had died of cancer, and he'd been left with two small kids and a stressful job. His sister, a solicitor in Cardiff, had moved to Pembroke to live with him. A complicated life that you couldn't just reveal to a woman you'd only met twice.

He hesitated over the contacts page showing on his dashboard, dithering over who to ring next. In the end, the choice was made for him. His dash lit up with an incoming call from one of his DCs, Siân Lewis.

'Got any news for me?' he asked her.

'The post-mortem is scheduled for Saturday morning. Would you like me to attend or would you rather—'

'You do it, as I'll have my hands full, but call me as soon as you can afterwards. Any update on where Heledd had been the night before?'

'A call came in this evening from a local who says he saw her at the bus stop at Haverfordwest station last night, around eight p.m. We've checked CCTV on the trains and there's nothing showing, which suggests she didn't get to the station by rail. I've got someone going over the cameras outside the station now to see if there's any evidence of how she arrived at the bus stop. The shelter is just about visible from the camera.'

'How far will the bus have taken her?'

'To the village, Penterry, near where her cottage is. She'd have had a twenty-minute walk from the bus stop in fair conditions. It could have taken her double that last night.'

'But we think she arrived there before the snowfall? That's a shame. Footprints or tyre marks would have been good.'

'I know. Her cottage is about half a mile from the field where she was found. She would have passed it, so it's possible she fell or went to sleep there.'

Harri frowned. Unless she was incredibly drunk, he doubted Heledd would have just fallen down in the field. 'Anything else?'

'That's it for now. We've conducted as much of a door-to-door as we can, considering the nearest neighbour to the farm is half a mile away. News had got round already and reporters were arriving as forensics were still on site. The weather is a nightmare and I'm frozen stiff.'

'Go home and get some rest. God knows what the weather will look like tomorrow.'

'I'll wait for you if you don't mind.' Siân paused. 'Do you think it's connected to Huw Jones's death?'

Harri suspected he'd be asked the same question over and over again in the following days. On the one hand, it made complete sense. A small child had died and the community had never forgotten, as Heledd had unfortunately found out. On the other hand, he didn't need the waters muddying if it was a case of murder. Heledd sounded on the cusp of a new life and the clothes she'd died in suggested the possibility of a new man. The team would need to identify him first and not worry about any residual resentment that locals might feel for a woman whose son had died twelve years earlier.

'I don't know but don't worry about that now.'

Harri was desperate to get off the phone so he could pull over and relieve himself. Despite hanging back on the drink at Mallory's, he still couldn't make an hour-long trip without having a piss. He'd probably picked up some weird infection, which meant a trip to the doctor's. Another thing to worry about. Checking there were no lights behind him, Harri put on his indicators and pulled over.

When he'd finished, he pulled out the scrap of paper Mallory had thrust at him. He dialled her number and she answered on the first ring.

'You're on for tomorrow.'

5

After speaking to Harri, Mallory resisted the temptation to open her computer and begin searching the death of Huw Jones. She wouldn't get far with a stinking cold, and her injuries had taught her that she needed to indulge in some self-care when she was feeling tired. She ran a hot bath, adding some expensive scented oil to soothe her joints, and settled back in the steam.

It had been a surprise to see Harri on her doorstep, but flattering he wanted her expertise. Her job at the cathedral was interesting enough, but hardly tested her investigative skills. A key part of her role was giving information about the cathedral to tourists. She'd had to mug up not only on the city of St Davids, but also on wider church history. She'd soon realised that visitors either knew hardly anything on the subject, and any information she gave them was better than nothing, or they were experts and nothing she told them was new. It had left her feeling inadequate and underqualified. Getting involved in this case would give her the opportunity to do something she was trained for. She hadn't actually agreed to help Harri, though, and part of her was infuriated he'd taken her consent for granted. It was pointless brooding over it – she was intrigued and Harri had spotted this.

She wasn't particularly surprised that she hadn't heard of Huw's death before. Her busy job had left her with precious little time to read newspaper articles about other tragedies. Harri, however, was right to be interested in local gossip. She was pretty sure it wasn't a coincidence that Bethan Rees and Gruffydd Ellis had unexpectedly appeared at the cathedral the afternoon following Heledd Jones's death. It was out of the usual order of things for two people to be having an unscheduled meeting in the building, and they both had a connection to the night Huw died. She wondered why they were meeting Canon Stack. Mallory sighed and sank further into the bubbles. For the moment, there was nothing she could do about the pair. The meeting would, she presumed, be finished by now. It was a job for tomorrow's afternoon shift, when she might be able to winkle out information from another volunteer.

A thud from the flat upstairs broke into Mallory's thoughts. Her neighbour Ffion was moving about. Mallory had passed her at the ice-cream shop earlier that evening and she'd been deep in conversation with the assistant there. More intrigue?

Mallory got out of the bath, pulled on a pair of jeans and a jumper, and climbed up the steps to the flat above. As she knocked, the smell of beef stew wafted under the door. God, she should get herself a slow cooker and start doing this. She had no excuse, except laziness and the fact she never felt hungry in the morning. Ffion opened the door in bare feet, her flat as warm as Mallory's.

'Hi – is everything all right?'

'Am I interrupting dinner? I could come back later if you're eating.'

'Just finished. Come on in.'

Ffion opened the door wider for Mallory to step inside. The two apartments had been renovated at the same time and had identical fittings. Ffion had purchased the flat, and spent time putting up pictures and hanging plant pots from macramé holders. It made Mallory's flat look sparse, but both places had the same all-encompassing warmth.

'Do you want a glass of wine or something? I've got a bottle of red in the kitchen.' Ffion ran her fingers through her tight curls.

'I'm fine, thanks. Could I ask you something?'

'Sure.' Ffion took Mallory into the living room, which was dominated by a huge widescreen television. The Welsh TV series *Pobol y Cwm* was showing; Mallory recognised the distinctive theme tune.

'So, what can I do for you? It's not my TV, is it? I try to keep the volume low.'

'Not at all. To be honest, I've just bought a new set myself but I'm waiting for someone to connect it. My son is coming to visit and he'll be bored stiff as it is.'

'That's all right, then. What can I help you with?'

Mallory kept her eyes on the screen, embarrassed now by her presence in the living room. 'I know this is going to sound a bit odd but when I got home this evening, I was told the news of the death of Heledd Jones. I wondered if you'd heard.'

Ffion froze and spun around to look at Mallory, her eyes wide with shock. Whatever she'd been chatting about in the ice-cream shop, it wasn't this.

'Heledd Jones? Mother of Huw Jones?'

'Yes, I'm afraid so.'

'You sure?'

'Absolutely. I have a friend in the police force who's just visited me. He told me about it but the way he was speaking, it was as if he expected me to know all about

37

Huw's death. I know you're local so I wondered if you could fill me in.'

Mallory hoped she was taking the right approach. She needed to show that she wasn't just communicating idle gossip, while expressing ignorance of the case to ensure Ffion was willing to pass on what she knew.

'I think I'm going to open that bottle of wine,' said Ffion.

Mallory stayed on her feet as Ffion disappeared into the kitchen. She made a show of looking at an advert on the television but from the corner of her eye she could see Ffion typing into her mobile. Harri had been wrong. The news hadn't made it to everyone in St Davids.

Ffion came back into the room with a glass of wine in her hand. 'Sure you don't want one?'

'Positive.'

'I can't believe it. I've had the telly on all evening and I didn't pay any attention to the news.'

'I'm not sure the identity of the victim has been released to the public yet. You knew Heledd?'

'Everyone knew of Heledd Jones. You know the story of how Huw went missing?'

'My friend told me the bare bones of it.'

Ffion winced at Mallory's description. 'Christ, once this gets out… It's not a secret, is it? Do you mind if I make a quick call?'

'Go ahead.'

Ffion looked like she wanted to go to the kitchen but took out her mobile in front of Mallory, who continued to listen as the phone rang out. Ffion forced a smile. 'No answer.' She took a gulp of wine and sat down on the sofa. 'You said the police visited you. What did they want with you?'

'I'm an ex-murder detective, they just wanted to chat about the death.'

Ffion's eyes widened. 'She was murdered?'

Mallory made a face. 'Sorry, I didn't mean to imply that. At the moment, the death is unexplained. That's what I have experience in.'

Anyone with a knowledge of police procedure would have wanted to know exactly why Mallory, working as a retail assistant, would be able to help an active investigation. Ffion, however, was prepared to take Mallory's story at face value.

'What did you want to know?'

'Anything you can tell me about it. Sorry, I'm working at the cathedral tomorrow afternoon, and visitors and staff might mention it once it's in the public domain.'

'Well, I was a teenager at the time so there's not much I can tell you about it. You know there was a party, right?'

'In the street opposite the Jones's house.'

'Mallory, in *this* street.'

'Here?'

'Didn't you know? Of course, you didn't. Why would you? Jack and Heledd Jones lived about five doors up. It was a house like this, a small terrace. The houses opposite are detached and Eleri Tew lived in one of those.'

'Eleri Tew? The name rings a bell.'

'You know who I mean. The politician whose face is permanently frozen. The press calls her the MP with the trout pout although, to be honest, the swelling has gone down a bit now.'

'Of course. I knew I recognised the name.' Eleri Tew was a petite woman, with blonde hair styled into a rigid bob which reflected her inflexible attitude. She was a Conservative politician known to be on the right of the party. Pro–Brexit, libertarian, but had made a name for herself championing legislation to regulate the beauty industry. A failed procedure had left her with a frozen forehead and enlarged lips, although Mallory thought 'trout pout' was a little harsh. God, she wished she'd brought something to write down some notes. She'd need to look up Eleri again.

'You used to see her a lot around town when she was a councillor, but then she got elected as an MP and now she spends a fair amount of time in London. She's usually back here for her Friday surgeries, though. She won't be happy that Huw's death might be raked over.'

'Perhaps her constituents won't make the connection.'

'Believe me, they will. It's also bound to make the papers, because Heledd was at a party at Eleri's house when her son went missing. The press will have a field day with that.'

'Eleri wasn't an MP then, though, surely.'

'Of course not, but she was on the way up and a big name in local politics. We all thought she'd get involved in the Senedd. She's always been hot on promoting Welsh interests but she had her sights set on a UK stage, so she put herself forward as a parliamentary candidate when the last MP stood down.'

Mallory thought of the task Harri had set her. Find out the local reaction. She was pretty sure Eleri Tew would have a very good alibi for her whereabouts last night. Her life would be significantly easier, and press attention easier to manage, if she was in London and not Pembrokeshire on a Tuesday evening.

'I believe people blamed Heledd for the fact her son went missing. Do you think that's a fair assessment?'

Ffion scowled and took another gulp of wine. 'No, that's not a fair assessment. Who the bloody hell has been telling you that?'

'Sorry, my friend just said something. I didn't mean to upset you.'

'After her son was found, there was a lot of talk. I mean, how did Huw get to St Non's?'

'You mean how could he have walked through town, down to the cliffs?'

'Exactly. It made no sense at all unless he was carried down there. I've never believed the official verdict that it was an accidental death. Surely someone would have seen a little boy walking on his own? And, if he was carried there, the first people you suspect are the parents, aren't they?'

'Wasn't his dad with some friends and looking after him?'

'That's right, including Eleri, but they were all exon-erated.'

'Did Heledd get much support from the community, though? She was in and out of mental health institutions.'

'I don't remember but what I do know is that she called her son a horror on the evening he went missing.'

'How do you know that?'

Ffion put down her glass. 'Because I was there.' She caught sight of Mallory's expression. 'Don't look so surprised. Around half this place had an invite, and the other half probably intended to turn up anyway. That's the way it works around here.'

'And you can remember what happened?'

'Of course. I was thirteen and wasn't particularly chuffed to be there. You never are at thirteen, are you? But I found a friend and we necked two glasses of cider in quick succession until my father caught us at it. After that it was bottles of Pepsi.'

'And when Huw disappeared?'

'It wasn't that late. Around six, I think. The party started to get weird, with people searching the house and lots of strangers coming and going. I asked what had happened and heard Huw was gone.'

'Did you join in the search?'

'My dad wouldn't let me. A child was missing and the first thing everyone thought was paedophile alert.' Ffion took another sip of her wine. 'So, I was bundled off home.'

Their eyes strayed to the television as a news report flashed onto the screen. A woman's face, her fair hair tied back away from her face, looked out from the screen, her expression impassive.

'Is that Heledd?' asked Mallory.

Ffion nodded, unwilling to tear her eyes away from the set. 'You know, I never believed the official verdict. I'm positive Heledd knew more about that evening than she was saying and now look what's happened.'

6

Harri kicked open the door of his office and pulled off his coat, spreading it across the surface of the radiator that was continuing to pump out heat. The station hadn't yet got the memo to turn down the temperature a degree or so to save money. He hoped his coat would be dry before he set off home. Even a morsel of warmth might make him feel a little better. He looked out into the CID room, where the duty officers were getting stuck in for the night. Steph, although clearly concerned about the discovery of Heledd's body, hadn't hung around for him to update her. His boss must have something on this evening, as it was unlike her to miss out on a briefing. No doubt she'd continue to pester him by phone if she was so inclined and he suspected he'd be getting a few more calls before the night was out.

Siân knocked on his door and came in carrying a mug of tea.

'Thought you might need this. You look terrible.'

'Thanks.' Harri took the mug, which had a picture of Andy Capp emblazoned on the front. 'Where the hell did you get the mug from?'

'From the kitchen. Why? Does it belong to someone?'

'I assume one of our esteemed colleagues is having a joke. Andy Capp is a cartoon character who likes a beer, gambling and occasionally beating up his wife.'

43

'Well, fuck that.' Siân leant to grab the tea back from him but Harri had already taken a gulp.

'I'll throw it in the bin afterwards,' he promised. 'We'll see who comes looking for it, shall we?'

Siân sat in the chair opposite him and opened up her tablet. She was one of the new generation of detectives for whom everything was digital. She probably didn't write anything down, which was fine, but what happened when technology failed? His kids would call him a dinosaur but blackouts did occur when the weather turned. Look at what had happened last year on Eldey, when Mallory had been trapped on the island with a killer. He saw Siân's mascara was smudged, giving the mistaken impression she'd been crying. Harri guessed she'd been rubbing her eyes, as he'd seen her do many times before, while staring at the computer screen.

'What have you got for me?'

'We've already interviewed the bus drivers for the route that might have taken Heledd from Haverfordwest back to Penterry and we think we've identified which bus she got on, the ten past eight. The driver remembers her sitting at the front and getting off at the village. The only problem is that his camera wasn't working; there's an issue with them on the buses, apparently. Kids like to vandalise them at the back so they can lark around.'

'Do we know why she decided not to drive? The car's at her cottage, isn't it?'

'I don't think it's that suspicious. Heledd, by all accounts, liked a drink but if she had alcohol issues, she functioned pretty well. It wouldn't have been much fun if she lost her licence. She was probably just playing it safe.'

'Any idea who she might have been meeting in Haver-fordwest? They might be able to give us more info on how she was getting home.'

'The station CCTV isn't much help so we're looking at cameras nearby to see if we can identify car owners who might have a connection to Heledd.'

'Can you do that as a priority tomorrow, please? What about next of kin, after the fiasco of us ringing Jack Jones? What's her sister's name?'

'Becca Jones.'

Harri frowned. 'I thought Jones was Heledd's married name?'

'Married and maiden name. Not a wide range of surnames in Wales, DI *Evans*.'

Harri laughed and gulped down the rest of the tea. God, he was thirsty. 'Point taken. Where does Becca Jones live?'

'Welsh Hook. She owns a mill there, Felin Wen, that she opens for tourists, and she lives in an apartment in the building. She's been told of Heledd's death and has taken it surprisingly well. I suppose you do when someone has been on the brink of self-harm for years.'

'Let's not start with a presumption of suicide, though.' Harri stood and rested his back against the radiator. 'I've got authorisation for someone to give us a hand on this. Do you remember Mallory Dawson, from the Eldey incident?'

'I remember.' Siân's tone was flat.

Harri glanced across at his detective constable. 'You don't have a problem with her, do you? She did a good job on that island, with no backup.'

'Five people dead. Great job.'

'That was hardly her fault, was it?' Harri's headache was making him crabby. 'And one of the dead was the killer. Look, she's got murder experience and you know the push is for more civilian investigators. It's a damn sight cheaper than training and recruiting actual detectives.'

'We'll be in the minority before long.'

'We need more hands on this and I don't want to go through that agency we use when we're short-staffed. I want someone I know and trust. You got a problem with that, Siân?'

'No problem, boss.'

'Good. Mallory wants to visit the farm where Heledd was found tomorrow morning. Will you meet her there?'

'Me?'

'I want to visit Heledd's sister tomorrow so I'm tied up.' Harri saw she was waiting for him to pass the job onto another member of the team. No chance. He wasn't setting a precedent for his staff to pick and choose their assignments.

'Shall we say ten a.m. at the farm?'

'Sure, boss.'

'Good. We're going to get all the paperwork signed off quickly. Orders from above, which have also given me permission to share the statements from Huw's death in 2011. They'll be in the file. Can you send them over to Mallory?'

Siân frowned. 'Are you sure that's allowed?'

'The Super's agreed to it.'

'Do you want me to send every statement from that night through?'

'They're just computer files, aren't they? Send through the lot. Mallory's experienced and I've given her the names of the six friends at the Jones's house that evening.

She'll know to make them a priority. I've a horrible feeling that something from that night is going to come back to haunt us.'

'Feeling?' Siân winked at him. Harri remembered his old DI when he had first become a detective. His stomach had turned to jelly every time he'd been called into his superior's office. The new generation didn't care for such niceties. Even calling him 'boss' had a slightly ironic ring to it.

Harri picked up his empty mug and threw it into the wastepaper bin under his desk. Siân had put too much milk into the brew and it had made him feel slightly queasy. 'I've got a bad feeling about a lot of things today.'

They both jumped at the shrill ring from Harri's desk phone. He picked it up and listened to the desk sergeant. His eyes met Siân's.

'Keep him there, would you? I'll come and get him myself.'

Harri replaced the receiver.

'Someone's in reception, says he's driven down from London to see us.'

'Don't they have phones there?'

Harri shrugged, wishing he had a dry jumper he could put on. 'I dunno but he says it's important. I'm prepared to give him ten minutes of my time.'

'He has information about the death of Heledd Jones?'

Harri shook his head. 'No. About the killing of Huw Jones. That's right. He said *killing*.'

7

Mallory opened the curtains and stared at the street. The small patch of garden outside her front door glistened with the sparkling whiteness of fresh snow. Mallory was sure she'd heard that it never snowed by the sea, due to coastal temperatures, but here was proof that such pronouncements were a load of nonsense. The weather was an issue for her – it had been bad enough climbing up the hill after work last night. She now needed to get back to the cathedral car park to pick up her car and drive over to the farm. The glass of wine she'd drunk at Ffion's had left a nasty tang in her mouth. She toasted two slices of bread and spread them liberally with Marmite to take away the taste of alcohol.

The chat with Ffion had been interesting but she'd not been able to press her about the six friends who had congregated at the Jones's house. The only one she'd really learnt about was Eleri Tew, but Ffion hadn't given her any information that wasn't in the public domain. She'd have liked to have pressed Ffion more about the other friends but her neighbour, her eyes straying to her mobile phone, had been anxious to get Mallory out of the flat.

Ffion's revelation that she'd been at the party suggested that Mallory would have her work cut out. A lot of people had been either at the party or later involved in the searches, an embarrassment of witnesses. The only thing of substance Ffion had told her was that the streets had been quiet enough when she had walked to the party and a young child might, just might, be able to make it to the cliffs without anyone noticing them. Mallory still wasn't buying it.

As she was leaving the house, she heard the door open above her and Ffion appeared on the landing. 'I heard you were up and about. Do you want these?'

She brandished a pair of walking poles, the type used by hikers. Mallory climbed the stairs and took them off her. 'Got a pair of skis to go with them?'

Ffion grinned. 'I'll be thinking of you, out in this weather.' Her smile faded as she looked at Mallory, last night's conversation on her mind. 'Don't mind my ramblings of yesterday, will you? It was a shock when I heard about Heledd. Best leave the past be.'

'Of course,' lied Mallory.

The poles were a revelation. Mallory had always been a bit sniffy about hikers hunched over their sticks, giving themselves backache. She kept her posture straight and took some tentative steps out of the front gate and onto the pathway, the going treacherous as layers of snow had fallen onto ice. The town was still waking up and hers were the only footprints as she walked along the streets that Huw Jones must have passed through. As she reached the top of the slope, she stopped. It had been a clear night that New Year's Eve, according to Harri, and she wondered if the cathedral lights had been on. If not, there would have been only the twinkle of lights from houses and yet he had taken the road in darkness down to the ruins. Mallory would need to pay a visit but his attraction to the place, despite his mother's story of mermaids, was difficult to fathom.

Mallory made it down the slope in one piece, resisting the temptation to slide down on her bottom. She threw her poles into the boot of the car and started off. The roads were treacherous but Mallory was a confident driver and she'd programmed the farm's destination into her satnav. As she neared Middle Mill, she saw a stream of vans and cars parked on the verge. She slowed down until she reached the police tape, where a lone uniformed offer stood shivering in the cold. Mallory wound down her window.

'My name's Mallory Dawson. I arranged with DI Harri Evans to visit this morning.'

The officer nodded towards a woman standing next to a red Yaris. 'DC Siân Lewis is waiting for you.'

The woman, dressed in a huge, quilted coat that reached down to her ankles, peeled away from the car and came towards Mallory. Her face was hard and Mallory could guess why. The first twenty-four hours of any investigation are crucial in shaping its outcome. Siân would want to be on the inside, progressing an important line of inquiry. Showing an ex-copper around a crime scene didn't quite cut it. Mallory held out her hand.

'Mallory Dawson. I don't think we met last year, did we?'

'I didn't have that pleasure. The boss speaks highly of you.' Her mood was sour.

Mallory adopted a conciliatory tone. 'I'm a bit at sea on this one. I won't take up much of your time. I just want to see where Heledd died and how the location fits into her walk home.'

'Sure.' Siân spun round, gesturing towards a mean one-storey cottage with cracked render. 'The farm's owned by Catrin and Thomas Cross. "Farm" is a little grand for what's in essence a small cottage and two fields.'

'They work on the land?' Mallory followed Siân down a track, wishing she'd taken the poles from the boot of her car. She hadn't wanted to lower herself in Siân's estimation any further.

'Catrin does. Thomas has a job in the local bar. One of them needs a regular income and it's Catrin who comes from a farming family.'

They arrived at the field, where three goats were feeding in a rusty metal trough. A woman in a battered Barbour jacket was leaning on the fence, watching the work of the forensics team, their white overalls blending in with the landscape.

'This is Catrin Cross,' said Siân.

Catrin, probably in her late twenties, turned her head to assess Mallory before dismissing her. 'More forensics?'

'Something like that,' said Siân. 'Catrin found the body yesterday morning when she went out to feed the goats. The red coat Heledd was wearing was easy to spot from this distance.'

Mallory guessed it was probably around fifty metres to the top of the field but a red coat would be a vibrant image against the snow.

'Did you immediately think it was a body?' Mallory asked Catrin.

'Not a body. We had a tourist last year fall asleep near the same spot and he was fine. I hoped that if it was a person, they'd still be alive.'

In this weather? Mallory cast a glance at Siân. 'And were there any footprints when you walked across the field to see who was there?'

'Nothing, but then snow fell all night.'

'And did you recognise her?' asked Mallory.

'Of course. Heledd Jones was well known around here.'

'Because of what happened to Huw or because she was a neighbour?'

'Both.' Catrin's tone was flat. 'I've given my statement to the police.'

'Of course.' Mallory moved away.

'You can't go into the crime scene,' said Siân, following close behind.

'It's fine. I've seen what I need to. The road that runs along the side of the field. I assume that's the route to Heledd's cottage.'

'Yes. She'd have been coming down the slope. Her house is further into the valley, so she wouldn't have passed this cottage until she'd come to the dip in the hill.'

'You've ruled out Catrin and her husband's involvement?'

'They're alibiing each other from seven p.m. For once, Tom wasn't working at the pub and they spent the evening together. There's been no dispute with Heledd, as far as we can discover, and we know Heledd was alive around nine, because of the bus driver's statement.'

Mallory looked round. Harri had given her access to the site as a favour. He wanted her to look at Huw's death, not Heledd's. Was there a connection between the two? Mallory wasn't sure, but it was a miserable place to die. Mother and son had spent their last moments out in the winter cold. It was a tenuous link but somewhere to start.

8

'There's something else.' Siân looked relieved to have got Mallory's visit over so quickly. 'We had a visitor in the station last night. The boss wants you to hear him out.'

'Visitor? In relation to Heledd's death?'

'No.' Siân hesitated, wondering – Mallory guessed – how much to tell her. 'You know what it's like in the early stages of an investigation. We get loads of calls – the legitimate, the crackpot, the deluded. This witness turned up at the station late last night. He'd driven from London after seeing the news of the discovery of Heledd's body.'

'Why did he come all the way here?'

'He's got a story to tell about the night Huw died and the boss now wants you to hear it from the horse's mouth too, as it were. You're at the cathedral this afternoon, aren't you?'

'Yes, but I'm working. I won't be able to get any time off.'

'Sorry, but Harri's already sent him up to St Davids. He'll probably be waiting for you when you get in.'

Mallory swore. Harri had clearly never worked in a shop. You don't have time to interview witnesses *and* serve customers. Great. Mallory caught a flash of amusement in Siân's expression.

'Fine,' she said finally. 'I'll find time to speak to him. Do you know what he said?'

'I do, but I'm not sure I'm prepared to give it any credence. You listen to what the chap has to say. His name's Gavin Lavine.'

—

After standing outside at the miserable farm, Mallory was desperate to get into the warmth of the shop. However, when she tried the door, she saw it was locked. A note pinned to the glass said the shop would be closed until midday. While the morning shift hadn't made it in, clearly Mallory had been expected to turn up. Mallory pulled out her keys and opened the door, turning on the lights. There was no sign of any visitor waiting for her, which was a relief. Her mobile rang as she was putting the float into the till: it was her manager, with a change of plan. The volunteer who had opened up the cathedral that morning had to leave and there was no one to replace her. Could Mallory keep the shop closed and the cathedral open until the replacement arrived?

'I can manage.' Mallory squinted at the rota. Midday prayers were due to start in ten minutes. 'Who's coming in to help out?'

'Bethan Rees, one of our lay helpers. She'll lead the service and stay on to keep the building open. Do you know her?'

'Yes, fine, I'll hang around the nave until she arrives. Leave it all with me.'

Mallory braved the weather once more and saw that the volunteer had shut the inner door. A man was waiting outside but it wasn't the elusive Gavin. Jeff, as far as Mallory could tell, came to every midday service and clearly a foot of snow wasn't going to make any difference to his habit. She unlocked the door and pulled it open.

'I think you might be our only worshipper here today,' she said, looking at her watch. 'Even the clergy haven't yet arrived.'

'They don't have far to come.' He looked around. 'What about the volunteers?'

'They had to go. Bethan Rees is coming, as long as she can make it in, of course.'

'Bethan will be here, don't you worry.'

'Does she live close by?' Mallory shut the door to keep in the meagre warmth.

'In Solva but she'll be able to get in – I've heard the road is clear.'

'I met her last night. I'd forgotten she interviewed me. She seems very capable. Does she have family?'

Jeff turned and looked beyond Mallory, to the door, to check that Bethan wasn't coming in. 'Single,' he whispered, as if it was a crime. 'She was engaged to Reverend Gruffydd but it came to nothing.'

'Gruffydd Ellis?'

'That's it. A wedding date was set but the engagement was broken off.'

'Gosh that must be awkward, working alongside your former fiancé. I'm not sure I'd fancy that. Has he married?'

'Oh yes, he has two children but his wife is a bit...' He tapped his temple.

'When—' They both jumped at the door opening and Jeff scuttled to his seat.

Bethan Rees came into the cathedral, shaking off an umbrella. Just what I'd use in snow, thought Mallory sourly, although she had to admit Bethan looked more presentable than she did.

'Hope it wasn't too late a night for you,' said Mallory. She saw Bethan frown.

'What do you mean?'

'You were last to leave here and now you're here again. You must feel like you never left.'

Bethan shot Mallory a glance and didn't dignify her with a reply. Mallory made herself scarce now Bethan was here and opened up the shop. It was Mallory's first-ever retail job and the least stressful role she'd ever undertaken. She was left on her own to open up the till, serve customers, restock shelves and cash up at the end of the day. She supposed it'd be different if she worked in a supermarket but there was little to worry about when selling china imprinted with images of the cathedral, cards wishing you Happy Easter and miniature statues of St David.

At half-two, a man came into the shop, the first customer Mallory had seen that day. In his forties, he had sandy hair that was thinning at the crown, which gave him a monkish appearance.

'Gavin Lavine.' He held out his hand. 'I guess you're Mallory.'

Mallory shook it. 'I was told you were coming to see me.'

'Quite a man, your detective inspector.'

'What do you mean?'

'Gave me a grilling and, I dare say, I deserved it. What can I say, except I did what I thought was for the best at the time.'

'Look, I've not actually spoken to Harri about this. I got a message through DC Siân Lewis.' Gavin grimaced, suggesting he hadn't had a much better reception from Siân. 'He's not given me any clues about what this is all about. You're going to have to tell the story all over again.'

'Here?' Gavin looked round.

'I need to shut the shop, although I'm not supposed to. We can go to the refectory, which hasn't opened today. We'll at least get some privacy.'

Mallory steered Gavin into the cathedral and up the stairs to the refectory, which bore no sign of a meeting having taken place there the previous afternoon. She saw, however, that the place gave you plenty of privacy. Gavin appeared unconcerned at the no-frills setting, settling at one of the tables.

'DI Evans said you were a consultant, is that right?'

'I'm helping him with a line of inquiry: anything relating to the death of Huw Jones in 2011. I believe you have some information in relation to that?'

Gavin frowned and pulled a water bottle from his orange rucksack. 'The thing is, I've sort of forgotten a lot of what I'm about to tell you. I think it's a case of convenient amnesia, if that makes sense. I had an accident, which caused a head injury. I'll come on to that in a minute, but the essence is that sometimes parts of my memory are a complete blank and the bits I forget are the most traumatic aspects of my past. You'll have to bear with me.'

'I'm fine with that.' Mallory had interviewed road traffic victims who'd struggled with the same problem. It was a case of listening, asking the right questions and not pushing when answers didn't come easily.

'I hardly know where to start but once upon a time I worked here, like you do.'

'In the shop?'

Gavin laughed. 'No, I had a much loftier role. I was employed here as a stonemason in 2015.'

'In 2015?' Mallory frowned, wondering where this conversation was going. A witness four years after Huw's disappearance?

'I arrived in the summer of that year. The diocese had contracted out various pieces of work and the company I co-owned won the contract to undertake minor repairs to the cathedral. It was fairly basic stuff but it was a glorious summer and I loved it here.'

'I'm yet to experience anything like summer in West Wales.'

'Just you wait. You're in for a treat. Anyway, while I was here, I was asked by Cadw, the Welsh heritage organisation, to undertake some minor repairs to the ruin of St Non's Chapel.'

Mallory's heart missed a beat. 'St Non's. OK.'

'You must have been there.'

'I've heard of it in relation to Huw's death but haven't yet been to see it. My son's due to visit soon and I thought I might take a walk down there with him sometime.'

'St Non's is considered to be the birthplace of St David. There's a modern chapel next to the rectangular ruins of the original.'

'How old is it?' asked Mallory, wishing she'd made them both a cup of tea in the shop. The cold was beginning to seep into her bones.

'They don't really know. St David is reputed to have been born there in the sixth century, so it's possible the chapel dates back to then.'

'And it's in ruins?' said Mallory.

'Exactly. It's had a chequered history. It was a place of pilgrimage for centuries until the Reformation, after which it became a house until it fell into disrepair. A stone with a cross within a circle was found nearby. It could have been a grave marker or perhaps a feature of the interior of the chapel. Anyway, they've propped it up in the corner of the ruins.'

'Propped? That doesn't sound very safe.'

'Perhaps you're right. One July Monday morning, I got a call. At some point over the weekend, someone had attempted to vandalise the cross. Probably kids larking about, who'd tipped the stone onto its front. It was lying face down on the ground.'

'Sounds like the usual mindless vandalism. They wanted you to take a look?'

'Exactly. Cadw were going to send an archaeologist up to assess the situation but they asked if I could go there in the meantime and make sure no more damage was done. I spoke to my bosses here and they were happy for me to go. I got in the van and drove down there. Sure enough, the stone was lying face down on the ground. It must have taken a few of them to tip it over.'

'Was there anything you could do?'

'The stone just needed putting back in place but I needed help, so I rang and said I'd wait for the archaeologist to arrive to give me a hand. While I was waiting, I had a root around the stonework which is usually hidden behind the cross. When things fall or are damaged, it's a good time to check out stonework that isn't usually on show. That's when I found the note.'

'A note?'

'I had my soft brush out with me and I was just giving the stones a wipe down. I didn't want to do anything more substantial without permission but I figured it was part of my remit to check the stonework hadn't been damaged by the antics of the vandals. I saw what I thought was a sweet wrapper, as we often find things like this. The nooks and crannies are a great place to stuff a crisp packet or piece of chewing gum. When I pulled it out, I saw it was a small bag, like the ones you use to store food in the freezer, and in it was a note.'

'What did it say?' God, he was frustratingly slow. Maybe it was the head injury but she wished he'd get a move on.

'I wasn't sure about opening it at first. It could have been a prayer or votive offering. People do push stuff like that in cracks in old buildings too. Anyway, curiosity got the better of me and I opened it up. On a piece of scrap paper, the message said, *"All six of us lied. Six lies killed Huw Jones."*'

9

'All six of us lied?' Mallory stared at Gavin. His face was flushed, as if he had a fever, but he met her gaze readily enough.

'Did you know about the death of Huw Jones when you read the note? Had people talked about it here at the cathedral?'

'Yes, but I didn't know much. On one of my first days here, someone had told me about St Non's and said something along the lines of "that's where the boy died".'

'Did they say the child's name, Huw Jones?'

'I don't remember. I didn't make the connection when I read the note, certainly.'

'So, what did you do? Show it to someone?'

'I put it back.'

Mallory wanted to laugh. There was something so solemn about Gavin that she didn't want to mock him, but he'd done the absolute opposite of what she or, she suspected, Harri would have done. No wonder Harri wanted Gavin to tell the story to her face. It would have sounded ridiculous coming from any other person.

'Why did you put it back? OK, you've said that you sometimes find bits of paper and so on, but you were cleaning up the area. Why put it back?'

'It's part of my superstition, I suppose. Don't disturb what's gone before you. Masons are one of the oldest trades in the world and there are plenty of customs that go alongside the profession. I don't always pay any attention to them but one thing I try not to do is disturb what's already there. The note wasn't a random piece of paper. It was as if someone had made a confession. It felt unlucky just to throw it away.'

'But didn't you want to show it to someone? Surely finding an intriguing note like that you'd have wanted to show it to the archaeologist from Cadw.'

Gavin turned his gaze away. 'I didn't show it to anyone. I put it back in the place where I found it, pushing it a little further into the spaces in between the stone. When the archaeologist arrived, we lifted the cross stone between us and restored the site to its original state.'

'So how did the writer get the note there in the first place?'

Gavin sighed, taking another sip of water. 'Go and have a look at the site. It's a stone propped up against the wall. You can put your hand behind it. Whoever put it there was following a centuries-old tradition of making a confession in a place of worship. Anyone could have left the note.'

'And you never told anyone about the message?'

'This is where things get a bit hazy… I had an accident here. After weeks of unbroken sunshine, we had a few wet days. It didn't stop me working, we just needed to be more careful. I was on the roof of the south transept, which was still treacherous from the rainfall. I slipped and banged my head and had a serious bleed on the brain. My colleague noticed quickly enough and I was transferred first to hospital in Haverfordwest and then to a London specialist centre. I remember very little from that time and it's only after piecing together bits and pieces from stories my family told me that I know what went on in those first few weeks.'

'So is the story you've told me something you've just remembered or something you've pushed to the back of your mind?'

'The latter. I honestly don't think I thought of the note for the first year after my accident. I was traumatised by my situation, not helped by the fact that money was tight. It was only as I began to get back on my feet that I allowed myself to think of those days in St Davids. I began to pick over the accident and, very occasionally, I'd think of the note that I found behind the stone cross.'

'And what made you call DI Evans?'

'I saw a news report about the death of Heledd Jones and it talked about her being the mother of Huw, the boy who died. That's when I made a connection with the note, and I jumped in the car and came here.'

'Why not telephone the team?'

Gavin flushed. 'Since my head injury, things haven't really been the same. I forget words, get fatigued easily. That sort of thing. I feel sometimes I'm easy to fob off. I wanted to tell my story in person.'

Mallory could see this. 'Are you sure you've got the form of words right. We're talking about years ago.'

'Pretty sure.'

'Six lies killed Huw Jones.' Mallory looked at Gavin. 'Do you think the note might still be there?'

–

Mallory was glad to have a companion to accompany her to St Non's, as the sharp winter air and draw of the sea made her shiver in her thick coat. They walked in silence down the narrow road with the sliver of water visible in the distance. The ocean frightened Mallory, which was no surprise considering she nearly died in it last year. The swish of waves in the distance, however, had a compelling regularity to it that was reassuring and she was drawn to the sound.

Gavin had wanted to stretch his legs after the long drive from London and Mallory wasn't much inclined to drive her car down the icy road. A year ago, the mile or so walk would have been impossible to complete due to her injured leg. Only a slight limp made it obvious she wasn't completely fit but Gavin, if he noticed, didn't comment on it.

As they left the town and the shelter provided by the houses, the wind grew sharper. They put their heads down and battled on, Gavin pointing out buildings in the distance.

'The structure to the left is a retreat centre,' he said. 'It was there in 2011 but empty at the time. Next to it is the modern chapel, with its Celtic cross on the roof. We're making for the ruins to the right.'

Mallory followed Gavin down a path that led to a stone arch with a statue of a female standing inside it, her arms clasped in prayer. The religious imagery left her cold, although Gavin appeared moved.

'This is St Non's Well. It's probably what drew pilgrims here and the reason the chapel was built in such a remote spot. Just a little further to go.'

He led her to a rectangle of stones enclosed by a wooden stake fence.

'This is the original chapel?' Mallory couldn't hide her disappointment. She'd conjured up an enchanting ruin but this was little more than a pile of stones.

'Exactly that. The modern building was put up in 1934. It's a nice design but of little archaeological interest. This is where it's all happening.'

Mallory surveyed the landscape, keeping her back to the crash of the waves below.

'What's that?' She pointed to an upright rock in the distance.

'One of the standing stones, which may denote an Iron Age settlement. I told you people have visited here for centuries. Have you spotted the cross?'

Propped up against one of the corners was a roughly hewn stone. Onto its surface was etched a round circle at the top, with a long cross struck through it. Mallory, who had been used to the stunning intricacy of the cathedral's stonework, was disappointed by the rough carving and the casual way in which it had been placed into the ruined rectangle.

Gavin saw her expression and smiled. 'A cathedral is a funny place to be working if you don't appreciate the variety of church architecture. This is still a place of pilgrimage and I get a buzz when I touch the stones.'

Mallory walked across the floor of the former chapel and inserted a hand into the space behind the cross. Her fingers touched moss and rough stone. There were plenty of crevices to hide a note but she couldn't identify anything that felt non-organic.

'I don't think it's still here. Can you help me move the stone?'

'I don't think that's a good idea. What if we're spotted?'

Mallory stood and looked around. In the distance, she could see a dog walker with his back to them. The place was otherwise empty.

'Give the stone a pull and I'll search behind. It'll take five minutes max.'

Unable to hide his disapproval, Gavin pulled the slab, grasping it with both his arms.

'Hold it steady.'

Mallory bent behind the cross and began to search in the crevices where render had fallen away. 'Can you remember where the note was?'

'Third or fourth layer from the bottom, I think. Look, you hold the stone and I'll find it.'

Mallory took over from him and watched his tall frame bend over the stonework. He used his long fingers to burrow deep into the fissures but shook his head.

'It's gone. I've looked in every possible place. Someone has found it.'

'Found it?' Mallory helped Gavin replace the stone. 'It's not something you just find, is it?'

'Why not? I did.'

Mallory wasn't so sure. If it was a tourist rooting around then it was likely to be lost forever. But surely if you found a note with that message, a quick internet search would identify who Huw Jones was and the tragic fate that had befallen him? If it had been her, she was pretty sure she'd have handed over the note to the police. The fact that nothing of the sort had been received suggested another possibility. That the note, assuming it existed, had been discovered by someone who knew exactly what the message meant and its removal was to ensure no one else read its contents.

Frustrated, Mallory left Gavin, who was checking they hadn't damaged the cross with their investigations. She was inexorably drawn to the sound of the waves beneath them but the height of the cliffs made her head spin. She concentrated instead on what a place like this might feel like to a three-year-old out in the dark. To her ears, the noise of the sea sounded nothing like mermaids singing, as much as you could conjure up the sound of an imaginary creature. If Heledd was such a good storyteller, however, perhaps she'd given the rasp of the waves a different meaning. St Non's was, as far as Mallory was concerned, a miserable place to die.

Gavin joined her and together they looked at the jagged rocks below them. 'You do believe me, don't you?'

Mallory kept her expression neutral. Did she believe Gavin's story? She didn't think he was a fantasist who had made up the existence of the note but she had to be mindful that he was the victim of a head injury. He might have in some way skewed the message in his mind in the years after the accident. If she were still a copper, she'd want stronger proof of the note's existence before she set the hare running, but it did fit into the role Harri had asked her to undertake. She was to look again at the death of Huw Jones and key to that would be the movements of the six people in the house from which he'd disappeared.

'I believe you.' She saw he looked relieved.

'Have I helped your investigation or made things more difficult?' he asked her.

Mallory pushed her hands deeper into her coat pockets. 'I'm having trouble getting my head around it all. It sounds fantastical. You seriously find these sorts of things occasionally in the buildings you work on?'

'Now and then, yes. You know, stone has a special place for us masons. We work with it, fashion it to our designs and use the fabric to pass on our own message. Have you ever heard of a mason's mark?'

Mallory frowned. 'Not really but I assume it's where you put some kind of signature on the stonework.'

'Exactly, but it can have all kinds of meaning. It can simply be to tell people you were involved in the building of a particular edifice, but a mason might want to make a mark for superstitious reasons or to give an apology to a divine spirit. Whoever wrote the note might have been offloading their repressed emotion... What's the matter?'

He'd noticed her frustration. While she'd need to consider the motivation of the writer of the note, it wasn't something she wanted to go into now. Instead, she wanted to tell him that life would have been much easier if he'd told the police about the note when he first discovered it hidden behind the cross. By leaving it *in situ*, if Heledd had discovered the note's existence or at least its contents, he might have unwittingly set in motion a chain of events that had led to her winding up dead in a field. And that was very hard to stomach.

10

Harri's alarm went off just as his son was coming home from his night out. He staggered out of bed and went down into the kitchen to turn on the kettle, his mouth parched. Ben had his head in the fridge and was rooting around its contents.

'Bloody hell. You seriously just got in? What've you been doing out on a night like this?'

Ben withdrew his head and frowned at him. 'Dad, there's nothing in here to eat.'

'There's bread in the bin. Make yourself some toast. Auntie Fran will be going shopping today.'

Ben groaned. 'She never gets me what I want. It's all stuff I have to cook. What about when I'm hungry like now?'

'If she bought you the junk food you want, it'd be demolished in an evening. The shop's got to last us a week. Think of the cost of living.'

Harri pulled a jumper over his head. Ben had let in the cold when he'd slipped in through the back door. He watched as his son stuck a couple of slices of bread in the toaster, yawning as he scratched his neck. Like most of his friends, Ben didn't drink alcohol. Harri, who'd spent most of his teens and early twenties with his face in a pint of lager, couldn't understand why the next generation didn't drink. Drugs were more popular but Ben said he

69

didn't touch them either, and Harri had seen enough addicts to believe him. He wondered what he and his friends did all night but didn't like to ask; the camaraderie between the pair of them meant more to Harri than the need to pry into his son's affairs.

Ben, as if suddenly aware of the hour, gave his dad a closer look. 'What you doing up so early?'

'A body was discovered yesterday. It was on the news – a Heledd Jones. Did you see it?'

'Haven't seen the news for a few days, Dad.'

Ben was putting enough butter on his bread to make a swimming pool in the middle of the slice.

'It doesn't matter. She was involved in an old case and some people in the area will be talking about it.'

'Hmm.' Ben's eyes were closed as he savoured the toast.

'When you wake up, will you do something with your sister while Fran goes to the supermarket?'

'Like what? Ellie will want to go round the shops and I'm not spending the afternoon in Claire's Accessories.'

Harri reached in his pocket. 'Take her out for lunch or something. Watch out for cars, because people who drive like idiots don't suddenly change their behaviour in the snow. Despite the weather, I'd rather you were out and about than at home.'

Ben looked at the two twenty-pound notes Harri had left on the counter. 'What's wrong? You're not normally like this.'

Harri thought of a little boy lying beneath a cliff while parties in the town above him carried on regardless. If he'd lived, Huw Jones would be only a little younger than Ben and maybe the life of his mother, Heledd, would have been different.

'Just take her out, would you?'

–

Harri had a shower and called the Family Liaison Officer sitting with Becca Jones, Heledd's sister, who confirmed that she was up and dressed. Harri took his car and drove it out of town, wishing he'd invested in better tyres. There were few vehicles on the road so at least he didn't have to contend with the county's idiots, but the driving conditions made for a stomach-clenching journey. Passing through a village, he saw a lone dog walker whose pet didn't look best pleased to be out in this weather, the movement of its paws reminding him of a circus pony. At a bend near Carew, his car went into a skid. He was driving slowly enough but he heard the crumple of the metal of his front wing panel as it hit a tree. Swearing, he got out and saw a dent that would need beating out, but no serious damage had been done. He reversed slowly and carried on.

Felin Wen, the woollen mill Becca owned, was down a narrow driveway that had been gritted with impressive efficiency. The white building came into view and the front door opened at the sound of his approach. A tall man with a beard, the FLO, waited for him to arrive.

'Had an accident?' The man was looking at his car, probably worried about his own trip home.

'Don't ask. How is she?'

'Generally fine. She's shocked and upset but funda-mentally OK. She hasn't been to bed, although I did try to persuade her to get some sleep. There was no way I was driving home in the dark in this weather.'

'When did your shift finish?'

The FLO looked at his watch. 'I should have left two hours ago but it's fine. I knew it was going to be a long one when I drove over here. If it starts snowing again, I'd get going or you'll be spending the week here.'

'You can get off now. I'll talk to Becca and make sure she's OK before I go. Anything of interest you want to tell me?'

'She's worried that Heledd took her own life. She'd been threatening it for years but Heledd had changed in the last six months. For the better, I would say, so there's a discrepancy between Becca's concern that Heledd died by her own hand and the fact she was looking and feeling better. One to probe. I couldn't get to the bottom of it.'

'Thanks.'

'The flat is up the stone stairs to the left of the entrance. It's got a sign marked private at the bottom.'

Harri grabbed the rail as he trudged up the steps, his energy deserting him. The door led straight onto a vaulted living room with a thick brown carpet. On a plaid sofa sat a large woman in her early forties with burgundy dyed hair who bore little resemblance to her sister.

'Who are you?' she asked.

'DI Harri Evans, the senior investigating officer for Heledd's death.'

'Bit important to be seeing me, aren't you?'

Harri smiled and took a seat opposite the woman. She wore a knitted jumper with a sort of hatching at the bottom. Fran, a mean knitter, would have known what the proper name for the pattern was.

'Are you planning to open the mill today?'

'I think, given the circumstances, I can shut it this weekend. I'm not someone who can just put on a show. Customers aren't going to like seeing me with reddened eyes.'

'You know, news of Heledd's death will be around the community by now. You might have to put up with some intrusive questions when you open up again.'

'I'm ready for that. Used to it, let's say. It's been the same since 2011.'

'I thought I should warn you.' Harri looked round for the door to the kitchen. 'Can I make you something to drink?'

'I've had endless cups of tea. What do you want?'

'I've read your statement and I have a few questions to ask you. Can I just clarify a few things?'

She gave him a sharp glance and settled back in her chair, picking up her knitting. 'All right.' A dog padded into the room, a small border terrier, and settled himself in front of the fire.

'You say in the statement that you saw Heledd about a month ago in Pembroke and that this was unusual, as she rarely made it out of Penterry.'

'Rarely, as in never. Every time I wanted to see her, I'd have to drive up to Penterry, unless she was in hospital, that is. Then it'd be an even longer trip to Haverfordwest.'

'She was in hospital a lot?'

'Every couple of years or so she would be admitted to a psychiatric unit there.'

'Were you involved in the decision to section her?'

'Never. She was under the supervision of the community mental health team and it was them who'd make the call, usually after a crisis.'

Becca sounded weary, after a lifetime of waiting for a phone call to say Heledd's issues had started all over again.

'Did you know we still had Jack Jones as Heledd's next of kin?'

Becca put down her needles. 'No but it doesn't surprise me. I mean, Heledd had nothing to do with the police, as far as I was aware, since Huw's death. How were you to know she and Jack had divorced? With the hospital, it was a different matter. I insisted they call me if there were problems.'

'You say you saw her in Pembroke around a month ago. Was it planned?'

'Not at all. I was down there meeting a client. I had a commission for ten blankets for a new complex of self-catering cottages near Brecon. Money no object. We met in Pembroke to discuss designs and afterwards I went for a walk around town. I saw Heledd in a cafe and was shocked at how well she looked.'

'Did she say why she was in Pembroke? Do you have any thoughts why she might have been coming into town?'

Becca shrugged. 'I think there was a man involved.'

'Why do you say that?'

'She had on a new dress and had cut her hair short. It suited her. She looked, for once, like she wasn't a victim.' Becca laughed. 'I guessed she'd started seeing someone.'

'Did you ask her about him?'

'God, no. Heledd was touchy at the best of times. Ever since Huw died, she'd kind of withdrawn into herself. We had a fragile relationship at the best of times and I'd do anything not to jeopardise any truce. I just told her she was looking nice and she was pleased with the comment. We had a coffee together and I offered her a lift back but she said she had her own car with her.'

'You've no idea who she might have met?'

'None whatsoever.' Harri saw a fraction of hesitation. Not enough for him to pounce on, but it was there.

'Can we go back to Huw's death? There was an investigation which essentially held up the truthfulness of both Heledd's and Jack's accounts. There was a very short period when Huw might have got himself out of bed and wandered down the street, possibly looking for his mother.'

Harri saw Becca was shaking her head. 'You don't agree with it.'

'I agree that Heledd had nothing to do with Huw's accident. I'm not so sure about Jack. He and that group of friends of his caused Heledd a lot of anguish. They seem honest enough but what do I know? When it came to repercussions, they made sure it was Heledd who got all the flak.'

'You're saying they were involved in the rumours that portrayed Heledd as a neglectful mother?'

'They didn't do much to defend her. The big sin was that for the first time in years, she went to that party by herself. Huw was a beautiful boy, with fair hair and huge blue eyes. He was fractious, though. He'd had a lot of tantrums when he was two and three, and Heledd was worn out.'

'It's a common age for these things to happen.'

'Right, and Heledd and Jack knew that. They were waiting for the difficult years to pass. The thing is, what Huw would have done if he'd woken up and realised his mother wasn't there was throw a wobbler. You'd have been able to hear his shrieks across the road.'

'It was New Year's Eve.'

'And I'm telling you that boy had a pair of lungs on him. If you don't believe me, fair enough. No one else did but I'm telling you Huw would not have opened the

75

front door and walked down the street without hollering for help.'

A wave of nausea washed over Harri. What the hell was wrong with him? He got up and looked out of the window. The snow was coming down in fat lumps. It'd be hard work getting to HQ today and he certainly didn't want to get stuck there. He hoped the duty pathologist could get to the hospital to undertake the autopsy, otherwise he could add that to his list of headaches. He turned his attention back to Becca and asked the question he was sure would bring him no joy. Everyone had a view on Huw Jones's disappearance so he might as well hear his aunt's thoughts.

'So, what do you think happened the night Huw went missing?'

'I don't know but I think one of those six had a hand in his disappearance.'

'Their alibis checked out.'

Becca gazed at him, her expression full of disappointment. It irritated Harri, who had seen that look before. A member of the public telling him their theory despite no evidence whatsoever to back it up.

'It is possible he walked down to the sea on his own.'

'Why? Why does he do that? He wakes up and looks, presumably, for his mother. She's out but his father is in the living room. So why doesn't he go to him? You're trying to tell me that, instead, he opens the door and deliberately heads towards St Non's. What I want to know, and it's the question I've asked time and time again, is why did he do that? The conclusion I come to is that he didn't.'

Stumped for an answer, Harri kept quiet. Becca had thrown her knitting to one side and stood, brushing down her skirt.

'Heledd's dead and she finally doesn't have to listen to the sly whispers about her leaving Huw on his own, when it was Jack who was the neglectful parent.'

'Isn't neglect a little strong? Jack thought Huw was safely tucked up in bed. It sounds like a tragic accident.'

Becca ignored the comment and continued, 'You know what the strangest thing was about the whole thing?'

'What?' asked Harri.

'The people who were the nastiest to my sister were those at the party at Eleri Tew's, where they saw with their own eyes that Heledd was always in plain sight. Imagine that. The people who know you to be innocent are your worst accusers.'

11

Mallory was exhausted by four o'clock. She could understand the need to keep the cathedral open during the
day but the shop had taken barely any money and her
hour's absence had gone unnoticed. She picked her way
across the cathedral precinct, spotting Bethan outside on
the snow-covered lawn making a phone call under a light
thrown by a yellow streetlamp. She had her hood pulled
up, as Mallory had seen her the evening before, and her
voice was raised, although her words were indistinguish-
able. She ignored Mallory, which was fine by her. She
needed to formulate a strategy to consider each of the six
friends in light of Gavin's revelations. She still hadn't quite
worked out how she was going to treat the story of the
note and she needed time to think. Annoyingly, Gavin
had proved to be difficult to get rid of after their visit to
St Non's, wanting to linger around the cathedral. She'd
been saved by her single customer of the day and, as she'd
turned her attention to his request, Gavin had disappeared.

Mallory had made it to the top of the hill when her
phone shrilled in the bitter evening air. Thinking it was
her son, she reached into her pocket.

'It's me, Harri. I'm sitting in the bar in the Grove Hotel.
Want to meet me here? I have the witness statements for
you.'

'You brought them yourself?'

'I've discovered we're not allowed to send them to an external email address. Until you have one of ours, it's hard copy only.'

'Give me ten minutes. It's slow going up the hill.'

Mallory's leg injury throbbed as she slipped and shuffled to the hotel. She hadn't been inside the building before – drinking alone wasn't really her thing – but the bar was a blast of warmth when she flung open the door. Harri was sitting in the corner, watching the entrance for her arrival. Mallory had pegged him as a man who drank pints, he looked the type, but he nursed a single gin and tonic as he listened to Mallory's account of the visit to St Non's.

'Think he's a reliable witness?' asked Harri.

Mallory picked up her glass of white wine. 'To be honest, I'm not sure. The tale rings true, at least in his own mind. I don't think he's giving us the runaround but I'm not sure about his recall. I don't think, for example, his account would stand up in court. We really need more evidence that the note actually exists. I think that's why he was disappointed the message wasn't still there. I think he was expecting me to doubt his story.'

'I wish he'd come to us sooner.'

Mallory shrugged. She agreed with him but not everybody ran to the police every time something odd happened to them. Harri must know that too.

'Are you going to proceed on the basis that the note, wherever it may be now, contained a germ of truth?' asked Harri. 'That all six friends in Y Bwthyn lied and that one of them, for reasons that aren't clear, wrote a note and shoved it in a bunch of stones.'

Mallory smiled. 'You have a way with words, you know. We're talking about a centuries-old tradition of leaving notes, confessions if you like, in religious buildings. According to Gavin, it's a worldwide phenomenon and not just for Christians. Think of prayers left in the Western Wall in Jerusalem. St Non's was a place of pilgrimage and, while travellers often leave stones along the way to symbolise shedding their burden, a message written on paper might serve the same purpose.'

'So, you *do* think it was there.'

Mallory sighed. 'I'm keeping an open mind. What I want to do is see those statements.'

Harri pushed over a buff-coloured folder.

'There you go. Something to read this evening. The accounts of six paragons of virtue who never put a foot wrong, if you believe their statements. Read them again, set against the message Gavin found, and you might come up with something different.'

Mallory resisted the temptation to open the folder and begin looking through the accounts. Harri's mind was still on the message.

'If the note's genuine, I wonder who wrote it. Got any ideas?'

'Harri, I know hardly anything about the six friends. Let me look through the statements and then ask me again. The question is not only if the message exists, but what relevance it has to Heledd's death. That's why I'm being brought onto the team, isn't it?'

'I've been doing some thinking.' Harri stared at his glass and made a face. 'I don't like this idea of a note that's no longer there. It's giving me three possible scenarios. First, we're talking about the St Davids headland and it's blustery even in the summer. A wind could have dislodged the note and it's been lost to the sea.'

'It's a possibility, but Gavin says he put it back deep into the stonework and then covered it with the cross. I don't think that's what happened.'

'The second possibility is that it was found by anyone, perhaps someone who was going to place a note of their own into the space behind the cross. For whatever reason, it was kept or discarded without the owner realising its significance.'

'Again, it's a possibility and if that's the case then there's nothing we can do.'

'The third scenario is that Heledd removed the note.'

Mallory felt her head begin to ache. 'Which means that someone must have told her of its existence. It's not something you discover by chance. Gavin says he's never discussed it with anyone so the only other person who knew of its location was the writer of the message.'

'One of the six.'

'Exactly. The message says "all six of *us*". One of the six was the writer and that person might have told Heledd.'

'Maybe,' said Harri, 'but it's not making any sense. Why reveal the whereabouts of the note? Why not just visit Heledd and tell her to her face that all six of them told a lie the evening Huw died?'

'Maybe the writer wanted to maintain their anonymity. If Heledd discovered the note, perhaps she was given a tip-off.'

Harri didn't look happy with her explanation and she couldn't blame him. It was just too tenuous. Until she started her investigation, they were simply speculating. She had little insight into the personalities involved and, again, it was the statements that would help.

'Let me read the witness statements first. Then what about me getting in touch with the six?'

'I'm speaking to HR in the morning and I've the go-ahead to get the contract to you as soon as we can. We're pushing this through fast. You're a civilian investigator, which will open some doors for you but not all. Please don't contact Eleri Tew. Leave her to me and Siân.'

'Any of the five you want me to look at first?'

'Start with Jack Jones. He's playing ball at the moment because he's on holiday with a cast-iron alibi for Heledd's death. Once he's back at work, he'll be harder to get hold of.' Harri picked up his G and T and drained the glass. 'He's also an experienced solicitor. He won't be worried at coming up against a civilian investigator so his defences will be down. See if you can unpick his statement. If we find a chink in the facts as laid out by him, it might give us an inkling that the writer of the note was telling the truth.'

Harri dropped Mallory at her apartment and hurried off. She sat at the living-room table and opened the file, without taking off her coat. Inside there were seven typed transcripts – those of the six friends who had been in Y Bwthyn and Heledd's own account of her movements that evening. Nothing more. There would, of course, have been many more interviews. Fellow partygoers who could corroborate statements, citizens of St Davids who had seen something, or more worryingly nothing. Harri either hadn't had permission to give her these or, more likely, wanted her to concentrate on the accounts of the key players. He had already told her that the investigative team had been unable to disprove the accounts of the six.

Mallory started with Heledd Jones's statement, which she thought would be the most difficult read. She slipped down the rabbit hole to a time when the Black Eyed Peas were in the charts and David Cameron was prime minister. It felt like yesterday and she had to remind herself that twelve years earlier, Toby had been a toddler, and she and Joe had been discussing having another baby.

The statement made her head ache. Police language had its own style and it was sometimes hard to unpick the emotions underneath the bald facts. Heledd had been at pains to emphasise she hadn't really wanted to go to the party and had been glad to return home. Her horror at the realisation that Huw was no longer in the house was still palpable, along with her conviction that he was likely to have headed for St Non's. She was sure that Huw had taken himself off and said he'd occasionally done so in the past. Heledd clearly blamed herself for the accident. She'd told her son stories about mermaids from St Non's, gargoyles coming to life on the cathedral wall and hidden people who lived in tree hollows. Huw had apparently loved all the tales but the one he wanted to hear over and over again was the story of the mermaids.

She appeared to bear no ill will towards Jack and his five friends, blaming herself for going to the party when she'd have rather been at home. It made difficult reading and the only comment that jarred was that Heledd had thought there was an air of intrigue about the evening.

Mallory moved on to the statement from Heledd's husband, Jack Jones, frowning as she read it through. She detected in Jack more than a whiff of her own ex in the tone he'd adopted in his statement. There was no admission that having a mini party at his own house wasn't a particularly good idea, with a sleeping child upstairs. He was a lawyer, of course, and Mallory wondered what it must have felt like being questioned as a potential suspect.

It didn't appear to have done his career any harm, if Harri was correct. He'd progressed from a provincial solicitor to a partner in one of Cardiff's top practices.

Going through the statements, Mallory was struck by how confident each of the friends was about their absolute right to be in the Jones's house. It suggested an arrogance born out of an expensive education and social status. Eleri Tew, of course, had since become a renowned MP, while Gruffydd and Bethan were connected to the cathedral, the former as a member of the clergy. She picked up her mobile and googled Duncan Lyall. He was a prominent tour operator in West Wales, a successful businessman. His LinkedIn profile showed a perma-tanned man in his thirties with an insincere smile. Gemma Bowen – the final statement that Mallory looked at – said in her account of the evening that she was a trainee doctor. A quick Google search found a Pembrokeshire GP of that name. Six friends with respectable jobs. Mallory wondered how much that had played into the ease with which the police accepted their version of events.

Mallory jotted down a timeline of the events that night.

4:00 p.m. Heledd leaves Y Bwthyn for the party (Jack Jones alone with Huw)

4:10 p.m. Duncan and Gruffydd leave party for Y Bwthyn (Jack, Duncan & Gruffydd in the house)

4:40 p.m. Gemma arrives at Y Bwthyn

4:45 p.m. Bethan arrives at Y Bwthyn

4:50 p.m. Duncan and Gruffydd leave for off-licence (Jack, Gemma and Bethan remain)

5:05 p.m. Eleri arrives at Y Bwthyn (Jack, Gemma, Bethan and Eleri in the house)

5:05 p.m. Duncan and Gruffydd return (all six now present)

5:30 p.m. Heledd returns to find Huw gone

Mallory guessed her timeline must resemble that of the original investigators. It threw up nothing of significance. One by one, the friends had drifted over to Y Bwthyn and enjoyed what must have been the last carefree New Year of their lives. From then on, the celebration would have a particularly grim association. Mallory's stomach began to rumble; she needed to put the statements to one side and concentrate on her domestic arrangements.

Her son, Toby, was coming to visit the next morning and she needed to get the place ready for his arrival. She'd taken the flat because, in addition to the main bedroom, it came with a box room big enough to put in a single bed and chest of drawers. It wasn't ideal but it was better than her sleeping on the sofa when he came to stay. A Christmas get-together had been difficult to arrange. Mallory had been busy with her new job and she was too remote for Toby to visit for a day or two. It had been agreed that she'd have him for a week in half-term, although plans had been finalised before she'd realised she'd be helping the police investigate an unexplained death. She decided to stay shtum about it when she spoke with her ex. Although a copper himself, he never understood those who left the force but remained on its periphery. For Joe, once you were out, you were out.

Mallory made up the bed and waited for the supermarket delivery packed with food that Toby liked to eat. The company had assured her they'd be able to get through this evening. She left the front light on to guide the driver to the doorstep, her mind still worrying away at the events of 2011. On the surface, it seemed an easy case to take on. Events firmly in the past but what tangle of secrets was she about to unravel? Not so long ago she'd put her life in danger trying to get to the bottom of a decades old mystery, and accepting a case when Toby was about to visit was foolhardy at best. With a sigh, Mallory sat down and began to read through her notes again.

12

Joe, Mallory's ex-husband, insisted on driving Toby all the way to St Davids, although he could easily have got the train as far as Carmarthen. It didn't bode well. Joe clearly had something on his mind but he'd declined to join them for lunch, saying he'd have a walk around St Davids to stretch his legs before driving back home.

Mallory sat in the pub and watched as Toby picked at his hot dog, extracting the pickles and grilled mushrooms he'd specifically requested as extra toppings. She quelled a surge of irritation at his fussiness, as she remembered her own mother complaining about her pickiness. What goes around comes around, thought Mallory. She took a swig of her Coke and looked out of the window. The snow was in that strange stasis when temperatures were too cold for a thaw but no fresh flurries were forecast. It felt as if time was standing still, waiting for something to happen, and Mallory suspected Toby would be bored stiff during his time here.

'It'll be good to have you in the flat. You'll like the room I've made up for you. There's also a surprise waiting for you when you get home.'

Toby stuck out his bottom lip. 'You'll be working, though, won't you? At the cathedral. Are you taking any time off?'

'Of course.' Definitely not the time to reveal details of her other job. 'I'm going to organise a coach trip so we can see the peninsula together. Then, while I'm at work, you can explore the place on your own.'

Toby stopped playing with his food. 'I'll find something to do with my time.'

He put down the mangled hot dog and began to shred his fries. He had the same long fingers as Mallory, but the skin stretched over them was almost translucent. She watched as he began to decimate the food. Aware of the fragility of the connection between them, Mallory ploughed on.

'You can have a look around the cathedral. I've had to study the history of the place and it's got some interesting stories.'

His face adopted a scornful look. She supposed, for Toby, her job was a comedown, from detective to tourist guide. 'It's only temporary, don't forget. Maybe in the summer, I can think of getting something more permanent. Perhaps you can spend next Christmas with me.'

'I want to spend Christmas with Dad.' Toby's voice was flat but his fingers continued to work the fries.

'Of course. Boxing Day perhaps.' Mallory was careful to keep the hurt out of her voice. 'All I'm saying is that I could make sure I'm not working next Christmas.'

Toby nodded and pushed away his plate. 'Shall we say bye to Dad? He said he'd be back around two.'

'Sure,' said Mallory, trying to ignore the pinch of anxiety on her son's face. Plans for both her and Joe were loose arrangements and she was surprised to discover that their son kept time to the minute.

They stood on the corner of the high street as they waited for Joe to arrive. Toby's baseball jacket hung off his bony shoulders and he shivered in the cold.

'There's Dad.'

Mallory followed Toby's gaze and saw Joe's Range Rover mount the pavement, ignoring the double yellow lines. She suspected he hadn't gone for a walk but had idled in the car while she and Toby ate lunch. Anything to avoid sharing a table with her. Mallory turned to give them some privacy – Joe wouldn't want to talk to her – but she heard the window being wound down. 'Hold on a minute.'

Mallory tensed as Toby gave her a surprised look. Joe opened the car door. He pulled out his wallet from his back pocket and gave Toby a ten-pound note.

'Go and get me a sandwich from that deli, Tobe. I'm starving. Just a plain ham roll, nothing extra on it.'

Toby, eager to please, took the proffered note and disappeared into the small shop opposite the pub. Some of Joe's cheer disappeared with Toby, but not all.

'How are you doing, Mallory?'

Mallory shrugged. 'Better, thanks. You?'

Joe made a face, not looking at her. 'All right. How was lunch with Toby?'

'It was fine. You know how it is.'

Joe looked at the floor. 'He's become very insular recently. I don't know what the matter is but he doesn't talk to me either so don't take it personally.'

'He looks like he's lost weight.'

'I think he's redistributed it. His arms and legs have become muscular. He lifts weights in his bedroom and he's started jogging.'

'Jogging?' Do teenagers jog? she wondered. 'If that's something he's interested in, maybe he could join an athletics club.'

'I offered to buy him gym membership but he wasn't keen. He's at that difficult age where he doesn't know what he wants.'

Mallory looked across the road. Through the deli window, she saw Toby had ordered and was waiting for the sandwich to be prepared. He was looking at them both, his face anxious in the reflected glass.

'Look, I'll keep an eye on him,' said Mallory. 'Teenagers don't talk to their parents. Is there something more specific you're worried about? I mean, exercise is a good thing, isn't it?'

Joe shrugged. 'He's changed in the last few months. You saw him on that island last autumn. He was fine then. Your escapades got him a bit of notoriety at school. He seemed to bask in it. Now he hardly says anything. Can you see if you can work out what's wrong?'

Mallory nodded. 'I'll try. I've taken as much time off as I can from work and I'll make sure he doesn't spend all his time online.'

'Couldn't take the whole week off?'

'I'm sorry. I'm relatively new in the role. I'm doing what I can.'

'Doing what you can? It's always about you, isn't it, Mallory?'

Mallory made an effort to keep her temper. 'I don't think that's exactly fair, is it? When we split up, Toby wanted to live with you and I could see why that might be best for him. That's hardly making it about me. What more do you want from me? I have to get on with my life and earn a living,'

'The custody arrangements are that he can stay with you every weekend. Or he could do, if you lived nearer.'

'But he didn't want to, did he? That was the point. He never wanted to visit. You expect me to live my life waiting for the odd Saturday when Toby actually wants to see me? What do you want me to do for the other hundred and sixty hours in the week?'

'You could come back to London anyway. There are jobs there.'

'None that I want to do.' She pointed to her leg. 'I'm not exactly employable.'

'You know your problem? You can never forgive people's failings. Not even your own.'

Mallory took a step back. 'Don't take your anger about Toby out on me. Whatever the problem is, if it's to do with the divorce, we're both equally to blame.'

13

Harri was off duty on Saturday but finding it impossible to relax. Becca Jones's worry that Heledd's death was due to an act of suicide might be a conviction genuinely held but didn't ring true. Harri suspected that the root of this belief was that Becca had seen Heledd at her lowest, following the death of Huw. But it was Becca who had said that Heledd was looking better in recent weeks, and Heledd had presumably spent the evening with someone. The post-mortem was taking place that morning but unless the pathologist found something immediately suspicious, they'd be waiting for further tests. Piecing together Heledd's movements in the days before her death would be key. He hoped he wasn't sending Mallory on a wild goose chase by asking her to focus on Gavin Lavine's story and everything that happened twelve years earlier.

He tried to remember what he'd actually been doing in December 2011, but the whole period was a blur. Paula had died in the October of that year and the priority had been to sort out his home life so he could continue to work and support the family. Fran hadn't needed much persuasion to leave her job in Cardiff and come to Pembroke. He remembered his surprise when he learnt she was planning to live with them rather than buy a house nearby. It made sense, of course, and suited him fine. It meant he didn't have to call her to pick up the kids or make arrangements when he needed to stay late at the office. She was always there for the children but it had put paid to any privacy or love interest Fran might have had. He watched her making coffee.

'A day for staying indoors,' she said, looking out of the window. 'Will you be all right?'

She knew him well enough to appreciate his restlessness at the enforced inactivity.

'I might ring round to see if any garages are open. The front of my car took a battering yesterday.'

'On a Saturday?' She sat opposite him. 'Save your phone calls until Monday, when everything's open. I've seen the damage and the car's still driveable. Do you want to chat about the case?'

He shrugged. 'What's there to say? The tragedy feels both close by and removed. I mean, I never actually met Heledd in real life.'

'True, although it's a case of six degrees of separation or, more relevant for round here, probably two degrees. I mean, you're going to find links everywhere. I used to work with Jack Jones, for example.'

Harri sat back and regarded his sister. 'You did? I don't recall you mentioning that.'

'Why would I? He joined my old practice in 2012 and at first, I couldn't work out how I knew his face. Then a colleague told me about the tragedy involving his son.'

'What was the feeling about him? I mean, did he ever speak about what happened?'

'Of course not. I used to talk to him occasionally but only to pass the time of day. I certainly don't have anything to add to your investigation. In any case, I left shortly afterwards to come here. He's doing very well in my old firm, but then you probably know all that.'

'You haven't kept in touch with him?' Harri reached over and pinched a slice of toast from his sister's plate.

'On and off over the years mainly through mutual friends. I sent him an email last year when I heard he was getting remarried. I had an invitation to the evening reception but I didn't fancy it. It was when July was at its hottest, if you remember. The thought of being in a boiling room crammed with people didn't appeal.'

'Know anything about his new wife?'

'Only that she's French and he met her on a skiing holiday. I was glad he'd found happiness again. Is he out of the frame for Heledd's death?'

'He was in his French chalet all week and it all checks out.'

'No reason for him to kill his ex-wife, anyway, is there?'

Harri made a face.

'Why the shrug?'

'Heledd, we think, had started seeing someone. Why not her ex? It does happen.'

'I think you'll find Jack's gone up in the world since his St Davids days. I've heard his new wife is just what you'd expect from one of Cardiff's top solicitors. You're barking up the wrong tree there, I think.'

'Sure,' said Harri, who still had his doubts. Old bonds and allegiances could be hard to break. He was saved from continuing this conversation by the sound of his mobile ringing. Fran raised her eyebrows as she passed his phone to him.

'Hello.'

'It's me, boss. The PM has just taken place and the pathologist says results are inconclusive, just as you

94

thought, boss. We'll be waiting back on histology and toxicology work and—'

'Don't tell me, they're short-staffed. Did they even give you an approximate time frame when we might know more?'

'Sorry but, you know, fourteen days is realistic. She doesn't think it's suspicious.'

'Who? The pathologist?'

'No, my mother.'

Harri glanced across at Fran, resisting the temptation to laugh.

'She's treating the death as unexplained but told me it looks like suicide. Smell of alcohol coming off the organs. She thinks there'll be traces of diazepam or maybe temazepam in the bloods.'

'So Heledd, what, gets drunk and decides to kill herself, taking herself to a remote field to do so?'

'I know it doesn't sound right, boss, and I've got something that might interest you. We've just had an ID on the car we think might have dropped Heledd Jones at Haverfordwest station. You know we were looking at nearby cameras to see if any of the registrations fitted known acquaintances of Heledd. Well, one blue Mercedes was captured driving towards the station at quarter to eight. Male driver and there's a passenger in the front that looks like a woman. The car is registered to Duncan Lyall. Ring any bells?'

Harri stood, wiping his clammy hands on his trousers. 'Of course. Duncan Lyall was one of the people at the house the night Huw Jones disappeared.'

'Exactly. Do you want to come with me to the interview? He's a big noise round here and might open up to someone higher up in authority.'

Harri snorted. 'Are you ill?' Siân liked to conduct interviews, said she was good at them and Harri was inclined to agree. She was more than capable of handling Duncan Lyall, whatever his status might be in polite society.

'All right, I'll do it myself.' Siân's tone was icy. She liked to give it but wasn't always able to take Harri's jokes.

'Don't be daft. Let me grab my coat.' He cut the call and finished his coffee in a gulp.

Fran looked in distaste at the trench coat he was shrugging on. 'You're not going out in that, are you?'

'What do you mean? You don't like my mac?'

'Have you seen what the weather's doing? That won't keep you warm.'

'It's a house visit not a trip to the Antarctic.' Harri thought of the dent in the side of his car. 'As I've been invited along to keep up appearances, I think I'd better borrow your car.'

14

Toby's eyes widened when he saw his late Christmas present.

'PlayStation 5.' He stroked the box as if it was a cat. 'I've been on at Dad to get me one of these but he said my PS4 was still good.'

'I've got the TV that is the most compatible with the technology.' Mallory pointed at the widescreen monstrosity that dominated the room. It had taken the handyman a good hour to get it fixed to the wall. 'I bought it at the same time, as part of a deal. Cost me an arm and a leg but I reckon I can take it with me when I move.'

'I need some games.'

Mallory brandished two presents inexpertly wrapped. 'They can get you started. If you get bored or finish them, we can order some online. OK?'

'Thanks, Mum.' Toby grinned at her and she saw how thin his face had got. It was good to see him smile, though, and he'd relaxed once his father had left. Mallory would have to dig a little into that relationship at some point in the coming week without appearing to criticise Joe. She didn't want to put Toby on the defensive.

'Um, I got it all installed but don't ask me about setting it up because I've no idea. You need to add your account or something.'

He had the console in his hand. 'I got it.'

97

Mallory left him and opened her laptop. At least she'd earned herself some brownie points by buying him the PlayStation. Long may it last. She typed out an email to Jack Jones, introducing herself and asking if she'd be able to talk to him. Given he was a solicitor, there was no way she could fudge her current status as a nearly employed civilian investigator. She openly admitted she was waiting to sign her contract but she'd appreciate a general chat about the night Huw died to see if it bore any connection to Heledd's death. Mallory hoped the reference to Heledd would put his mind at rest. He had an alibi for that one. With the email sent, she looked at the other names on the list. If all the friends were still in touch, and she knew Bethan and Gruffydd were, then once Jack received the email, there was always the possibility that he would forewarn the group. By the time she came to interview them all, they'd have got their stories straight.

Mallory sat back in her chair and thought about Gavin Lavine and the note. If she were to start with the presumption that all six lied, then the lies might have been co-ordinated. If that were the case, then she'd never get to the root of the note.

Perhaps there was another way. If she could identify one lie, that might give validity to both the existence of the note and its contents. If one person lied then perhaps it was true of all of them. She picked up the folder of witness statements and regarded the list of names on the front.

Duncan Lyall was a local tour operator. Although if she bought herself a place on one of his tours, he wasn't going to be driving the actual bus, she might still be able to get some gossip about him from the driver. She opened the

Lyall's Tours website and looked for something that might entertain Toby.

'Do you fancy looking for seals while you're here? I could book us a tour if you fancy it.'

'If you like.' He sounded distracted, concentrating on the screen that was showing an update patch download.

Mallory raised her eyebrows. Progress. She booked two tickets for a mid-week tour, noting that capacity was limited. Duncan's business was going well. She looked at the next name on the list. The two friends connected to the cathedral presented more difficulties. Bethan Rees she knew, which didn't help much, as the woman was tight as a clam. Gruffydd Ellis lived in a nearby parish but she might be able to catch him at the cathedral. He'd at least been friendly to her the night she'd heard of Heledd's death. Eleri Tew was out of bounds, which was a shame, as she fancied meeting the woman with the frozen face. Gemma Bowen was a GP, which gave her an idea. She clicked on the medical practice website and downloaded a new patient form. Since her move to Wales, she'd not bothered registering with a GP. The last few years had been filled with hospital appointments, first because of the injuries sustained in the line of duty and then after her poisoning on Eldey. Coughs and colds, she was willing to put up with. She filled in as much of the form as she could and made a note of the practice opening times. On Monday, she'd make an appointment to see Gemma Bowen.

She was about to shut down her laptop when she saw she had a new email. Jack Jones had replied straight away. The interview was on.

15

Lyall's Tours were founded by Duncan Lyall's father in the 1970s, when he was an enterprising young student. He realised there was a market for vehicles smaller than the huge coaches operated by other tour companies. His first vehicle had been a yellow ten-seater and had operated from a garage outside St Davids, taking tourists to coastal villages and beaches down roads that the larger coaches couldn't get through. The tour had developed a good reputation, more coaches had been bought and the itinerary expanded. During Harri's childhood, he'd often seen the buttercup-yellow vehicles driving around the countryside, usually packed with holidaymakers. When Duncan had taken over the business, he'd updated the fleet, still keeping the distinctive yellow colour.

Duncan was a different character to his dead father. While Alec Lyall had been about reputation and quality, there was a sharper entrepreneurial edge to his son. Over the last three years, reports had been received of passengers charged unofficial prices for extra trips not on the itinerary and young women pestered by drivers. Complaints had been investigated when reported, but Harri suspected they were the tip of the iceberg and cases had not proceeded to court due to lack of evidence. The business remained popular but when Harri saw the little yellow coaches on the road, he thought of girls his daughter's age being pestered by an older male driver and he wanted to punch someone.

He'd met Duncan twice, the first time in his younger days, when attending an accident involving one of Lyall's coaches. Duncan had arrived at the scene almost as quickly as the ambulance and had hovered as paramedics checked for casualties. As a young copper, Harri had put the worry down to concern about his staff and passengers. Now, he wasn't so sure.

The second meeting had taken place at a fundraiser for a local nursery that had been threatened with closure. Both Ben and Ellie had attended the school and he'd donated 200 pounds, which had felt a lot at the time. The fundraiser had taken place in the grounds of Duncan's house and Harri had been blown away by the opulence of the place. Duncan Lyall was doing well. Very well.

Siân had suggested ringing ahead to arrange a meeting with Duncan but Harri wanted to see his reaction to their unexpected presence. He lived in a house on the outskirts of Haverfordwest and Siân was waiting along the street. When she saw Harri pull up beside her, she opened the door and climbed into his passenger seat.

'This'll be interesting.' She looked across at him. 'That mac warm enough?'

Harri ignored her and drove to the entrance of the Lyall residence. The gate had an intercom, which Harri remembered from his previous visit, and it was Duncan who answered the ring.

Harri leant forward towards the speaker. 'It's DI Harri Evans from Dyfed Powys police. I have with me DC Siân Lewis. We wondered if we could have a brief chat with you.'

There was silence as, presumably, Duncan weighed up his options. Finally, the gates began to open, Duncan clearly not demeaning himself with a reply. Harri inched the car up the drive where the snow had been cleared into heaps lining the path. The front door opened and Duncan stood on the steps in a thin jumper. Whoever had done the work, it wasn't him. His expression was neutral, his focus on Harri.

'Have we met before? Your face is familiar.'

'At the fundraiser for Ysgol Bryn. You put on quite an event.'

'Of course, I remember. We saved the school, didn't we? Come into the warmth.'

The house was 1930s red-brick, solidly built without much design flair. Duncan had left the frontage largely untouched but had extended into the garden, and it was to one of these back rooms that he took Harri and Siân. The kitchen was cavernous, with a huge glass window over-looking the lawn where the tent had been erected when Harri had last visited. Duncan pointed at an industrial-sized machine.

'Would you like a coffee?'

Siân glanced at Harri, clearly craving her caffeine shot. 'Why not?' he said.

'Good.' Duncan rubbed his hands, pulled out a grinder and tipped in some beans. 'Take a seat while I rustle them up. What can I help you with?'

'We're working on the investigation into the death of Heledd Jones,' said Siân.

Was it his imagination or did Duncan relax? Whatever he thought the visit might entail, it wasn't this.

'Heledd, yes. Hold on a minute.' The noise of the grinder echoed around the room. That was the problem with these huge spaces: every sound would echo. He made coffee for the three of them and joined Harri and Siân at the table.

'Very sad about Heledd. Thirty-eight is no age.'

'Can I ask,' said Siân, 'when was the last time you had any communication with Heledd?'

'Of course. On Wednesday morning, she called me, wanting to meet. I was a bit surprised because, before that, it had been years since I'd spoken to her.'

'How long exactly?'

'I don't know. Maybe six, seven years. I see her sister Becca occasionally because her mill, Felin Wen, is on one of our itineraries. Tourists want to see a genuine Welsh blanket being made and Becca does them beautifully. If I remember rightly, Heledd was there one time I went to the workshop. That must have been the last time I saw her before Wednesday.'

'How was she with you?' asked Siân.

'Stand-offish, nervy. You know I was at their house when Huw disappeared?'

Harri nodded.

'So maybe that's why she didn't usually want to speak to me. I probably brought back bad memories.'

'You must have been surprised to get a call,' said Harri.

'Completely, but she sounded different. The Heledd I knew was shy, insecure. When she was married to Jack, I thought she was a bit of a drip. On the phone, when she rang me, she was calm and determined.'

Siân looked around the room. 'So why did you decide to meet her, given your social circles were so different?'

'Not that different. I'm still part of the old gang, even if we've gone our separate ways and our fortunes have differed somewhat. My wife and I went on holiday to

France with Heledd's ex-husband Jack and his new wife this summer. Left the kids with their grandmother and walked the Alps. Gemma I saw when I had to take one of the kids to A & E and we had a chat then.'

'I thought she was a GP?'

'She is now. I got the impression she didn't settle into hospital working. It was good to catch up with her when I saw her. As I said, we're all sort of in touch in some way or other.'

'Even with Eleri Tew?' asked Harri.

'Even Eleri.'

'So can you tell me exactly what Heledd said on the phone?' Siân had her tablet out and was typing into it.

'She asked if we could meet and I was happy to, for old times' sake. We met in the lobby of The River Hotel in Haverfordwest. I didn't particularly want her coming to the house. My wife is away with our children in Spain for half-term and bringing a woman back here would land me in hot water, however innocent it was.'

'They've gone away without you?' asked Siân.

'Can't spare the time.' There it was again, Harri noticed. That flash of discomfort.

'So, you met her at what time on Wednesday evening?'

'We were due to meet at seven p.m. Heledd wasn't there when I arrived so I had a G and T and waited for her.'

'How did she seem when she arrived?' asked Siân.

'Friendly, on the ball. It was quite a surprise. In fact, she reminded me a little of her sister.'

'What do you mean?' asked Harri.

'Becca's a good businesswoman. If you look under-neath the red hair and hippy clothes, she runs that mill as a profitable enterprise. It's not easy making money from artisan crafts. In the summer you get the tourists but who wants to buy a thick blanket in the heat? In the winter, many of the tourist attractions shut down but not the mill. Becca manages to keep going because she's got grit. I saw some of that determination when I spoke to Heledd.'

'What was the content of your conversation?' asked Siân.

'She wanted to go over the night that Huw disappeared. To be honest, it was what I was expecting and I'd have been surprised if we had anything else to say to each other.'

'Presumably, she'd asked for your account before.'

'Of course. When Huw was found dead, she'd gone to each one of us and questioned our exact movements that night.'

'Why would she do that? Presumably, she was distraught after the death of her son. Why did she feel the need to question you?'

Duncan flushed. 'How the hell should I know? I told her exactly what was in my statement. That I'd gone over to the house around ten past four, was told Huw was sleeping upstairs and, apart from a trip to the off-licence with Gruffydd around ten to five, that was it until Heledd came bursting in.'

'And she was happy with your account?' asked Siân.

'Of course she was, because it was the truth. What the hell are you getting at?'

'We're trying to get some insights into Heledd's state of mind,' said Harri, watching the flush on Duncan's face creep down his neck. 'So Heledd questioned you about your movements on the night Huw died. Then you don't see her for years, until she contacts you to go over everything again. Would that be an accurate timeline of events?'

Duncan sniffed. 'That's about it. I don't know what the hell the issue was. You gave us a good grilling at the time, so don't think you didn't do your job properly. I just wondered whether Heledd was trying to find that gap in the evening when Huw slipped out.'

'Did you have any ideas?'

'Of course not. I was pretty plastered that evening.' Duncan looked down at his hands. 'It's always been an issue for me and I finally kicked the habit ten years ago. I'm completely dry now but there are holes in my memory. I told all of this to Heledd.'

'Did she say why, after questioning you when Huw first went missing, she then left a gap of more than a decade before seeking you out again?'

'Not until I asked her. It was the first question I had. Why resurrect it all now? We'd passed the ten-year anniversary of Huw's death, which was on my mind a lot, and I never heard from her.'

'And her answer?' asked Siân.

'She said she was working something out.'

'Working what out?' asked Harri, his mind on Gavin's story.

'She wouldn't tell me but I got the impression she'd learnt something that had got her rethinking that night.'

'Was she accusing you of being complicit in what happened?'

'No!' Duncan took a deep breath. 'She wanted me to go through everything again and tell her as much as I remembered, which actually isn't that much. I mean, I can recall vividly the shock that he was missing and the search for him. You know how that ended. But the hour or so we were in the house? Not much, I'm afraid.'

'What did you remember?'

Duncan waved a hand. 'This and that. The problem is, when you're questioned years after an event, it's never clear if these are actually your memories or what you've told yourself about what happened over the years. Add in the amount I'd drunk that night and...' Duncan raised his hands.

'Did you get an impression of why Heledd might have been questioning you?'

'She was good at a poker face, I discovered. There wasn't any part of my narrative where I thought she was listening more intently, if that's what you mean.'

'And how did she seem when you'd finished going through your account again?' asked Siân.

Duncan stood up and picked up his coffee cup, depositing it in the sink. 'She asked outright if I'd withheld anything from the police.'

Harri and Siân exchanged glances. 'And had you?' asked Harri.

'No, of course not.'

Harri stared at the man. He must have a sunbed in one of the rooms, as his skin had a light tan to it. He thought of Gavin, telling Mallory of his discovery of the note, and of Heledd asking Duncan if he'd withheld anything. A connection, surely.

'How did Heledd take the news?'

'I assumed I was still off the hook, as it were. She asked...'

Duncan stopped, looking as if he regretted starting the sentence.

'She asked what?' said Siân.

'She asked if I ever wrote anything down.'

'Did you know what she was talking about?' asked Harri.

'No idea. I wondered if she was writing her memoirs. I mean, people do, don't they? And it would account for her change in appearance. Trying to make sense of the past and all that. She didn't push it – we finished our drinks and I drove her to the bus stop, as the night was getting wild.'

'Did she say how she'd be getting back from where the bus dropped her at Penterry to her house?'

'I didn't ask. She wasn't that drunk, you know. It never occurred to me to worry about her.'

'And what did you do after dropping Heledd off?' asked Siân.

'I came back home. I'm afraid there are no witnesses, as I'm on my own, but Heledd was alive and well when I last saw her.'

'And she gave no indication of her private life? Whether she now had a boyfriend, for example?' asked Harri, remembering Becca's view that there was a man involved.

'She said nothing about that. I doubt there was a man in the background. She was still obsessed with her son's accident and, rightly or wrongly, it's what ate her up. I can't imagine anyone putting up with that in a relationship. I know that's what broke up her and Jack.'

'Did she ask you about him?'

'She never mentioned a word, which is just as well, as I don't play piggy in the middle with exes. Jack's a very old friend. I was fond of Heledd back in the day but it's been a long time.'

'And you can't say, for example, if she might have spoken to someone else who was there at the house that evening?'

'I really couldn't tell you. She never mentioned anything.' Duncan looked at his watch. 'I'm sorry but I have an online meeting at four. I'm going to have to get ready for that.'

Harri and Siân rose. Back outside in the cold, Harri pulled up the collar of his too thin mac.

'What do you think?' asked Siân.

Harri shrugged. 'Why would Heledd start with Duncan if she's got questions about Huw's death? He's not exactly the most approachable of the six. My guess is the others have been contacted too.'

16

Jack looked at his wife's tear-ravaged face and knew he'd never be able to comfort her, despite the desperate grief he was struggling to contain. Heledd had brought beauty to the marriage and that attribute he had thought so important to a respectable county solicitor: a willingness to fade into the background. He knew his friends had been astonished by their wedding but had any of the women he hung around with before he met Heledd really expected to drag him to the altar? He'd slept with all of them at one time or another but Heledd's luminosity and clear adoration had been hard to beat. Huw's arrival, however, had produced a seismic shift in their relation-ship. His evenings at work had become more frequent, so much so that Heledd and Huw were often in bed by the time he returned home. The connection between him and Heledd had been stretched to breaking point and he wondered what the death of his son would do to their marriage.

Huw was dead. The reality of this was mind-numbing, and part of him rejected the knowledge as monstrous. His body felt as if he was covered in a layer of ice, which had nothing to do with the cold. He knew he should say something to Heledd, to comfort his wife, but his emotions were frozen and he was drawn to Duncan, who looked suddenly sober. Jack watched as Duncan was led by a uniformed officer into the back room. Each of them was giving an account of the hour or so before Huw disappeared.

Eleri had insisted on being interviewed back in her own home and Jack guessed, judging by her expression, this house of grief repelled her. Eleri, of all of them, had the most to lose, he guessed. She was leader of the local council but had her eyes set on a bigger stage than Pembrokeshire afforded her. Unlike Eleri to be away from the action, though. She'd want an account of what had gone on in the house while she was absent, he was sure.

Bethan and Gemma were huddled with their arms around each other. It surprised him, as he wasn't aware the women were close, but they must have been drawing comfort from each other. Neither made any attempt to comfort Heledd, whose grief appeared to be embarrassing them. He wished the officer trying to comfort her would take her upstairs, but that was out of bounds. The forensics team was scrutinising Huw's room, although God knows what they were looking for. He had been in the house the whole time Huw was here. That he had never heard his son leave was something he knew would haunt him for the rest of his life.

It was the story of those bloody mermaids, he was sure. Huw, physically resembling his father, had taken after Heledd in his love of all things strange and wonderful. He'd loved her stories of the *Mabinogion* and, after exhausting them, Heledd had begun to make up her own tales. St Non's, that godawful outcrop looking out to sea, had been a magical place for Huw, as had the gatehouse leading to the cathedral. Why the bloody hell hadn't he made his way to the latter? He'd have been spotted in town straight away and would be back lying in his bed with no harm done.

Gruffydd was trying to catch his eye but Jack had no intention of discussing his son, or his raw grief, with him. Of all the friends, he had least in common with Gruffydd and it had been an irritation when he'd turned up with Duncan. He paused. He'd already been spoken to by officers but it would soon be time for an official statement. Perhaps not everything needed to be revealed. Perhaps some things just didn't matter.

17

The First Lie

Jack's face appeared on Zoom and Mallory's impression was that he was the epitome of a successful lawyer. He had fair hair going grey that was cropped short to his head. His face was slightly burnt, with the telltale white marks of skin shielded by sunglasses. A skier's tan. In the background, Mallory could see a woman carrying a box of vegetables into the kitchen. She set it down on a shelf already laden with gym weights of different sizes. Jack clearly liked to keep himself toned, even off the slopes.

'Sorry about the commotion behind me,' said Jack, not looking the slightest bit bothered. 'Marie-Axelle is just back from the market.'

'Your wife's French?' Harri hadn't mentioned that, although she supposed it didn't matter.

'She is. Our chalet is in the village next to the one where she grew up. It reminds me a little of West Wales. All the locals know each other, a big influx of tourists in high season. Except here in France it's in winter, when everyone comes for the skiing.'

'You live most of the year in Cardiff, though?'

'Right. We're leaving tomorrow to go back to Wales before half-term starts. Things get a bit busy during the school holidays.'

'You don't have children yourself?'

Jack winced. 'Only Huw. Marie and I only got married last year but she's five years older than me. We've decided not to try for them. We are in complete agreement about this but our reasons are very different. I hate the thought that I'd be somehow replacing Huw.'

Jack, Mallory suspected, had also had a raw deal when it came to the death of his son. Mallory had been left with the impression that, while Heledd had shouldered the blame, Jack had waltzed off to the Welsh capital and begun a new life. But perhaps that was an inverted form of sexism, assuming men picked up their lives after a tragedy. It didn't sound like this had been the case with Jack at all.

'I know you've spoken to the investigating team at Carmarthen and provided them with a statement. As I mentioned in my email, I've been contracted by the police to help them with the investigation. Can I ask if your specialism is criminal law?'

'It isn't, so you have nothing to worry about on that front. I work in intellectual property and don't usually deal with the police.'

'Can I start with your former wife, Heledd?' Mallory wondered if it was a difficult subject, with Marie in the background.

'Of course, although I can't help you very much. I haven't seen her at all since our divorce.'

'And you say she made no attempt to contact you.'

'None whatsoever.'

He paused, giving Mallory time to reply, but she stayed silent. The pause, however, allowed the sound from Toby's computer game to seep into the room.

'Sorry,' said Mallory. 'I bought my son a PlayStation 5 for Christmas and I'm already regretting it.'

'How old is he?'

'Fifteen. I'm sorry, I know he's around the same age Huw would have been. I want you to know that's been on my mind a lot as I've been reading over the notes.'

'How are the teenage years? Every year, on Huw's birthday, I wonder what he'd have been like as a teenager.'

Mallory grimaced. The simple answer was that she wasn't sure, but she was hardly going to discuss Joe's concerns with this witness. 'Toby and I don't live together. He lives with his father, which is his choice. It means when I see him, we generally rub along fine.'

Jack frowned. 'Complicated families.'

'Exactly.' Mallory looked down at her notes, although she didn't need them. Everything she wanted to ask was buzzing around her head.

'The reason I've got in touch with you is that, as I explained in my email, I'm being brought into the team investigating Heledd's death.'

'Which I can't help you with.'

'Exactly, but we're looking at any potential links with Huw's death in 2011.'

'Which was ruled accidental.' Jack leant into the screen. 'Are you telling me that wasn't the case?'

It was Mallory's first glimpse of the force of personality behind Jack's charm. 'Not at all, but first Huw dies in tragic circumstances and then Heledd. We'd be remiss not to look into any potential connection.'

'OK.'

This was where Mallory had a choice to make. Whether or not to reveal the note's existence. There was still no evidence that Heledd knew of the message. She made a decision. 'We've had someone come forward with evidence that all six of your statements to the police in 2011 were factually incorrect.'

'Factually incorrect.' A flash of fury crossed Jack's face. 'What the hell does that mean?'

'As you are a solicitor, I don't think I need to explain the term to you.' Mallory paused. She would leave it at that. The message had said 'lies', which suggested a deliberate withholding of the truth, but given that Jack was already wound up, she'd see what he came up with.

'Factually incorrect.' Jack's face was stony. 'I'm a solicitor, for God's sake. I don't make false statements to the police, as that would be a good way for me to ruin my career. I was completely honest in my statement at the time so I don't know what you're talking about.'

Mallory made no attempt to mollify the man. He might be out of the frame for Heledd's murder but there were ten minutes or so when he was alone in the house with Huw on the night of his death. Not long enough to take him to St Non's and back, but the others might have been accomplices. No, Jack Jones still had some answers to give.

'If I sent you a photograph of your original statement, would you have a look at it now? I'll stay on the call while you do.'

Jack gave an exaggerated sigh. 'Well, OK.'

'Sending it now.'

He turned his head away from her as he picked up his iPad, opening her attachment and reading it through. As he finished it, she thought she saw relief in his face. It would have been the first time he'd seen the statement since he first signed it, although he'd have been questioned about its content time and time again. His expression, however, suggested the essential facts held true.

'I stand by everything I said here.'

Mallory's mood sank. She'd believed Gavin's story, whatever doubts she had about his reliability after a head injury. There was no doubting Jack's relief on reading through his statement. She hadn't been able to find any discrepancy herself. Jack said he'd watched the football results show, and turned the TV off when Gruffydd and Duncan arrived. Perhaps she should move on, forget about the note, and question Jack about his friends' accounts. If they were still in touch, however, he was unlikely to give up any information. So Mallory tried a final stab at Jack's own account of the evening.

'What about what's *not* in the statement?'

'What do you mean?'

He was being deliberately obtuse. 'I'd like you to think about what you might now add in, with the benefit of hindsight. Say, something you missed out.'

An omission wasn't the same as a lie but Mallory was clutching at straws.

Jack shook his head and looked at his watch. 'I tell you, it's all as I recall it.'

Frustrated, Mallory leant in towards the screen. 'Please look again.'

With an exaggerated sigh, Jack picked up his tablet once more. I'll go through it sentence by sentence if I have to, she thought, but she noticed he briefly stopped, before carrying on reading.

'What is it?' she asked.

'It's a minor thing.'

'Go on. Please.' Mallory held her breath.

'I said I was sitting in the house watching TV when Duncan and Gruffydd turned up out of the blue. I let them in and asked them to be quiet. I think the phrase "out of the blue" isn't technically correct. We'd kind of planned it.'

'Planned what?'

'That Duncan would join me at the house. I never told him to bring Gruffydd, so I don't know why he came along, but I suggested Duncan should come over and keep me company while Heledd was at the party. The rest of the gang turning up was completely unplanned and it was them that I was thinking of when I said "out of the blue". It was a tiny omission.'

'Duncan and you had already decided on the get-together. Did you text to arrange it?' Mallory knew they hadn't; the phone records of people present in the house had been checked.

'I told him in the pub the previous evening that I'd be on my own from four for about an hour, until Heledd came home, and he gave me a wink saying she wouldn't mind if I had a bit of company.'

'And you were surprised when he came along with Gruffydd as well.'

Jack shrugged. 'A little.'

'And what about when the others turned up?'

'Again, I was surprised.'

Mallory kept her expression neutral. Of course, he bloody wasn't. The group ran around as a gang. Safety in numbers. She looked at the list of names on the front of the folder Harri had given her: Duncan Lyall, Gruffydd Ellis, Gemma Bowen, Bethan Rees and Eleri Tew.

'Do you think,' she asked, 'it's possible that your friends all made a similar, um, omission?' She had failed to keep her tone neutral and she saw Jack's expression harden at her acidity.

'I can't answer for them, can I?'

True. He couldn't, but now she'd managed to unearth his lie, however accidental it might have been, the contents of the note seemed more realistic. Of course, Jack was trying to downplay his failure to tell the team that the evening at his house had been planned. Jack might think it a small omission, but to the ex-copper in Mallory it said one thing: the visit was arranged, which meant someone possibly had time to plan.

18

Mallory saw that while she was on her Zoom with Jack, she'd missed four calls from Harri. She wondered why people did that. Continue to call when she didn't answer. One missed call would have sufficed to let her know he wanted to speak to her. She rang him back and he picked up immediately. She listened as he updated her on the meeting with Duncan Lyall.

'So Heledd was asking Duncan about his movements in 2011? What was his reaction to her questions?' asked Mallory.

'A sort of resignation, but Heledd asked him if he wrote anything down. Duncan took this to mean a memoir, which is a little odd, but I'm wondering if it has any connection to the note found at St Non's.'

'So, you do think it existed?'

'I'm keeping an open mind but there's a possibility Heledd either discovered the note or its contents.'

'Gavin was adamant he didn't tell anyone else about it.'

'But one of the six wrote it, didn't they? Maybe they told Heledd about its existence. Hold on.' Mallory waited while Harri covered his phone and spoke to someone. 'Sorry about that. Look, I've got an appointment in half an hour that I can't miss, so I'll have to be quick. I'm trying to imagine someone telling Heledd about the note but leaving her to do the interviewing of the six friends. That doesn't sound right.'

No, thought Mallory, it doesn't. 'Do you have an alternative scenario? One person wrote the note and another told her about it?'

'Christ. You're tying me in knots, Mallory. What did you think of the statements?'

'In themselves, there's nothing to get excited about. However, I've just finished speaking to Jack Jones.'

'And?'

'I've managed to winkle out something that wasn't in his statement. What he didn't reveal to detectives that night was that it was planned that Duncan would join him at Y Bwthyn while the others were out.'

'And?'

Mallory suppressed the instinct to throw her phone across the room. The noise from Toby's game was beginning to jar on her and now she had a monosyllabic DI to deal with.

'And nothing. That's it, but it's still an omission. At the very least, Duncan knew he'd be at the Jones's house.'

'But, so what? If we're going to prove that one of the six had a hand in Huw's death, we need to concoct a scenario that begins with one of the six intending to do harm to him.'

'Well, let's start with Duncan. You've just interviewed him. Did he give anything away?'

'He was supremely unconcerned about any questions involving 2011. I can't help you but you're welcome to interview him yourself. I was questioning principally in relation to the death of Heledd Jones.'

'Right. I'll be in touch with him because I'm going to proceed on the presumption that the note was genuine and all six did indeed lie in their original statements. And I think I'm going to discover more than Jack Jones's minor omission. Do you mind if I visit Heledd's home, near where she died? I want to have a hunt round to see if I can find evidence of the note.'

'The house has been searched but you're welcome to look. I don't think the cottage is kept locked, unless one of my team has decided to shut up things properly. The cottage certainly wasn't locked when we visited it on Thursday.'

'Was the place rented?'

'No. According to Becca Jones, Heledd bought the place for a song with her divorce settlement. It's surprisingly in good shape, given Heledd struggled to look after herself, but maybe I'm making unfair assumptions about her.' Harri paused. 'So, you believe that the note's genuine?'

'Why not? I've nothing else to go on.'

'But maybe Duncan's lie is the same as Jack's. I mean, there's no mention of a premeditated get-together in his statement either, is there?'

'No. The note said, "six lies killed Huw Jones". That means there are six lies to find.'

'OK, OK. Be careful, though,' said Harri.

'What do you mean?'

'I think Heledd was murdered and I'm proceeding on that basis. If there's a killer out there, they won't like you unearthing long-buried secrets.'

'I'll bear it in mind.'

Mallory shut her computer and wandered into the living room. 'Toby, I'm going out for an hour. Do you want to come? I just need to drop by somewhere.'

Toby paused the game he was playing and stood up, brushing down his trousers. 'I thought I'd go for a run.'

Mallory glanced at the grey sky. 'It's miserable out. Won't you freeze?'

Toby smiled. 'Once I start, I'll warm up. I need to work off my breakfast.'

She'd made them both a bacon sandwich, which was hardly a feast. 'Well, OK. I won't be long.'

—

Mallory's assumptions about the life Heledd had led following Huw's death were swept away when she saw her house. It was a two-storey cottage that showed signs of recent repair to the stonework. The front door was flanked by two pots of holly, their leaves neatly clipped into a globe, with the red of the berries peeping through a layer of snow. The cottage had new doors and windows, suggesting money had been spent on the place recently.

The front door, as Harri had guessed, was unlocked. In the hall, the cottage retained its original flagstones, which had become uneven with wear. The walls would originally have been whitewashed but Heledd had painted them a heritage dark cream. The room was bare, except for a wooden bench with a rail of pegs above, from which two coats hung. They were everyday jackets – one waxed and the other quilted. Heledd's choice of a red woollen coat for a cold February night suggested it had been mainly for show. She had known she would have to make a return journey in a bus of dubious quality but had nevertheless gone for style over comfort.

The downstairs rooms had a stillness to them broken only by the ticking of a mantlepiece clock. Each was sparsely furnished but gave a clue to Heledd's personality. A row of fantasy novels with colourful spines sat on the oak side-table above a basket of knitting holding a striped piece of work in progress. A new Apple TV had been mounted to the wall. The kitchen threw up no clues but the contents of the fridge suggested Heledd cooked from scratch. Mallory, who lived on a diet of fresh seafood and ready meals, frowned. Trauma victims often failed to look after themselves, but here was evidence that Heledd saw the importance of putting nutrients into her body.

Something wasn't fitting. The accounts she'd heard – from Harri and from Ffion upstairs – suggested a woman barely surviving. Here was the living accommodation Mallory aspired to. The house of someone winning at life, or at least more than Mallory currently was. She idly wondered how much the house might fetch if her sister decided to put it up for sale. Mallory doubted her finances would stretch that far but it might be worth asking the question.

Upstairs, Mallory searched through the bedroom but saw no evidence of a note. There were also no signs of a man's presence, unless he was someone very good at covering his tracks. In the bathroom Mallory rifled through the cabinet and saw no birth control pills or other contraception. As she was shutting the glass door of the cupboard, she heard tyres on the gravel outside. Moving to the landing, she saw a red Yaris parked near the front door and Siân stepped out into the February morning. Despite her official presence on the case, Mallory felt like a guilty intruder, although her own car was parked clearly enough on the driveway.

The front door opened and Siân hollered, 'Hello!'

Mallory stood at the top of the stairs and looked down. 'It's me, Mallory.'

A look of annoyance crossed Siân's face. She adjusted her handbag on her shoulder. 'I've come to get Heledd's computer.'

'I've had a look round but I've not seen one. Do you know what you're looking for?'

'A MacBook Air, according to Becca Jones. Heledd bought one about six months ago.'

Mallory came down the stairs and followed Siân into the living room. 'A new laptop, a new-ish TV, well-kept flowers in the pots, a fridge stocked with food. This doesn't sound like the Heledd I've been hearing about.'

Siân was opening cupboards and rifling through them. 'She bought this place in 2013, just after her divorce. It's only in the last six months that the house has been renovated. It was in decent nick when she bought it but needed new windows. I got in touch with the builder who did the work. She paid him in cash, which isn't that unusual around here. Some farmers still prefer the notes under the bed.'

'What does her bank account look like?'

'The residue of her divorce settlement – Jack Jones came from a wealthy family so they must have helped – and she took a small salary from Becca for putting her wool products online. And I mean small. Nine hundred pounds a month.'

'So, where's the money for the renovations coming from? Did Jack pay her any maintenance?'

'Nope. Clean break, although he did give her the proceeds of the house sale when they divorced. If you're thinking blackmail or something, forget it. I've had a quick go at the sums and I don't think Heledd spent anything meaningful in the nine or so years since her divorce. The money just mounted up but six months ago, she finally decided to spend it.'

'Do phone records throw up any clues?'

'Locked. Can't access it. Tried various combinations and ran it through coding. Can't unlock it.'

'Have you tried fingerprints?'

Siân wagged her finger at Mallory. 'Not allowed but the pathologist said it wouldn't work anyway. Something to do with the electrical conduction when we're alive. We do have the phone records, however, which we're going through, but what we really want is access to WhatsApp, Messenger and the like. And that's harder.'

'The phone was on her when she died? It suggests if there's a killer, they weren't particularly bothered whether we accessed it or not. If there was incriminating evidence, the first thing I'd do was take the phone.' Mallory glanced around. 'I'll leave you to look for the laptop but my guess is it's gone.'

'It hasn't. I've found it.' Siân was on her knees after retrieving a silver laptop from underneath the sofa. 'It's where I put mine when I've finished with it at night.' Siân lifted the lid. 'It's switched off. I'll take it straight to the digital forensics team. What are you going to do next?'

'Me? I'm going to see Becca Jones.'

19

It had been five years since Harri had last visited the doctor, and things had got a little more stressful in the surgery. Taking a break in the middle of a case wasn't ideal but since he'd hit forty, his mortality had been weighing heavily on him. It took him three early-morning Monday phone calls to finally secure a much-coveted appointment with a locum. Harri presented himself at the agreed time and explained his symptoms.

'Tired all the time?' The doctor was looking at his computer screen, typing in Harri's notes. Harri would personally have preferred some eye contact but understood that, for once, he wasn't the professional in an interview situation. 'It says here that you're a lone parent to two teenage children. That can't be easy.'

'It's a damn sight easier than when they were small.'

The locum raised his eyebrows. 'You've been on your own for a while?'

'My wife died of cancer when they were young. I've brought them up on my own, with the help of my sister who moved in with me.'

'That working out all right?'

'It's been over ten years. It's fine.'

'What about your work life? Do you have a stressful job?'

'I'm a detective inspector. It's very stressful.'

The locum stopped typing and turned to Harri. 'Detective? My father was a policeman. Retired early with high blood pressure.'

'Is mine high?' asked Harri.

'Not especially. I tell you what, we'll take some bloods from you and run a range of tests. It could be something like anaemia or B12 deficiency. You're not overweight, so that's something in your favour. Let's start by ruling out the obvious.'

A warning bell tolled in Harri's head. Rule out the obvious? It suggested there were other, less obvious, causes as to why he might be feeling tired all the time.

'You don't think it's serious, do you? My kids have lost one parent already.'

The doctor smiled but refused to be drawn. 'Let's see what your results bring.'

'Can you take my bloods now?'

'I'm afraid not. You need to make an appointment with the nurse.'

'Look, I'm leading an investigation into an unexplained death. I don't have time to wait a week, or probably longer, until a nurse can fit me in. Can't you take them?'

The locum looked pained. 'Give me a second.' He disappeared and came back a few minutes later with a nurse, and then left the room.

'Don't doctors know how to draw blood?' asked Harri.

The nurse leant over him. 'Probably can't remember how to do it,' she confided.

'Please tell me he's qualified,' said Harri.

'GP trainee. Don't worry, he's being supervised by one of the partners. Ready – sharp scratch.'

Harri was glad to get out of the practice, with its wipe-down seats and antiseptic smell. Not much different from an interview room, he supposed. What he wanted to do was go home to bed and climb under the covers. He couldn't understand where this lassitude came from. Paula had been this tired towards the end but that had been after two years of chemotherapy that had slowed down, but failed to eradicate, her disease. He couldn't actually be dying of cancer this quickly, surely. A lie-down was impossible: he needed to speak to his boss because the next person on the list he wanted to interview was Eleri Tew.

–

'No way.' Steph smoothed down her hair that had been gelled and scraped back into a bun – or was it scraped back and gelled into a bun? Harri didn't know. He'd have to ask Ellie, who was an expert in these things. It was pointless asking his sister, who was as clueless as him about hairstyles.

Harri's eyes slid to a plaque Steph had on her desk. It had appeared after the Christmas break and it read: 'Queen of fucking everything'. He wondered who'd bought it for her. Maybe her husband, as he was sure she didn't have any kids. The words summed her up, although what the message didn't say was that her successes were achieved off the back of other people's hard work. There was, below her, a hierarchy of disgruntled employees sick of their solid skills being appropriated for her CV, even though she'd toast the success of her 'team' at the end of each case.

'There were a lot of people at the party that New Year's Eve. Why are you focusing on Duncan and Eleri?'

Oh, *Duncan* and *Eleri*, was it? Harri kept his gaze steady. If Steph was stymying his investigation, he'd go over her head. There were processes in place for bent coppers and he'd take that path if he had to. 'I'm not focusing on them. We've interviewed Duncan Lyall as he was one of the last people to see Heledd alive. There's a possibility Heledd made contact with all the friends present in her home in 2011. I assumed you'd want us rather than Mallory to speak to Eleri Tew, given the fact she's an MP. If you've a personal interest in this, ma'am—'

'What do you mean?' she asked, her voice sharp.

'I noticed you used their first names. I know you're professional enough to declare any connection to the suspects.'

'Are they suspects?'

'All right, witnesses, but the process is the same.'

Beneath her angry stare, Harri saw a flicker of discontent. Steph was rattled.

'I don't know either of them more than you do. Duncan, I mean Mr Lyall, said you'd met on a previous occasion.'

Two, thought Harri, but no need for you to know that.

'I understand why you want to speak to Eleri Tew and, of course, it's in the public interest that she's interviewed in the same way as any other witness. Please bear in mind, though, she's a master of PR and if we put a foot wrong, it'll be all over the news. Who else is Heledd likely to have spoken to about a note that may or may not exist?'

'Possibly Gemma Bowen, a GP.' Harri thought back to his recent appointment and made a face. 'And two members connected to St Davids diocese, Gruffydd Ellis and Bethan Rees. These are all people who attended the New Year's Eve gathering and have remained in West Wales.'

'What about the people who haven't?'

'Jack Jones says he hadn't been contacted by his ex-wife – in fact, he claims he hasn't spoken to her since their divorce.'

'And what's Mallory Dawson up to?'

'Looking at 2011. We need to get her contract signed as soon as possible, so she can talk to the others. She's keen to get started but I've told her it'll be us who will speak to Miss Tew.'

'Don't be calling Eleri "Miss". She's married now, even if she's kept her name. OK, I'll give you the designated power to sign the contract for Mallory. Don't bother me about it unless there's a problem. I want you to report back to me once you've spoken to Eleri. Don't focus on the note too much. I remember 2011 well enough. Everyone had a view on how Huw had ended up at St Non's.'

'What do you think happened?'

'I think it was a tragic accident and, frankly, in relation to Heledd's death, I've heard over the years that she wasn't coping.'

'You think it was suicide, then?'

'I bloody well hope so, Harri, for all our sakes.'

–

The opening of a new ward at the local hospital had saved Harri and Siân a trip to London to interview Eleri. The forthcoming unveiling of the renovated wing had been reported in the *Western Mail* and Harri, spotting the article, had called her office to arrange an interview. Whatever knock-back he had been expecting hadn't materialised and they'd been asked to present themselves at Eleri's constituency office at nine o'clock on Tuesday morning. It had been six days since Heledd had made the fateful trip to Haverfordwest but it had been too much to hope that Eleri had been in West Wales the previous week. In fact, she had been giving a speech to the Royal College of Surgeons about her own experiences of plastic surgery.

Eleri looked younger and prettier in real life, an observation for which his daughter would have called him a chauvinist if he'd dared to articulate it out loud. Her face had a slight sheen to it, which must be a result of the fillers she continued to use, if press reports were correct. However, her previously inflated lips now just looked unnaturally full, as if they'd been stung by a bee. He thought she'd have been much better looking if she'd left her face to nature, but no doubt Ellie would have called that comment sexist too.

Unlike Duncan Lyall, Eleri was not relaxed. It might have had something to do with the solicitor sitting next to her, who would have briefed her to keep everything as concise as possible. There was a third person in the room, to whom he hadn't been introduced.

'Ms Tew, I'm more than happy to have a solicitor present in what is only an informal chat but I'd prefer that to be it.' He looked pointedly at the tall man with a crew cut, who held his gaze. Ex-military, Harri guessed.

'This is George Hansen.'

The name meant nothing to Harri. 'And?'

She didn't like his tone, colouring slightly. 'He's my husband and chief of staff. He wants to hear what I have to say.'

I bet he does, thought Harri. Chief of staff was a grand title for what must be basically her office assistant. Eleri was a Member of Parliament but held no ministerial role; her only other work in the Commons was on the

Medicines and Medical Devices Select Committee. Her diary, although busy, hardly warranted a chief of staff.

'So,' Harri said. 'This is an informal chat, with your solicitor and your chief of staff in attendance.'

'Something like that.' She'd kept her composure. 'How can I help you?'

Harri sat back and let Siân ask the first question. This surprised George Hansen, who caught his eye with an unsmiling gaze.

'Ms Tew—' said Siân.

'I prefer Miss.'

So, Steph had been wrong about that, thought Harri.

'Sorry, Miss Tew. Can you tell me the last time you had communication with Heledd Jones?'

Eleri glanced down at the sheet of paper in front of her. 'Saturday, 11 February.'

Rather cleverly, Eleri had written down the key dates she needed for the interview but had not brought along anything more substantial, such as a diary or notebook, that might be appropriated as evidence.

'And how did she communicate with you?'

Eleri glanced at her solicitor. 'She rang me on my mobile.'

'Your personal or work one?'

'They're one and the same.'

Harri leant forward. 'Who pays the bill? You or your parliamentary office?'

'As I said, they're the same thing. I pay it and claim the cost back through my parliamentary expenses. It's standard practice.'

'OK,' said Siân. 'Is your number easily obtainable?'

'Not particularly but colleagues, friends and family have it. I suspect Heledd didn't have to look far to find the number.'

'You didn't ask her how she obtained it, though?'

'I did not.'

Harri inwardly groaned. It was like getting blood out of a stone. Siân, however, remained cool.

'What did Heledd Jones say to you?'

'She asked for a meeting and said that she had some information as to what happened in December 2011.'

'The night her son, Huw Jones, died?' said Siân.

'Yes, exactly.'

'Did she say what this new information was?'

'No. I asked her but she wanted to meet me in person to discuss it.'

'And what was your response?'

'I told her that if she had new information about the death of Huw,' Eleri stopped, her lips working, 'then she should telephone the police. I thought that was the proper way to go about what might be important evidence.'

'And what was her response when you suggested it?'

'She said, "Thanks very much," and cut the call.'

'She gave no indication what the evidence might be?' asked Siân.

'None whatsoever.'

'And how did you feel about the call?' asked Siân.

'You don't have to answer that,' said Eleri's solicitor. 'Let's keep to the facts, shall we?'

'I don't mind.' Eleri looked across at her husband. 'It stirred up a lot of old memories for me. I love my constituency. I'm a Pembrokeshire girl to the bone and I've tried to do right by all my constituents. But when you've been born and bred somewhere, you come with history. My history is Huw Jones and the fact I was hosting the party that Heledd attended when Huw went missing.'

'You were also at the Jones's house,' said Harri.

Eleri flushed. 'Very briefly.'

There was a short silence no one sought to fill.

'Prior to that call,' said Siân, 'how long was it since you'd spoken to Heledd?'

'Probably a few years after Huw's accident.' She glanced down again at her piece of paper. 'I think it was around 2014. I was at the Carmarthen Show presenting a prize and I saw Heledd. She looked a little lost. I went up to speak to her but she didn't really respond. I got the impression she was heavily sedated and I later saw her at her sister's stall.'

'You know Becca Jones?'

'Becca's the same age as me and I know her to talk to.'

'And you haven't spoken to Heledd between 2014 and now?'

'I've had no contact with her whatsoever.'

'Did she say in what context she wanted to talk to you?' asked Harri.

'What do you mean?'

'Well, you're both an acquaintance and her Member of Parliament. Was she going to you as someone she once knew or did she want help in an official capacity?'

'Definitely the former,' said Eleri, shooting a glance at George.

'How do you know that? The response you gave her was one of officialdom. Follow the correct procedures.'

'I hope other friends and acquaintances would have given her the same advice. It's not the time to play Nancy Drew when we're talking about the death of a child.'

'Is that what you think she was doing?' asked Harri.

'Look, I don't know, because we never actually talked about what she wanted to tell me.'

'Can I ask…' Harri took his time to formulate the question – he needed to pee, which wasn't putting him in the best mood. 'Do you have anything to add to the statement you gave to police on the evening of 31 December 2011?'

'Of course not.' Eleri's colouring was bright, no need for that expensive-looking blusher she'd put on her face.

'I can share with you a copy of the statement, if you'd like to take a look,' said Siân, taking a sheaf of papers from her bag.

Eleri looked at it as if it were a court summons. 'I don't have anything to add to my original statement.'

Her solicitor coughed. 'You might want to have a quick glance at it to refresh your memory.'

Eleri shot him a look but reached to take the paper. Her eyes skimmed over the page and she shook her head, handing it back to Siân. 'Everything is correct, especially, if you could note, my comment that I had only been in the house for twenty-five minutes.'

'Odd that you were there at all,' said Harri, 'considering the party was at your house.'

'I noticed that most of my friends weren't at the party and I guessed they had headed over to Jack's. I went to fetch them back. I hadn't spent two hundred quid on booze to have them drinking it elsewhere.'

'And you noticed nothing untoward?' asked Siân.

'I did not. Can I ask why you're asking me these questions now? Are you seriously implying that Heledd's death might be connected in some way to Huw's accident?'

'We have received an allegation,' said Harri, 'that all six of you lied in some way on that New Year's Eve night.'

'Nonsense.' Eleri glanced up at her husband. 'If I had a pound for every unsubstantiated allegation I've had to deal with over the years, I'd be able to afford enough Botox treatments for the rest of my life.'

She noted their surprise. 'Don't think I'm not aware of how I'm depicted in the press. Eleri Tew, she of the trout pout as a result of a dermal filler gone wrong. Well, I was in a position to do something about it and that's what I did. I helped bring in new regulations for the industry, but it's brought me enemies too. If someone says I lied, ask them to be specific. I stand by everything on that statement.'

'Anything that you want to add to it?' asked Harri.

Eleri stood, smoothing down her dress that was without a crease. 'Nothing whatsoever.'

20

Men, Mallory decided, had a very strange way of looking at women. She had relied on Harri's description of Becca, who'd been portrayed as part hippie, part cottage-industry entrepreneur. Becca's mill, however, was definitely a reflection of the latter personality trait. From the moment visitors arrived, they were led on a tour that took in Welsh knitting history, local wool manufacturers and cutting-edge design.

Becca, to be fair, did give the impression of not giving a shit what the world thought of her. She had deep mahogany red hair, which suited her, and dungarees with one shoulder flap undone. Her boots, however, were an expensive Australian make that Mallory had been craving for years but had decided the money would be better placed in the savings account for Toby's university fees.

'DI Evans said you'd be dropping by.' Becca swept a lock of hair from her eyes. 'Do you want a tour of the mill?'

Mallory looked at her watch. 'I can't. My son's waiting for me at home so this needs to be a quick visit.'

'Sure. Shall we go to the office? I'm glad, because I've a lot to do today.'

Mallory followed her to a room at the back of the building, aware that Becca had been keen to emphasise she was also busy. Mallory was inclined to consider this competitiveness a positive personality trait and she wondered about the dynamic between the two sisters.

'I know you've provided a statement to the police about Heledd but I want to ask you about my impressions of her cottage.'

'Go on.'

'I saw the house of someone who was making a life for themselves. I can understand that, following Huw's death, Heledd's grief might have been all-encompassing but I'm finding it hard to believe that this was still the case now.'

Becca gazed at her. 'You're not local, are you?'

'I've been here less than six months.'

'Then I need to tell you something. When people decide what you are, it stays that way. Heledd was fine when we were growing up but she suffered from depression after conceiving Huw and she never properly recovered. When Huw died, everything came to a head and, as far as I'm concerned, she wasn't treated in a competent manner by the professionals.'

'But this changed?'

'Stay with me, please. I can see you're champing at the bit but you need to wait. No, it didn't change. I was fighting a running battle with mental health services in this county. Her medication needed adjusting from time to time and, very occasionally, she became a danger to herself.'

Becca stopped and picked up a skein of wool. It was marl grey in colour, a shade Mallory usually hated, as it reminded her of her old school uniform. But here, it reflected the colours of the landscape. Becca smiled slightly as she saw Mallory looking at the wool.

'It's undyed,' she said. 'I could take you to the sheep, if you wanted. Anyway, I thought this would be Heledd for the rest of her life. Just about coping. Then, six months ago or so, everything changed.'

'Are we talking about July?'

'It was July when I noticed, but her improvement could have started before then. She came to see me here and I saw she was brighter, more focused. This had happened before, perhaps not to the extent I saw in July, but I was wary. I'd had too many false dawns with Heledd.'

'Did you ask what the cause of the change was?'

'Of course, but subtly. You couldn't just demand these things of her. She'd shrink away and the conversation would be at an end. No, I said she was looking well and jokingly asked if she had a man.'

'And what did she say?'

'She didn't say anything. She just smiled and changed the subject.'

'Which left you with the impression that she did have a man in tow.'

'Yes. As I also said, she changed how she dressed. She used to live in jeans and oversized shirts. It suited her – she never really knew how attractive she was – but it was as if she'd come alive. She bought new dresses. She had one on from Toast and it was from this season.'

'Have you been to her house recently?'

'Not since last summer, I don't think.'

'It has new windows, and appears recently decorated.'

Becca sat back in her seat. 'Well, there you are. If she's got a new man, she's going to spruce the house up.'

'New windows?' Mallory couldn't keep out the incredulity from her voice. 'It's the first time I've heard of someone going that far.'

'You know, I'll go and take a look at that place myself. It doesn't sound like I remember it. She'd made a *cwtch* for herself, true, but it was all very homely. You're telling me it's spruced up?'

'I am.' Mallory paused. 'I guess you'll inherit it from her now.'

'I have a copy of her will, so I know I'm the sole beneficiary. We made wills in each other's favour a few years back. If I'd gone first, she'd have got all this.' Becca waved an arm at the room.

'You'd say you were close?' said Mallory.

'Yes, I would. Things haven't been easy for Heledd but we were close.'

'Can I ask…' Mallory leant back in her chair. 'I know this is nothing to do with the investigation, but you're older than your sister and when you were born, they gave you an English name, Becca. Whereas Heledd's is Welsh.'

Becca laughed. 'You need to read up on your Welsh history. The Rebecca Riots, *Terfysgoedd Beca* in Welsh, were a populist uprising by tenant farmers against the taxes imposed by tollbooths. Many were already living in poverty because of high rents and tithe fees. They attacked tollbooths and their operators as a protest. Nothing wrong with the name Becca around here.'

Embarrassed, Mallory turned the conversation back to the investigation. 'Can I ask what else might have propelled Heledd into such a transformation? Say there isn't a man involved, what else might have given her a new lease of life?'

Becca frowned. 'Getting Huw back, I suppose, but I can assure you that wasn't going to happen. I saw Huw's body myself.'

'I read your statement. I believe you went down to St Non's with Heledd.'

'I was the first person Heledd rang when she realised Huw was missing. She wanted to check he hadn't come round to mine.'

'Was that a possibility?'

'It was, actually, as I lived in St Davids at that time. He'd taken himself off twice before. The first time, Heledd had been busy in the kitchen and he'd slipped out of the front door. She caught up with him pretty quickly and he said he was on his way to Auntie Becca. The second time, it was just before Christmas and he said he could hear the mermaids singing at St Non's. Heledd realised it was Christmas lights playing tunes in a neighbouring house.'

'Did Jack know about these wanderings? It seems an odd idea to get a mate round and start drinking if Huw had a habit of leaving the house.'

For the first time, Mallory saw a flash of discomfort. 'I don't think Heledd mentioned it. You know, Jack and his friends were from a different class to us. They all went to a private school out by the coast. Heledd and I went to the local comp and I know Heledd felt she never really fitted in with the gang.'

'And why might that have prevented her admitting to Jack that Huw occasionally left the house?'

Becca shrugged. 'I got the impression that the one thing Heledd was proud of was her son. Jack wanted a family and he was the first of the gang to settle down. If she admitted that Huw occasionally escaped from the house, it might dent her status as a good mother. Not that I believe all that claptrap. Kids have a mind of their own, but that was Heledd's thinking.'

'Which might also explain her excessive guilt when Huw died. She and Jack, however, didn't get divorced until 2013.'

'No, but their marriage broke down immediately. Jack left the family home within a month.'

'Where did he go?'

'He got a job in Cardiff. He said it was to get away from St Davids during the week but he rarely came home. The marriage was effectively finished from that night.'

'I'd like to come back to Heledd's transformation six months ago. Instead of her meeting someone else, do you think it's possible that Heledd discovered something connected to Huw's disappearance? A piece of knowledge that might have made her feel better about her own role that evening.'

'Like what?'

'She met Duncan Lyall the evening before she died. Did you know that?'

Becca stilled. 'No, I didn't. What did she want with him?'

'She asked if he'd written anything down about the events in 2011.'

Becca frowned. 'Any idea what she meant?'

'Do you?' Mallory was hoping Heledd had told her sister of the note's existence but Becca's bewilderment was clear. 'She never mentioned a note, for example?'

'No. Nothing at all.'

'It doesn't matter. I'm trying to make sense of a few things.'

Becca rose, signalling the meeting was over. 'Well, if you find out, make sure you tell me. I could do with of some of that sparkle dust Heledd had at the end.'

21

Mallory was glad to get out of the house the following morning. Anything to stop her continually refreshing her emails while she waited for her contract to arrive. Toby's initial enthusiasm for a trip out to the sea had dimmed by the time the day arrived. She'd had difficulty getting him out of bed and they were both bad-tempered by the time they boarded the little yellow coach from the marketplace in St Davids. Their destination was Strumble Head. Mallory had never heard of the place but according to Janey at the cathedral, it was the best place to look for seals. The bus had stopped to pick up passengers from other destinations en route, leaving them to take the two remaining seats. The driver, Polly, introduced herself and promised to point out landmarks on the way. Once they were out of St Davids, Mallory opened her bag and pulled out two croissants, handing one to Toby.

'I'm not eating that. It's going to have fluff all over it.'

'It has not. I've only just put it in there.'

Toby folded his arms. 'I'm not hungry.'

'I don't know where we're stopping for lunch. It'll be a bumpy journey and you need something in your stomach.'

Toby regarded the pastry for a moment. 'Fine.' He tore off a morsel and put it in his mouth.

Settling back in her seat, Mallory looked around. She guessed they were all tourists. There was a family of four, with two teenage girls who must also be on half-term. The other two passengers were an older couple who had a little spaniel with them. She hadn't expected animals to be allowed on the coach but it seemed Lyall's Tours had a relaxed attitude to dogs.

Toby finished the croissant and wiped his hands on his jeans. He turned away from her, his eyes on the scenery. The fields were still white, only spindly trees devoid of leaves providing any colour, but at least the roads were clear of snow. The downfall had been quick and the thaw was pressing up behind. When they arrived at Strumble Head, Mallory saw they would have to walk down a precarious path towards the lighthouse. Toby and the two teenagers took the lead, while Mallory brought up the rear, the wound on her leg beginning to pound. Polly, sensing her vulnerability, walked alongside her.

'Have you worked for Lyall's Tours for long?' Mallory asked her.

'Since December. They needed extra drivers for the Christmas markets. I was expecting to be laid off in the new year but I'm still hanging on here. It's a zero-hour contract so no guarantee of work.'

'Must be tough.' Mallory was beginning to limp and wasn't sure she'd make it as far as the lighthouse. She could hear Toby's laughter, which was a wonderful thing, and she didn't want to put a damper on things by having to go back to the bus.

'It is but that's the nature of tourism work, isn't it? What do you do?'

'I'm retired from the police.'

'Really?' Polly stopped. 'That is exciting. Was it an injury?' She looked down at Mallory's leg.

'It was. I'm now working at the cathedral, although it's been a quiet few weeks.'

'Wait until summer arrives.'

They walked in silence as Mallory picked her way across the path. She wished she'd brought the poles Ffion had lent her but she'd been convinced the day would involve nothing more strenuous than sitting on the coach. 'Have you met Duncan Lyall?'

Polly pulled a face.

'You don't like him?' asked Mallory.

'I haven't met him but I've heard...' Polly stopped. 'Never mind. I'd better go and check on the group.'

'Of course. I'm holding everyone up. I'll shuffle along and enjoy the scenery, and meet you on the way back.'

Mallory watched the girl skip forward and cursed having mentioned she was ex-police. It was probably that which had stopped Polly from gossiping with her. So, Duncan had a reputation. It would be interesting to hear what exactly it was.

—

They stopped for lunch at the Angler's Rest, a white-washed building facing the sea, and sat together at a long table, with Toby, to her surprise, taking the seat next to hers.

'You can sit with your new friends if you want.'

Toby curled his lip. 'They're not my friends.'

Mallory sighed, wondering if something had been said at the lighthouse. Toby ordered burger and chips from the menu and devoured it, pinching chips from her plate too.

'Fresh air given you an appetite?' she asked. She was scrolling through the emails on her phone, trying to see if the contract had come through yet. Toby's hand, hovering over her plate, froze.

She ordered more drinks for them and saw that Siân had sent her an email about the interview with Eleri Tew. As she was finishing reading the notes, the father of the teenage girls tapped her on her shoulder.

'I don't think your son's very well. He's got a touch of food poisoning.'

Mallory's heart sank. 'Is he in the bathroom?'

'I can hear him retching in one of the cubicles. I knocked on the door and he said he was fine. I thought you'd want to know.'

'Christ. Thanks for letting me know.'

Mallory knocked on the door to the gents and barged in, startling a customer who was zipping up his flies. 'Toby. Are you OK?'

'Mum.' Toby's outraged voice came clearly over the door. 'This is the men's toilet.'

'I heard you were sick. Open the door.'

Toby unlocked the cubicle door, his face pale. 'I think I ate something that disagreed with me.'

'It can't have been the croissant.'

'Maybe the burger.'

'Food poisoning doesn't work that quickly. How do you feel?'

Toby brushed past her. 'I feel fine. Can we just forget about it?'

She watched him wash his hands under scalding water, the steam rising from the tap. He poured soap into his palms and washed them again, before pulling a wad of paper towels from the tray on the wall.

'Are you sure everything's all right?'

'I said it was, didn't I? Can we please get out of here?'

Mallory followed him out of the toilet and past the table where everyone was finishing up. They climbed aboard the bus and Toby took the window seat, resting his head against the glass.

Mallory glanced down at his jeans-clad legs. They were stick-thin, and surely running should be turning them to muscle? As the bus started, she felt suddenly at sea, riding next to a boy she barely knew, investigating a case she couldn't get to the heart of and wondering what she was doing in this remote place. She put her arm round Toby's shoulders and squeezed him. 'Everything will be fine.'

He turned to her, his face full of misery. 'Will it?'

22

'So,' said Siân, doodling on a notepad, 'do we believe Eleri Tew?'

'You know, it was quite difficult to separate our questions around the death of Heledd Jones and that of her son ten years earlier. You managed it pretty well, Siân, but did you notice something?' asked Harri.

Siân didn't miss a beat. 'She was more relaxed about answering the questions in relation to the death of Heledd Jones than that of Huw.'

'Exactly,' said Harri. 'It suggests, naturally, that Eleri feels she has nothing to worry about in relation to the recent death, which is unsurprising, given her alibi.'

'It also suggests she is hiding something in relation to Huw's death, but I couldn't push it without revealing the existence of the note. We don't want to show our hand yet, do we?'

'No, but I also don't want to focus on just that message, in case it's some weird hoax. Kids get up to all sorts and don't forget the cross was tipped over in an act of vandalism. Leave it to Mallory. She can take it as far as she can.'

'Even if it's a hoax, I think Heledd discovered the contents of that message and she wanted some answers. All five of those original suspects had a vested interest in keeping the fact they lied under cover.'

'Six, including Jack.' Harri wasn't as willing as Siân to write off Jack Jones as a suspect.

'You know,' said Siân, 'when there's a group of friends, there's often an unofficial leader. The sort of coolest one or the best looking. They'd been friends since school, so the dynamic would have shaped itself in their teenage years and may well have hardened in their twenties.'

'Duncan Lyall, from my reading of it, was the most charismatic. I'm not sure I'd call him a leader, though. Each time I've met him, I've been struck by how much he's intent on self-preservation. Is that leadership?'

'Sounds like the Super,' said Siân.

Harri laughed but only after he'd checked over Siân's shoulder that Steph wasn't anywhere within earshot.

'You know who I'd first visit if I was wanting to dig deeper into 2011?' said Siân. 'Gruffydd Ellis. He's the type to write a confession of sorts. He's a vicar so he must have a conscience.'

'Don't you believe it,' said Harri, whose first job as a detective had been to arrest a priest on child pornography charges. 'Do what I say and not what I do.'

Siân looked shocked. 'They're not all like that. The minister at our chapel has been there thirty years. Not a blemish on her character.'

'I'm not saying they're all the same, but they're human beings with all their foibles, like us. What—' They were interrupted by the door opening. A uniformed officer was holding a piece of paper in his hands.

'Thought you might like to see this email we've just received.'

'What is it?'

Harri took the note with a frown on his face. Heledd had been high profile in the community, and they'd had a few calls and emails from well-meaning, and not so well-intentioned, members of the public with their views on what had happened. They were collated, investigated and largely discounted by members of the team. He read the note and looked up at the officer.

'Have you checked this out?'

'Yes, and it all adds up. Not sure why she didn't mention it before.'

'What is it?' asked Siân, who came around his desk to look at the message. 'Catrin Cross is the niece of Eleri Tew. Maybe ask yourselves how Heledd ended up in that field.'

'Eleri never mentioned it in her interview, did she?' said Siân.

'She'll say we never asked, but it never occurred to us, did it? We've assumed it's a random patch of farmland close to Heledd's house.'

'I wonder how important it is.' Siân frowned. 'You know, it's not that surprising Catrin and Eleri are related. I mean, Catrin's family have farmed there for years and we know Eleri was local too.'

'Which is fine. So why the bloody hell didn't either of them tell us?'

'It's pretty clear who will be easier to ask about all this.' Siân snapped shut her notebook. 'I'm on it. I'll drive over to speak to Catrin now. How's the car?'

'My mechanic says it's not worth fixing until after the snow clears. He thinks I might have another dent to match the one on the driver's side.'

'Confidence in you, then.'

'I just exude it, don't I?'

23

Gemma kept her arms around Bethan and pulled her closer. As a trainee doctor, she should have been offering to comfort Heledd or Jack but the female officer who'd led her back into the sitting room had made it clear she didn't want the friends speaking to each other until statements had been taken. Both of Huw's parents looked devastated. Heledd was the most obviously stricken. She was in deep shock, as Gemma had often seen in trauma patients after an accident. If she hadn't been a witness to Huw's death, she'd have suggested Heledd go to hospital. Jack was harder to read but he was also showing signs of shock. His skin was grey-blue and he was sweating profusely. Again, Gemma couldn't step into the role of medic but he needed checking over too.

She glanced around the room. The rest looked subdued. With the exception of Heledd, she'd known her friends since the first day at high school. The gang hadn't been formed then, though. They'd only started hanging out when they'd turned fifteen but, still, the bond was there.

Gemma rubbed her face. It had all seemed such a good idea to head over to Y Bwthyn when she realised that Duncan and Gruffydd had left. No one would miss her if she went over to join them, she'd thought but, of course, Bethan had spotted her absence and come over to join them too. It had turned into a jolly gathering. Just the six of them. Exactly like the old days.

Gemma looked up and saw Heledd's gaze on her.

'I'm so sorry,' she said across the room to her. 'I'm so desperately sorry.'

Heledd lowered her head, unable to reply. When Gemma first met Heledd, she'd been struck by her fragile beauty, in contrast to her own tallness, Eleri's hard edge and Bethan's composure. Nervy was what her own mother would have called Heledd, and it must have held some attraction to Jack. She wondered, however, how much he knew about the extent of Heledd's medical issues. When they were together as a group, he rarely spoke about his wife, leaving Gemma unsure what he knew and what he didn't. Heledd had made an effort this evening: she was wearing a dress that wasn't particularly flattering but didn't take away from her beauty. She was sitting next to Gruffydd who, she guessed, must also want to put some of his training to use. She didn't know much about the priesthood but they would be used to dealing with people under intolerable strain. Gruffydd, however, looked as shell-shocked as Heledd, leaving Gemma to wonder how suitable he was for his chosen profession.

'Why are they interviewing us all separately?' asked Bethan.

'It's procedure. They probably want to make sure our stories tally.'

'Tally?' Gemma watched as Bethan swallowed. 'We're not under any suspicion, are we?'

The girl was hopelessly naive. Huw was dead at St Non's and the police would be establishing the timeline to check whether or not his death was an accident. It was ridiculous. No one would want to hurt Huw and yet they'd now have their movements, conversations and friendships come under close scrutiny. She couldn't understand why Heledd hadn't just taken Huw to the party. It was only an hour, for God's sake, and most mothers would have woken up their children so they could enjoy some downtime together.

Gemma sighed and untangled herself from Bethan. 'Just keep to the facts. When you arrived and what you did. We'll all cover for each other. It's what friends do, isn't it?'

24

The Second Lie

Toby was still in bed when Mallory left the house. He'd left the door open to his room and Mallory stuck her head round to say goodbye. When she saw him lying on his stomach, snoring slightly, she decided to leave him be. She'd washed his running things from the previous day and he'd pulled them out of the drawer, ready for his next jog. She doubted he'd be up to it. That morning, the bathroom had a sickly smell that Toby had attempted to conceal by spraying some of her perfume around the space. Whatever he'd eaten was still disagreeing with him. Feeling guilty at leaving him, she slid into her car and started the engine.

The snow was in an eerie stasis state. The fall had stopped but temperatures were too cold for a thaw, leaving the town like a Hollywood stage set awaiting its ice princess. Mallory was pleased to see that the gritter had been out and the roads were in a decent shape. The surgery was a mile or so outside St Davids, in a newly built facility with plenty of parking. After receiving Mallory's new patient form, the practice had attempted to book her in with a male doctor. She'd already spotted that Gemma Bowen was the only female GP at the practice and had insisted on seeing her. Now Mallory was in the waiting room, she felt like weeping. The combined effects of first her attack while in CID, divorce, and then her poisoning on Eldey were finally catching up with her. She thought of the message in the note and tried to steel herself. She was here for a reason and she needed to see her plan through.

Gemma came into reception to collect Mallory who was reading on her phone an email from Harri updating her about his interview with Eleri Tew. Gemma was physically imposing, just under six feet tall, but clearly happy in her skin, as she wore boots with heels. Glad to leave the waiting room where a patient next to her had been coughing phlegmily into a handkerchief, Mallory followed Gemma into her office.

Gemma Bowen sat heavily in her chair. 'Thank you for booking an appointment. We like to see new patients when they register. Is there anything of particular concern you want to talk about? I can see from your notes you've had a time of it recently,' she commented.

Mallory saw the form she'd completed up on screen. 'I'm not sure. My leg wound has never properly healed. I was stabbed repeatedly when I was attacked in the force. The wound that gave paramedics most concern punctured my lung but that healed, eventually, after a prolonged stay in hospital. My leg is better than it was but I still walk with a limp.'

'Can I see? Do you want to come to the examination table?'

Mallory undid her trousers, pulled them off and sat down. Gemma snapped on a pair of surgical gloves and began to prod the red gash.

'It appears to be healing nicely, although I can see it's taken a while.'

'I had an issue last autumn, where poison was deliber-ately put into an ointment I was using for the wound.'

Gemma straightened and took off her gloves. 'I remember reading about the case. You're lucky to be alive, by all accounts. What are you doing in St Davids?'

'I've recently got a job in the shop at the cathedral.'

Gemma glanced at her in surprise as she sat back down in her chair. 'How do you find it?'

'Generally OK. It's a part-time job but I've actually just been offered some consultancy work for the police. They need an extra pair of hands for a case they're working on: the death of Heledd Jones. What can you tell me about her?'

Gemma flushed, looking down at her hands. 'I knew Heledd slightly. I was in St Davids the night her son, Huw, died.'

'I'm sorry if it's bringing back bad memories. I'm learning that this is a close-knit community. Everyone knows each other.'

'Is Heledd's death suspicious?' asked Gemma. 'I was sorry to hear that she died. I had assumed everything had finally caught up with her.'

'What do you mean?' asked Mallory.

'Well, she had a history of mental illness, as I'm sure you know. I was involved in her care when I worked at Larch House, a mental health facility.'

'When was this?'

'Just after Huw was born. She suffered from postnatal depression and was treated at the unit.'

Mallory zipped up her jeans and sat opposite Gemma, her mind turning over what the doctor had just told her. She saw the GP was agitated, and trying to hide the fact by typing notes into the computer.

Mallory said, 'I've been tasked to check if there's any connection to the death of Heledd's son in 2011.'

'Huw?'

'Yes, that's right.'

'Is that why you're here? To question me about that night?'

'What do you mean?'

Gemma turned her gaze fully onto Mallory. She had pale blue, almost grey, eyes fringed with dark lashes.

'I mean, if you want to question me about that night, I'd appreciate it if you contacted me outside of working hours. I'm very busy.'

Mallory realised that, behind her anger, Gemma was exhausted. Her skin had a translucent quality, with smudges of brown under her eyes.

'I'm sorry. I'm aware, of course, that you were present the night Huw died but I've done nothing further than read everyone's statements from that night.'

Gemma frowned. 'Everyone's?'

It was Mallory's turn to frown. She was missing something. 'Yes, that's right. I simply wanted to see what everyone said about what had happened the night Huw went missing in case it might shed light on Heledd's death.'

'In what way? This was nearly twelve years ago. What possible relevance could it have?'

'I don't know yet. Can I ask you... I've read your statement and you seemed convinced that Huw's death was an accident. What made you so sure about it at the time?'

Gemma looked up at the clock, clearly desperate to get rid of Mallory. 'It was a bit chaotic at the house that night. People coming and going. I'm afraid I don't think Huw was at the forefront of anyone's mind, except obviously Heledd's, but she was at the party. It would have been easy for a child to slip out of the house.'

'No signs of foul play?'

Again, Gemma's gaze turned on Mallory. 'Not one of us in that house would have done any harm to that beautiful boy.'

'I'm sorry, I'm not buying the conclusion he just wandered off. I think something else happened. Had Heledd been in touch with you recently?'

'I haven't seen her for years. Why would she contact me?'

'She'd been in touch with both Duncan Lyall and Eleri Tew. Why not you too?'

'I've not heard from her. What did she want with Duncan and Eleri?'

Mallory saw that Gemma was surprised by the news of Heledd contacting her friends. It suggested the GP wasn't in touch with either of them. 'We think Heledd had new information about the night Huw died and wanted it clarifying.'

'What new information?'

'She was particularly interested in the statements you all made about the evening. In particular, she wanted to know about any specific lies each of you might have told.'

Gemma stood, towering over Mallory.

'I think this has gone on long enough. I have patients waiting in the surgery. As I said, if you want to speak to me in an official capacity, I'd appreciate it if you contacted me in the evening.'

'There's nothing you want to add to your original statement? It's new to me, for example, that you saw Heledd in a professional context. There's no mention of that in your statement whatsoever.'

'I wouldn't have mentioned it. I'd have considered it part of doctor-patient confidentiality.'

'What nonsense. You know as well as I do that when a serious crime is suspected, it's within your rights to pass on any relevant medical information to the police.'

'But Heledd couldn't have killed Huw,' cried Gemma. 'She was at the party so his death had nothing to do with her.'

'That wasn't your call to make. When you were questioned, you said you hardly knew Heledd.'

'That was true.'

'But you didn't say that you had met her in a professional context. I'm asking you again, why not?'

Mallory's questioning was relentless and Gemma shrank from her.

'Because,' Gemma said finally, 'Heledd didn't want Jack to know about her depression. She came to Larch House without her husband's knowledge.'

Mallory stared at the GP. 'She never told Jack she was suffering from postnatal depression? Why keep something like that from him?'

'I don't know.' Gemma had reached the end of her patience. She strode to the door and flung it open. 'Ask him. I'm not privy to the dynamics of people's marriages.'

25

'We've had the results of the tests the pathologist ordered.'

Siân knocked on Harri's door as he was scouring his online diary, trying to find a spot when he could undertake his unconscious bias training. All three sessions were programmed for the coming fortnight and he had his hands full already with the Heledd Jones case. With a feeling of relief, he closed the window, the date not yet selected.

'Don't keep me in suspense.'

'Her blood alcohol level was forty-three per cent. We're talking serious difficulties walking and speaking. Given she was seen drinking earlier in the pub, the pathologist believes it was the contributory factor towards her death of acute hypothermia. Do you want me to spell out the science behind it?'

Annoyed, Harri folded his arms. 'How did I ever pass those inspector exams?'

'All right. In essence, there were high concentrations of something called catecholamine. It's a chemical present in most hypothermia deaths, as it's secreted in cold weather. It confirms the other signs found present during the post-mortem, including swelling of the hands and feet, and purple patches visible on the skin. Heledd froze to death.'

'What about the blood work? Any signs of a sedative administered?'

'Nothing. Alcohol was the major contributory factor. What do you think?'

'I think it's all sounding a bit bloody convenient. Duncan says she only had a drink or two and witnesses stated Heledd was perfectly able to walk when she got on and off the bus. Where did the other alcohol come from?'

'She possibly had a bottle of spirits in her pocket that she chucked when it was finished. We're checking shopping receipts now.'

'The route Heledd walked has been searched, though, and nothing's been found, and it doesn't sound like this new Heledd that had emerged over the last six months.'

'Perhaps she'd learnt something during her chat with Duncan that sent her over the edge.'

'He says not and, anyway, he dropped her off at the bus stop. There was no chance for her to purchase alcohol after that. What about your chat with Catrin Cross? What did she say about not mentioning her relationship to Eleri Tew?'

'She looked guilty, so I'd say it was a deliberate omission. I pressed her pretty hard and I also got her to admit she searched Heledd's body before calling us.'

'What the bloody hell did she do that for?'

'I guess to see if there was anything incriminating in relation to Eleri, although Catrin isn't going as far as to admit that.'

'You think it relevant to the case?' asked Harri.

'I'm not sure it is. The essential facts hold up. You find a dead body in your field and when the police come to interview you, your first thought is not, oh by the way, the aunt I never speak to was briefly in the house where the dead woman's son disappeared from over a decade ago. It's not exactly an organic conversation.'

'Bloody hell, she was giving an official statement. Where the hell do you get organic from?' Harri was sure it was one of those training courses. Organic, for God's sake. The fact that Catrin had searched the body suggested she had her wits about her well enough. Siân, however, did have a point, and it was Eleri who should have mentioned the relationship. The arrogance of the woman made his blood boil but he supposed it didn't really matter now, in any case.

After Siân had left, Harri sat thinking. Finally, he picked up his phone and dialled Mallory's number. 'You signed that contract yet?'

'Morning to you, too.'

'Listen, I've just had the results back from the pathologist. There was an excess of alcohol in Heledd's blood and I can't get to the bottom of it. Can you sign the bloody document? Do the electronic signature now and send it back to me, and I'll sign it this side. I want you in Carmarthen as soon as possible.'

'I could come down today, although I need to check in on Toby first. He wasn't well last night. I do have some information for you, though. I've just spoken to Gemma Bowen.'

'Save it for when you get here. Come down as soon as you can.'

Harri got up and stretched his legs. The headache that he had woken up with was getting worse and his mouth was parched. He took a long swig of water from a bottle and opened up his emails. Mallory had signed the document and he added his own electronic signature too.

As he stepped out into the open-plan CID room, he saw Siân talking to a uniformed constable near the window. They glanced over at him and he saw Siân nod her head.

'Everything OK?'

'Charlie, here, says we've been called by Lizzie Lyall, Duncan's wife. She's at the airport in Spain, as she's flying back this morning, and she says she can't get hold of her husband.'

Harri frowned. 'Why is she calling us? Perhaps he's in a meeting or out somewhere.'

'She says she's been trying since five a.m. our time. Duncan doesn't sleep well so he's up early every morning and uses the gym in the house. She expected him to answer her first call. He asked her to telephone him to make sure they made it to the airport in time for the early flight. She's tried every half hour since.'

Harri glanced up at the clock on the wall. Ten past ten.

'We've sent a patrol car to the property but they can't get beyond the gate. It's like Fort Knox there,' said the PC.

'Do you have a number for Mrs Lyall?' asked Harri.

'She'll be on the plane now. She gave us permission to enter the house, in case he's had a heart attack or something. We're waiting for the go-ahead from my sergeant but he thought it worth checking with you too. We know Mr Lyall was questioned in relation to the death of Heledd Jones.'

Harri glanced at Siân. 'I think, given the circumstances, we should have a look at the place. Can you radio the patrol car and say we'll join them?'

–

In the car, Siân was quiet, staring out of the window. Harri kept to the speed limit. One bump in his car was enough

164

in one week, but he could feel the pull of urgency. As they neared the house, Siân roused herself.

'What are we expecting?'

Harri pulled the handbrake and shrugged. 'Not sure, but I haven't got a good feeling about this.'

The immediate problem of entering the grounds was resolved by one of the patrol officers, who produced an Enforcer from the car.

'Do you think it'll work on an electronic gate?' asked Siân, who got a look of contempt from the constable. Harri watched as the spring from the device forced itself against the metal frame, causing the magnetic lock to break. With a sarcastic grin, the officer opened the gate.

Ignoring him, Harri and Siân got back into the car and drove up the driveway. A blue Mercedes was parked in front of the window, its body as dirty as Harri's car. After a brief glance inside, Harri rang the doorbell. Siân was peering through the downstairs windows, checking the rooms.

'I can't see anything,' said Siân. 'The funny thing is the curtains are drawn on the room on the left, which I think was the living room when we passed through the house to the kitchen. It suggests he hasn't got up to open the curtains yet.'

'What about upstairs?'

Siân stood back. 'One set is drawn, the rest open. He might still be in bed.'

That's not good, thought Harri. He turned to the constable and nodded at the white front door. 'You can have all the fun again.'

The door opened as easily as the gate and the two uniforms went in first. Glancing at Siân, Harri followed them. There was the smell they all recognised. Blood being warmed by the excessive heat emanating from the radiators.

'Don't enter anywhere. Go to the entrance of each room and look in.'

'Jesus Christ.' The officer who'd had a grin on his face a minute earlier looked like he was going to throw up.

Harri walked over to him, putting up a warning hand for the others who made to follow. At the sight of the blood and slaughter, he turned his face away.

'Call it in,' he said to Siân. 'Secure the room and get the team over here as soon as possible. This has happened recently.'

Harri stumbled outside and fought down the bile rising in his throat. It was years since he'd been sick at the sight of a corpse, but his own body was proving hard to predict these days. In the end, the cold wind sweeping across the front lawn revived him enough and he was able to pull out his mobile.

His last call had been to Mallory and it was her voice he wanted to hear. That was the problem with violent death. Not enough of your colleagues were acquainted with it. It left you an outlier, getting your respite from others who'd looked into darkness.

'What now?' asked Mallory.

Harri told her and heard her sharp intake of breath. 'Shit. I'll ring Toby rather than swing by the flat. I'll be down as soon as I can.'

'You won't get anywhere near the scene until later. Go and see your boy and keep in touch. You said you'd seen Gemma Bowen. Did she say anything that might link her to this?'

'The opposite, I'd say. She was surprised when I told her Heledd had met Duncan. I did manage to work out the lie, though.'

'And?'

'She'd known Heledd in a professional capacity but specifically withheld that information from her statement.'

'Why the deliberate lie?'

'I'm not sure.'

Harri heard a noise behind him and saw Siân in the doorway. 'Look, I've got to go. Good news you've worked out two of the lies. I think Duncan's might be a little harder to fathom now.'

26

Duncan was making a concerted effort to sober himself up to answer the investigator's questions. Parts of the evening were difficult to remember. When he looked at his watch, he realised it was only twenty past nine. Christ. What a New Year it was turning out to be. Eleri naturally had pissed off, leaving him to rack his brains to remember an order of events that hadn't been important to him at the time. He remembered arriving at Eleri's house with plans to slip over to see Jack once Heledd had arrived at the party. Not that Eleri minded that sort of thing. She liked him for sex but preferred him out of the way when situations arose where he might embarrass her. The funny thing was that it was he, not Eleri, who was Pembrokeshire establishment. Everyone knew Lyall's Tours and his father was a stalwart of the local Chamber of Commerce, whose current Chair was on the Conservative constituency selection committee.

Duncan drank a glass of water and glanced around the cornflower blue kitchen. That must be Heledd's work, not Jack's. God knows why the pair of them had tied the knot. What the hell had Jack been thinking? Heledd was pretty enough. All right, he thought about her sometimes when he was having sex with Eleri but, God, she was hardly their sort of person. The only good thing to have come from the marriage was Huw, a beautiful child adored by Jack. Together, they had watched his body being winched from the rocks, Jack rigid with shock. Duncan had spotted a tourist taking a video of the recovery on their mobile phone. He had left his best friend's side for a moment, snatched the phone and thrown it over the cliff. One look at his face, and the tourist had decided not to make an issue of it. Ghoul.

As he sobered up, Duncan could feel the beginnings of his own shock. Anger was starting to shapeshift into horror at what had come to pass, and he had an idea of the origins of a deception that might have led Huw to the bottom of the cliff. The main thing was that they all covered for each other. In truth, with the exception of Jack, none of them should really have been at Y Bwthyn. God, even the name gave him palpitations. The house wasn't even a cottage, so why name it Y Bwthyn, 'the little cottage'? Anyway, he would keep his statement as concise as possible. Not give anything away and blame any shortcomings in his account on the amount he had had to drink. No acting required there. He was certain everyone else would do the same. At least, they'd better do or it wouldn't just be the phone going over the cliff.

27

The Third Lie

Mallory stared at the imprint of where the body of Duncan Lyall had fallen, and shivered. She had never become inured to death, and each passing was a tragedy. This catastrophe, however, was dominated by the manner of his killing. The blood spatter suggested primaeval fury, which meant Duncan had seriously upset his killer. Forensics had finished their work. When she'd arrived, Harri had been champing at the bit to get a look at the crime scene, but now they were finally allowed into the living room, he was oddly subdued. He'd told Mallory he knew Duncan a little, which meant there was a part of the process that would involve him addressing his own grief.

Mallory was sorry she hadn't met Duncan in real life. He had been a man of many faces. She'd found his statement a little coarse, even when considering it had been mediated by police language. His account of that evening had felt matter-of-fact in the face of such a tragedy. Harri had described him as charismatic and charming, without being overly creepy, which was a difficult line to navigate. However, the coach driver she had spoken to had been less complimentary. She glanced around at the blood sprayed up the walls and decided it was lucky his wife and children had been on holiday in Spain. Given the frenzy of the attack, Mallory didn't think for a minute any of them would have been spared, if they had crossed paths with the killer.

Until now, they had been dealing with the tragic death of a child in 2011 and the unexplained passing of the boy's mother. Mallory had barely got going with her questions, and her suspicions that the two events were connected due to a series of untruths had sometimes felt nebulous. This act of violence, however, would blow everything out of the water. There would be a major incident team created and Harri might find himself sidelined as others took charge of the investigation. In Mallory's experience, they rarely appointed a DI as the senior investigating officer in a murder case.

Harri was standing next to Siân, looking like he wanted to be sick.

'No need to look,' she told Harri. 'The injuries will be detailed in the autopsy report.'

Siân glanced at the pair of them. She had the iron stomach of the young. 'The killer must have carried on hitting him long after he was dead.' She pointed a finger at the imprint of a hammer, lying by Duncan's side, which had been removed by police. 'Why leave the hammer for us? It gives us more forensic possibilities than if they took it with them.'

Harri stirred. 'If the weapon's found on someone, they've some explaining to do. If they dump it when leaving the scene, who's to say they're not caught on CCTV or a doorbell camera? Easier they leave it here, which also suggests it's not immediately associated with the killer.'

Mallory squinted closer at the outline. More mallet than hammer, she thought. The type campers used to pitch their tents. 'If it's a woman then maybe it'd be a heavy instrument to lug about. A male killer might not be able to take it away without a bag to carry it in.'

'So now you're officially on the team,' said Harri. 'Any theories as to what might have happened here?'

Mallory could feel the gaze of the two detectives, neither hostile nor exactly benevolent. It felt like she was on trial.

'You both saw him recently. Did he give you any suggestions that he was concerned for his safety?'

'Nope,' said Siân. 'Although, despite Heledd's recent death, we both got the impression he wasn't initially sure why we were here. It's possible he had something to be guilty about.'

'Something not connected to Heledd's death?' asked Mallory.

Siân shrugged. 'Just an impression.'

'In answer to your question, I don't have any theories. What are your thoughts, Harri?'

Harri shrugged. 'I don't know. Lyall's Tours are sound enough but the business was beginning to develop a reputation for sharp practices. It might have a bearing on this.'

'Could I dig around the house a little?' asked Mallory.

Harri nodded and pulled Siân aside. Mallory pushed open the nearest door, which led to Duncan's study. The forensics team had rifled through the desk and had presumably bagged up any documents that might be of use to the investigation. She wondered what they'd focused on. Perhaps financial affairs, although who kept paper bank statements these days? There was no evidence of a laptop, which suggested it had already been removed.

In a corner on the table, there was a photo of a group of friends, and she saw Jack and Duncan with their pals. It must have been taken a few years before Huw's death, as the group looked barely out of their teens. Gruffydd and Bethan looked younger and more carefree; Bethan was smiling into the camera with none of her usual reserve. Eleri stood back a little from her friends, asserting her independence from the group dynamics, possibly. Gemma Bowen was unsmiling but her eyes were on Bethan, as if checking her reaction to something said. There was no Heledd, unless she had been behind the camera. The three men, Duncan, Gruffydd and Jack, were standing at the back and had their arms around each other's shoulders. Bethan had one arm around the legs of Gruffydd. They must have been together for a few years before the night of Huw's death and they definitely looked like a couple here.

Mallory slipped the photo out of the frame and looked at the back. Nothing was written on it to suggest when it had been taken. She replaced the image but took a photo on her phone, in case she needed to refer to it again. The rest of the photos were of Duncan with his wife and children, two girls about six and eight. Lizzie Lyall had been met at the airport by a Family Liaison Officer who was now helping the family.

Mallory looked round in dismay. There was nothing here to hint at what Duncan might have kept from the original investigation. She left the study, padded up to his bedroom and had a cursory look in the bedside cabinets, which again had been checked through. A noise from outside made her look out.

'There's a car approaching,' shouted Mallory. 'Are you expecting anyone?'

'Shit.' Harri's voice floated up the stairs. Mallory watched as Harri stepped out of the front door and hurried out to meet the driver of the car.

It was a petite woman with a dark bob, who matched the photos on the desk. Duncan's wife had made it home.

Mallory hurried down the stairs and joined Harri outside.

'This is my house and I want to go in.' Lizzie was hysterical, tears streaming down her blotched cheeks. She wiped her nose on the sleeve of her coat. Mallory dug into her pockets and pulled out a packet of tissues.

'You don't want to go in there,' she said.

Lizzie took the packet from Mallory's hand and blew her nose. 'Who's she?' she asked Harri.

'A colleague,' said Harri. 'She's right. Please don't go into the living room until we've been able to clean up.'

The woman blanched. 'Oh my God. What did they do to him?'

'We can talk about that in a bit,' said Mallory. 'Where are your children?'

'With their grandmother. My mother, I mean, not Duncan's. We were met at the airport by two of your colleagues but I'm afraid I've given them the slip. They still think I'm upstairs, putting the children to bed. We had an early start this morning.'

Harri rolled his eyes and got on the phone. His colleagues were in for a rollicking, and rightly so, thought Mallory.

'Can I see Duncan, at least?' Lizzie asked Mallory.

'The body's been removed to the hospital, pending an autopsy.'

'Can I see it there?'

174

'It'll be up to the pathologist but I don't think that's a good idea. Let's sit in your car, shall we, and I'll get someone to accompany you back to your mother's after our chat.'

Mallory steered Lizzie back into her grey Range Rover. It smelt of orange drink and sweet wrappers. Lizzie must be an indulgent mother or perhaps she'd wanted to keep them quiet on the journey back from the airport. She saw Harri had finished his call and was coming to join them.

'Do you know who's done this to Duncan?' Lizzie asked Harri who, to Mallory's surprise, had slid into the back seat, leaving the passenger space for her.

'Not at the moment. Has your husband had any threats to his life?'

Lizzie paused, dabbing her eyes. 'Don't all successful businessmen have enemies?'

Not really, thought Mallory. 'Do you have anyone specific in mind?' she asked.

Lizzie shrugged. 'No one in particular.' She took a deep breath. 'Duncan began to take his security more seriously a few years ago. We had the intercom put on the gate and updated the house alarm.'

'He didn't say why?' asked Harri.

'The business was expanding and I got the impression we'd gone up in the world. You should have seen this house when we first bought it. It was stuck in the 1980s, with its burgundy bathroom suite and dado rails around the centre of the walls. We did it up ourselves. I suggested moving elsewhere as the business became more successful but he liked it here. I even suggested returning to St Davids but he wasn't having any of that. Too many memories.'

'Did you know...' Mallory paused to get her words right. She didn't want to antagonise the woman. 'Did you know that Duncan had a drink with Heledd Jones recently?'

'Her?' Lizzie turned to face Mallory, her expression horrified. 'Don't tell me she's responsible for this.'

'Heledd is dead.'

'Dead? How?'

Mallory glanced back at Harri. Duncan had presumably spoken to his wife in the last week and yet hadn't mentioned Heledd at all.

'We don't know,' said Harri, 'but there's a possibility that the deaths are connected. We interviewed Duncan about the night Heledd died and he was very open about his movements.'

'He met her the night she died?' Lizzie pulled down the sun visor and dabbed at the mascara streaking her cheeks. She was making an effort to pull herself together but Mallory thought the act was also defensive. By looking at herself in the mirror, she was avoiding their gaze.

'Yes,' said Harri, 'but as I said, he gave a perfectly good account of his movements that night. He wasn't a suspect.'

'That's all right, then.'

Mallory leant forward. 'Lizzie, did Duncan ever talk about the night Huw Jones died?'

Lizzie knew what Mallory was talking about straight away. 'Sometimes. When he'd had a drink, he'd become a bit maudlin. Actually, strike that, he was usually incapacitated but not in a nasty way. He'd get all sentimental and talk about his days in St Davids. The night of Huw's death came up a lot too.'

'He was sober the last few years, though, wasn't he?' said Harri.

'Went to AA and got clean.' There was pride in Lizzie's voice.

'Did he ever say anything specific about what happened?' asked Mallory. 'For example, things he wished he'd done or said.'

Lizzie frowned. 'Not that I remember. I got the impression he'd concocted this plan with Jack that the two of them would get stuck into drinking while they waited for Heledd to come home from the party. He was a bit annoyed the plan got hijacked by the other friends. You know what friendship groups are like. If one does something, the others have to follow.'

'You think that was the dynamic?' asked Mallory. 'The others gatecrashed an invite that hadn't been extended to them?'

'That's the impression he gave. Why are you asking me this?'

Harri spoke from behind. 'You asked if there was a connection between Heledd Jones's death and Duncan's. We're trying to find one.'

Lizzie pulled her phone out of her bag. 'I know Super-intendent Steph Morris. Would it help if I called her?'

'No,' said Mallory, before Harri was forced to answer. 'This death will be given priority, believe me. Please, Mrs Lyall, think. Was there anything Duncan was edgy about or didn't like to discuss further?'

'You don't think he could have had anything to do with Huw's death, surely?'

'I'm just trying to get to the bottom of what happened that night. We think Heledd was trying to do the same.'

Lizzie slammed up the sun visor and puckered her lips.

'Something went on the night Huw died. I don't know what, but Duncan was furious about it.'

'You mean,' said Mallory, trying to keep her voice even, 'something happened that resulted in Huw's death?'

'I don't know. I mean, I don't think so. Duncan didn't like to talk about it but I never thought he was responsible for the death of Huw.'

'What then? What happened?'

Lizzie turned towards her and Mallory saw how exhausted she was. 'Duncan, when he had a drink, got a bit free and easy with his fists. He never hit me. I promise you that. I'd have walked and taken the kids with me.'

'Who would he fight with, then?'

'Other guys he met outside the pub, taxi drivers when they tried to rip him off. Always men, he was never violent with women.'

'OK and you think he was violent that night?' Mallory turned to Harri, who was partially in darkness now that dusk had begun to fall. Someone had turned the lights on in the house and the windows glittered against the darkening sky. He was content to let her continue with the interview.

'One evening, when he came home plastered, he started talking about that night again. Only, this time he said, "I never should have hit him." When I asked him what he was talking about, he clammed up.'

Mallory shivered, the cold of the afternoon air seeping into her bones. 'Are you sure he didn't mean Huw? That perhaps he'd been crying and he hit him.'

Lizzie was shaking her head. 'I assumed it was one of the other men. Probably not Jack, as those two were thick as thieves. Maybe Gruffydd, as he was always, you know, the spare part. I assumed he meant Gruffydd.'

'But why would he hit him?' Mallory thought back to the statements. If the two men had scuffled then neither would have mentioned it to the police for fear of incriminating themselves. But the statements would likely have been given straight after Huw's body had been found. Any fight, if this was Duncan's lie, must have taken place while they were in the house together or shortly afterwards. She needed to find out more. Unless… unless… it had been tiny Huw that Duncan had hit. That would put a very different slant on matters.

28

Harri watched as Lizzie reversed the car and drove back up the driveway. She'd turned down the offer of an officer to accompany her, saying they could call for a statement later. The arrogance of the rich, he guessed. He was pretty sure that despite Mallory's words, she'd be on the phone to his boss soon enough. He doubted he'd be lead officer for this investigation, which meant a difficult interview with Steph tomorrow. Mallory, he saw, was looking at her watch.

'Need to get going?'

'It's not that. I've left Toby in town, as I'm sick of him sitting in front of the computer. I need to pick him up.'

'Why not come to ours for something to eat? He can meet the kids.'

'You sure your wife won't mind?'

The reference to Paula made Harri jolt, an unusual reaction, but perhaps it was because Lizzie's grief had reminded him of his own. No longer raw but still there if he picked at the scab.

'My wife died. I live with my sister.'

Mallory frowned. 'God, I'm sorry. Was this recent?'

'No. Ellie barely remembers her mum. It's not been easy but we do our best. Anyway, come along. We can't chat about the case in front of the kids but we can at least unwind. I'll follow you while you pick up your son then you can tail me back to Pembroke.'

'Well, OK.'

They drove towards Haverfordwest, where Toby stood on a street corner waiting for Mallory. Harri noticed that he had her dark hair and was tall, but his weight had some catching up to do. Once Mallory had pulled up behind him, they set off towards Harri's house. He hadn't gone half a mile before his phone rang. Mallory's name came up on the dashboard.

'What about I interview Gruffydd next? Maybe Lizzie was right and there was a fight with Gruffydd. I might be able to get to the bottom of that.'

'I thought we weren't talking shop tonight,' said Harri, conscious of Mallory's son listening.

'Don't mind me,' he heard the boy mutter.

'If you want to interview him in an official capacity, for God's sake make sure you frame it as if you are looking into the death of Heledd Jones. Don't mention Duncan at all.'

'Think I might be sidelined now? Get shunted off before I've even begun?'

'I don't know.'

Mallory cut the call and didn't ring again. He pulled his car into the drive and Mallory parked on the road outside his house. Harri was proud of his 1930s semi. He'd bought it with Paula when they'd got married and he was now well over halfway paying off the mortgage. Fran insisted on paying rent, which she could well afford, but he'd put that into a savings account for his two kids. They'd need all the help they could get when they wanted to get on the housing ladder.

Ellie was on the floor, reading a magazine, when they came in. She rolled over lazily, exposing her stomach, until she hastily pulled down her T-shirt as soon as she saw Mallory and Toby behind him. 'Dad, you never said you were bringing anyone with you.'

'Didn't know I needed permission in my own home.' Harri took off his jacket and hung it on a peg. 'Where's Ben and Auntie Fran?'

'Fran's on a Zoom call. Ben's out.'

'We're going to have a Chinese. I'll see if I can persuade him to collect it for me.' He turned to Mallory and Toby. 'Come in and sit down.'

Now he could study Toby up-close, he saw that the lad was rake-thin. He'd met him once before, on the case on Eldey, but hadn't noticed his gauntness then. He pulled out a menu from the shelf where a stack of flyers lay, something Fran always chastised him about. Apparently, you were supposed to use your iPad for things like that.

Ellie was already on it. 'Fran will have lemon chicken. She has it every time.'

He passed the menu to Mallory, so she could look through it, and took off his tie. He was dying to put on S4C, as he wanted to see what the reporters were saying. There'd be pictures of yellow buses, he was sure, but he wanted to see the tone of the news and whether any of Duncan's shadier side slipped into the reporting. Mallory was consulting with Toby about the menu and he wanted a prawn curry. When Harri couldn't get hold of Ben, he rang the Chinese and ordered a dish for him too that he could microwave when he got in.

While they waited, he saw Ellie get up and go upstairs, returning wearing a longer top. Fran followed her down, her eyes on Mallory as she came into the room.

'This is my colleague. I told you all about her.'

'You did.' Fran smiled across at the visitors. 'Having Chinese? Just so you know, I do cook but my efforts go unappreciated when there's a takeaway on offer. I thought you'd be late tonight?'

'The day's not finished for me, I don't think, but I need something to eat. So does Mallory.'

'I've been listening to the news online,' said Fran, perching on the armrest of the sofa. 'I just can't believe it.'

'Did you know Duncan Lyall?' Mallory asked Fran.

Fran glanced at Harri. 'I knew of him, of course, but I'd never met him. No reason to do so. I work in medical negligence and he certainly wasn't a client.'

Fran was settling down for a gossip and Harri wasn't sure whether to be relieved or concerned. His sister could be indiscreet when she wanted to and he hoped Mallory would bear that in mind if anything was revealed that might impact on the case. The gleam in Mallory's eye suggested she knew Fran could be a mine of information.

'Do you know any of the people who were in the house at the time of Huw Jones's death? Has Harri mentioned this to you?'

'We've chatted about it. I know Dr Bowen but she's not my GP. We're part of a professional women's network and have chatted in the past. She's a bit, I dunno, stand-offish, which has led me to wonder what she's like with her patients. And, of course, I know Jack Jones professionally and we briefly worked for the same firm.'

'She was invited to his wedding,' said Harri.

Toby had slid his phone out of his pocket and was flicking through some website. He looked up, his eyes shining.

'Mum, you never told me he was the owner of Lyall's Tours. We went on a trip with them the other day.'

Mallory rolled her eyes. 'Let's not talk about it now.'

'But he owned all those yellow coaches. You see them everywhere. Not just the one that picked us up. I look out of the window and see them pass by.'

'The business will carry on,' said Mallory, still looking cross. 'You can still bus-spot if that's what makes you happy.'

Toby made a face. 'You know, outside school there was an ice-cream van that was busted by the police and I thought of that when I saw the buses.'

Harri frowned, looking at the boy. Mallory had said her ex-husband was a copper too and it made a difference. He knew his own kids had an instinct for what constituted criminality, and many children of detectives entered the force as well. Mallory, he saw, had also turned to her son. 'What do you mean, Tobe? Why did it remind you of the ice-cream van?'

'I don't know.'

'Think.'

Toby folded his arms. 'I saw one at the sea's edge when I went for a run today. Maybe it was that.'

'They stop at the beaches,' said Harri. 'Nothing unusual there.'

Toby shrugged, embarrassed he was now under scrutiny.

'Seriously, Tobe. I believe you. Think again. What's the connection to the ice-cream van?'

At last Toby got it. 'There was a queue of people waiting for the bus to arrive.'

Harri looked at Mallory's face and frowned. 'What is it?' For God's sake, what were this pair up to? People queued to get on the coaches. So what?

'I presume,' said Mallory, 'that this is the same ice-cream van where the owners were convicted of selling drugs to your classmates.'

Toby shrugged, looking down at his dingy trainers. 'It was just what reminded me, that's all.'

Harri groaned. If it was drugs, not only would he be off the case, but then so would Steph. It would be the responsibility of the County Lines team. He caught Mallory's eye and grimaced.

29

Mallory left Harri's house, desperate for her bed after the Chinese meal she'd scoffed. Toby also appeared to have had his fill, dozing next to her as she navigated her car down the windy Pembrokeshire lanes. It was trying to snow, and she wove in and out of localised flurries that failed to settle on her windscreen. It had been an interesting day. She'd begun with that illuminating chat with GP Gemma Bowen and ended it looking at the room where Duncan Lyall had met his killer. She'd also managed to unearth Duncan's lie just at the point she'd thought he would take his secret to the grave with him.

An interesting, exhausting and confusing day. It was a shame she hadn't been able to sit and discuss everything with someone, like she'd been used to doing when in the Met. A trip to the pub to let off steam but also tease out some of the wilder theories. Nevertheless, it had been a good evening, with even Toby appearing to enjoy himself. In fact, Harri's domestic set-up had induced in her a pang of jealousy. Another one winning at life, although he'd undoubtedly experienced the tragedy of his wife's early death. Mallory's mother had briefly offered to move in when she'd split up with Joe but the suggestion had been half-hearted, and both had been relieved when Mallory refused. Harri's house looked chaotic but homely, a far cry from her sparse flat.

As they came into St Davids, the lights of the tiny city woke up Toby and he rubbed his eyes. 'Urgh, I feel sick again.'

'I'm not surprised. You were shovelling the food into your mouth as if you'd forgotten what it tasted like.'

'Leave it, Mum.'

Mallory frowned, surprised at her son's curt tone. 'We're both tired. Why don't you go to bed, rather than turn on the TV? Don't forget you've got to go back. We need to leave early to get you to Carmarthen for your train.'

'Sure.'

–

Toby spent an age in the bathroom. He took the portable radio in with him and Kate Bush blasted from behind the door, her voice distorted by the steam. The shower ran on for fifteen minutes, infuriating Mallory, given she was on a water meter. She nearly banged on the door but doubted he'd be able to hear her against the din.

Instead, she got out her notebook and jotted down what she'd discovered over the past few days. Leaving aside Duncan's death, which she would consider separately, she'd made decent progress on unpicking the message found by Gavin Lavine. She was proceeding on the assumption, without any corroborating proof, that both the note existed and that Heledd had discovered its contents. Heledd had asked Duncan and Eleri about the truthfulness of their statements that night, and that was too much of a coincidence. She hadn't, however, contacted Gemma, which was odd. Either she'd not got round to it yet or Gemma was lying. Mallory tapped the pencil between her teeth. Doctors lied, didn't they? Of course they did but what would Gemma's motives be for doing so? No ideas sprung to mind but she mentally filed away the possibility.

Next, the lies. She'd unpicked three of them. Jack had withheld from the police that he'd made arrangements for Duncan to visit. Mallory didn't think it was an innocent omission. For some reason, he'd wanted to deflect attention from Duncan. It might have something to do with what Mallory considered the third lie. Duncan's admission to his wife that he had hit someone. Had Huw fallen foul of Duncan's legendary temper that evening? It was possible he had smacked the child and no marks had shown up post-mortem, although she'd need to check that with the pathologist. The second lie – Gemma's omission that she had had contact with Heledd professionally – was also potentially game-changing. She'd been more than willing to tell Mallory, there in her capacity as patient, about Heledd's postnatal depression, so the reticence while speaking to the police made no sense. Patient confidentiality, my arse, thought Mallory.

The bathroom door opened, letting a blast of steam into the hallway. Toby hurried across the room with a towel wrapped around his waist and shut the door of his bedroom.

Mallory returned to her notes. She'd get in touch with Gruffydd next. She thought him the most likely candidate for writing the note and she also suspected, based on nothing more than their brief acquaintance, that he might be the most likely to crack under pressure. She would speak to him in the morning. She sat back in her seat. The Chinese had made her thirsty and she was desperate for some water. She went into the kitchen to pour herself a glass and returned to the table, wrinkling her nose. God knows how much of her shower gel Toby had used, the place stank of orange blossom.

Leaving aside the six lies she was trying to fathom, she turned to the killing of Duncan Lyall. If the businessman had been involved in drugs, Mallory had a pretty good idea it would be on the County Lines team's radar. News about potential sources of narcotics leaked out eventually and the team, with the right intelligence in place, would be the first to know. Mallory thought about the connection between Duncan and Heledd, which still couldn't be ruled out. Heledd lay dead in a field after meeting Duncan for a drink and, a week later, Duncan was savagely murdered. There was no evidence Heledd had taken drugs, which suggested that whatever connection their deaths might have, there were other links to untangle. Which brought her back to the letter.

A noise from Toby's bedroom interrupted her thoughts. She got up and tapped on his door. 'Is everything OK, Tobe?'

'I'm in bed, Mum. Don't come in.'

'Fine.' Mallory decided to have a shower herself before bed. A five-minute one rather than Toby's marathon session. As she stripped off, she became aware of a sickly nauseating smell underneath the scent from her shower gel. She grabbed her dressing gown and banged on Toby's door again.

'Have you been sick?'

'No, Mum. Go away, I'm trying to sleep.'

Mallory returned to the bathroom and sniffed the air. She was pretty sure Toby had been ill but couldn't understand why he'd lie. After a bout of food poisoning, it was natural he might still have a delicate stomach, so why try to hide it? She continued to worry as she prepared for bed and spent a sleepless hour wondering if she could get Toby an appointment with a different doctor at her practice. Concern left her exhausted until she rolled over, desperate to catch some sleep before she needed to face another day.

–

The following morning, as Toby dozed, she tried the number for the vicarage at St Madoc's, where Gruffydd Ellis was stationed. Actually, she was pretty sure 'stationed' wasn't the word for where a vicar earned a living. She would have to ask Janey when she was next on shift, as she couldn't risk embarrassing herself with the question in front of anyone else. The phone rang out unanswered, which was no bad thing, as she could drive to the village and wait for Gruffydd there. Now Toby was returning home to his father's, she'd have more time to concentrate on getting in touch with the remaining friends, but she woke feeling flat. Despite their cramped home, she'd got used to having Toby in his tiny bedroom and the drone of the computer game as she worked with her headphones on.

She was dropping him off that morning at Carmarthen. As Joe was working a morning shift, he didn't think he'd be able to drive there and back to pick up Toby, so he'd meet him at Paddington. As usual, Toby had left things to the last minute. It was five past nine and they needed to set off within the hour for Toby to make his train.

Mallory made a brew and pushed open Toby's door. The room was in darkness and he'd pulled the covers over his head. Mallory drew back the curtains and put the tea on the table next to him.

'Come on, Tobe, you need to get up.'

'I'm trying to sleep.'

'Tough.' Mallory looked around the room and saw his clothes strewn across the floor. She started to pick them up and fold them, ready to put in his rucksack.

'Leave them, Mum. I'm not going home.'

Mallory froze. 'What do you mean?'

'I'm not going back to London.' His voice was muffled under the duvet. 'I'm staying here.'

'Tobe, what's the matter?' Mallory crossed to Toby's bed and sat next to her son, feeling completely at sea. She was aware she didn't know her son as well as she might like. His insistence on living with his father after their divorce meant she had little idea about his worries and fears.

She heard him mumble under the covers.

'What?'

He threw the covers off. 'I just don't want to go back and you can't make me.'

'It's not as straightforward as that. Is it to do with you being sick?'

Her words infuriated him. He pulled a T-shirt over his shoulders, reached down to grab his tea and went into the living room.

'Toby, we need to talk. I need to ask you something. Are you deliberately making yourself sick?'

She'd at last articulated her fears from the previous night. One look at his face, and the fury and the shame she saw showed she'd hit the mark. Her stomach dropped.

'Look, Toby, maybe we can talk about this. I can talk to Joe. I don't want you going back to London today without sorting this out.'

'I'm not going back to London, full stop.'

'Christ.' She crossed the room and put her arms round him. She felt him tense but he didn't pull away. 'What's the issue with London? Is this why you've been making yourself sick?'

'I don't know.' His voice shook and she gripped him tighter.

'OK, look, let me text Joe and say there's been an issue. He'll be at work but as soon as he calls, I'll speak to him.'

Toby pulled away without looking at her. 'Thanks, Mum.'

Mallory found her mobile and sent a text to Joe. While she waited for him to pick up the message, she rang Harri, immediately feeling better when she heard his reassuring voice. It had been the same on Eldey, when she'd first met him. He listened as she told him about Toby.

'Kids. I had no problem with Ben, but Ellie went through a difficult stage when she was fourteen, so younger than Toby. I found she had a boyfriend who was undermining her confidence – a toxic relationship, I guess.'

'What did you do?'

'I went round his house and had a *chat*.' Harri's emphasis on the word made Mallory laugh.

'God, I'm going to have a difficult conversation with his father. Joe's not the most enlightened male. I don't think the possibility that Toby's bulimic even crossed his mind.'

'You think it's that bad?'

'I don't know,' said Mallory. 'I don't know anything anymore.'

After cutting the call, she could hear Toby speaking to his father. Joe must have got her message straight away and, realising her line was engaged, called his son. Mallory tried to hear how the conversation was going but Toby's voice was low.

She opened the back door to let some of the cold air in, feeling claustrophobic and depressed. She heard Toby come into the kitchen as she stood in the doorway, contemplating the small yard.

'Dad wants a word.' He gave her his phone and walked into the living room. She heard the TV switch on.

'What's happened?' demanded Joe.

'Hold on.' Mallory shut the door on Toby and told Joe what she'd discovered.

Joe was stunned into silence. 'Are you sure?'

'Pretty sure. He's been out running every day since he's been here, which I thought was odd, given the weather. Now, I'm worried it might be connected to his vomiting.'

'What's he been up to there?'

'I'd bought a PlayStation, as I thought it would give him something to do while I was at work but he hasn't moved away from it all week, except for his runs. I've had to drag him out on a bus trip. Has he said to you how long he wants to stay with me?'

'He told me he's not coming back here. That's all he'll say. I'm going to ring the school this afternoon and find out what the hell is going on there. They'll have to be informed because they'll want to know where he is. I'll use the opportunity to see if there's been any issues.'

'What about his friends? Do you know of any?'

'He hangs around with a group of them. Steve is one, Archie another. I don't know, there are about six or seven of them.'

'A group.' Mallory thought of the six she was looking into. 'That could be the problem. You know, the dynamics, and so on.'

'Tell me about it. Look, leave the school with me. You've got Toby so try and get him to talk. If he needs to speak to someone, a counsellor or something, I'll pay.'

'Do you think,' said Mallory slowly, 'that it's us? That our divorce has caused this.'

She could hear chatter in the background and felt for Joe. He was on duty and she'd probably caught him in his break. It was a nightmare taking personal calls at work.

'I don't know. I don't know anything about bulimia. Look, can I call you later? I've got to go.'

Joe cut the call, leaving Mallory staring in dismay at Toby's closed door.

30

Toby had put on his earphones and his eyes were fixed to the screen. In the game, a realistic-looking male prisoner was trying to break out of jail through a hail of bullets. Mallory knew how he felt. After the drama of the morning, she was exhausted, although it was only coming up to ten o'clock. Toby had his back to her and, for now, the conversation was clearly over.

Mallory was due to work at the cathedral shop at midday. She guessed, given Toby's mood, she could start early and see if she could knock a few hours off later in the week. She'd need to speak to her manager about her situation at home. Christ. She managed to catch Toby's eye and made an exaggerated gesture that she was going to work. He nodded, looking relieved, and turned away from her. Mallory stepped out onto the pavement and nearly lost her footing. Gusts of sea air blasted down the road, making her catch her breath. She turned towards the cathedral and saw Ffion walking towards her, hair slick from a swim in the sea. As Mallory approached, Ffion lifted up the hood of her oversized fleece.

'Hi Ffion.'

The girl walked past her without comment. Mallory whirled around.

'Is everything OK? Toby hasn't been playing his games too loudly, has he?'

Ffion stopped and hesitated. 'You never told me you were still working as a copper. I thought you had a job in a shop.'

Mallory wasn't sure if she could face another confrontation. 'I'm not. I'm retired but I've been asked to help with the investigation into Heledd's death. The request came out of the blue. I *do* work in a shop at the cathedral.'

Ffion turned and tightened the string of her hood. She looked freezing and Mallory promised herself she would never become one of those cold-water swimmers who didn't look any healthier than herself.

'When you came up to my flat the day after Heledd died, were you pumping me for information?'

'I was genuinely curious. The death of Huw Jones had been mentioned to me by the person who asked me to come into the investigation and I hadn't at that stage agreed to help them out.' A white lie that Mallory felt guilty for telling. There were enough lies in this case already.

Ffion shrugged. 'It's made a lot of people unhappy. We feel scrutinised again and I saw Duncan Lyall died yesterday. There's a killer on the loose, isn't there?'

'There is, but Duncan was killed in a targeted attack. I don't think it's a random killer on the loose.'

'What about Heledd?'

'It's too early to tell.' Mallory stepped towards her neighbour. 'Please, Ffion. Any investigations on my part are just about confirming what happened to Huw that evening and how it might relate to Heledd's death. There's no scrutiny of the local community at all. I can see everyone did their best and it was, after all, a member of the public who found Huw's body, wasn't it?'

Ffion relaxed a little. 'My friend who was at the party with me thinks we're all going to get interviewed again.'

'Is that who you called that evening I told you of Heledd's death? You were trying to get hold of someone.'

'Yeah. Trudy was the friend I was at Eleri's party with. We talk about that night sometimes. So, will the police contact us again?'

'Not unless something comes up that we need to check with you.'

'I've heard you're reinterviewing the people who were at Y Bwthyn that night.'

Have you? thought Mallory. So that had got round pretty quickly. She'd only got to Jack Jones and Gemma Bowen, and both had been in confidential settings. Jack was in France so she'd put money on Gemma sharing the news. So much for her emphasis on doctor–patient confidentiality. No, Toby would not be seeing Gemma – Mallory would make sure of that when she rang the surgery to make an appointment for him. Neither, in fact, would Mallory. From now on, any interactions with Gemma would be strictly business.

'Look, Ffion, do you have time for a coffee? I've got a problem with my son which I can't really talk about. I'm not due at work until midday – I need something to take my mind off things. Can I ask you properly about that night?'

'You do want to interview me?'

Mallory shivered. 'It's not an interview, I promise. I want to talk to you about Duncan's death.'

As she predicted, Ffion's eyes gleamed. The businessman's death, despite its brutal nature, appeared less of a tragedy than either vulnerable Heledd's or Huw's. Well, that was the order of things, so no surprise there.

'OK.'

—

They squeezed into a tiny coffee shop in the square, where the tables were huddled too close together to maximise revenue during the tourist season. Fortunately, they were the only customers, although the proprietor showed signs of wanting to earwig the·conversation. Mallory took a table by the window and kept her voice low.

'You are right: I've been speaking to the people that were at Y Bwthyn that night. The thing is, the essential truthfulness of each of those friends' statements has been thrown into doubt.'

'Essential truthfulness?' asked Ffion.

Mallory sighed. She'd slipped back into police speak quickly enough. 'We think that lies were told that evening.'

'Who by?'

'All of them.'

'I—' Ffion stopped, as a woman brought over their coffees. It was unexpectedly good and just what Mallory needed. As the caffeine coursed through her, she felt herself revive. Ffion lowered her voice. 'And do you think Duncan was killed because he lied?'

Mallory paused, the cup at her lips. Did she think that? It was possible but unlikely, unless Duncan hitting the child was the catalyst for something else. The pathologist's report had found no injuries on Huw that weren't consistent with a fall from a height. She met Ffion's excited gaze.

'It's possible. That's all I can say.'

'And how do you know that they all lied?'

'I can't say that either.'

Ffion sat back in her chair. 'So, what can you tell me? I mean, I'm asking all the questions here.'

'I know. Look, I discovered yesterday that Duncan had a temper. Had you heard something similar?'

Ffion hesitated.

'He's dead, Ffion. It might help find his killer.'

'I thought,' said Ffion, 'that you were looking at Huw's death.'

'I am. Did you hear any rumours of a fight that night?'

Again, Ffion wavered. 'Yes, but nothing to do with Huw.'

'What was it about, then?' asked Mallory.

'The thing is, Duncan was always ready with his fists. You know the type of thing. A gang of lads outside a pub after closing time. A scuffle breaks out and you could be sure Duncan would be in the middle of things.'

'I understand. And is that what happened that night? A scuffle.'

'Before Trudy and I were bundled into the car and taken home, we saw some pushing and shoving between Duncan and Jack.'

'Duncan and *Jack*? Not Gruffydd?'

Ffion frowned. 'Not Gruffydd, no. It was definitely Jack.'

'You're certain, even though it was dark?'

'It was near a street light. It was definitely Jack.'

'Do you know neither mentioned it in their statements?'

'Why would they? I mean, it was *after* Huw had gone missing. Why mention a scuffle that probably broke out in the heat of the moment?'

'Because these things matter!' Mallory's voice rose and she felt like weeping. A boy is dead and still people lie about their actions. She hated them all because she was now pretty sure that all six friends were covering up for each other. All protecting each other for no other reason than a warped sense of friendship. But Duncan was now dead and she had to be mindful of the possibility that one of those remaining five had silenced him for reasons that weren't yet clear.

Mallory, aware that the woman at the counter was gawping at them, lowered her voice again. 'Any idea what the fight was about?'

'No, I'm sorry.'

'It doesn't matter.' Mallory decided not to ask her about Gemma or, for that matter, Jack. She would speak to Gemma and press her again on what was going on.

'You're sure we're safe?' asked Ffion, draining her coffee. 'There's been some weird stuff going on and I want to know if I'm at risk.'

'Weird stuff? What do you mean?'

'I mean someone hanging around outside the house late at night. I've seen them a couple of times now.'

'Male or female?'

'I can't tell. It's always after dark but there's definitely someone there. I thought they might just be looking for empty holiday homes to break into so I've been leaving all my lights on. Now I'm not so sure.'

Mallory thought of Toby. If she'd brought danger to her doorstep then he shouldn't stay at the flat. But he'd made it clear he wasn't going anywhere. She would be more vigilant and, if she saw the figure, go and confront them. Because, if someone wanted to know what she was up to, it suggested she was on the right track. The thought gave her hope.

31

To his surprise, Harri was appointed SIO of the team investigating the death of Duncan Lyall. Steph argued that she wanted a murder detective leading the team, not someone with narcotics expertise. It was a point in his boss's favour. She pulled Harri aside before his team briefing, catching him in the corridor as he looked through his notes.

'There's something fishy going on, Harri, and I want to be kept briefed about this. I mean, every morning; you come and tell me progress. Get your pal Mallory down here too. I want to meet her.'

'Mallory? I've given her the task of pursuing the note found at St Non's. You want her brought into the wider team?'

'I bloody well do but I want to meet her first. Get her down as soon as you can.'

There was a buzz in the office when Harri walked into the meeting. Siân was at the front, alongside DC Freddie Carr, who'd relocated from Manchester to find the good life in Pembrokeshire. His eyes were shining, which suggested the good life wasn't what rocked his particular boat. The County Lines team was represented by a woman, who looked not much older than a teenager. He'd heard the team liked to put detectives *in situ* and she'd fit in very well. The rest of the team were members of CID pulled in from stations around the region.

'Right,' he said. 'Let's go.'

-

Harri was concluding the meeting when his mobile rang. They'd identified over forty lines of inquiry, looking into the personal and business interests of Duncan Lyall and Lyall's Tours. Personally, if Heledd hadn't died a week earlier, he'd have been inclined to think that Duncan's shady business dealings were finally catching up with him. Now there was a more complex web of old case and current investigation, and it was likely to be messy. The number calling his mobile was withheld.

'Mr Evans?'

There was a silence and Harri realised it was his personal mobile that had been ringing. His heart lurched. Not the kids, please, he prayed.

'I'm calling from the surgery. We've had the results of your blood tests and the GP would like to see you.'

Not the kids then, thank God, but what the hell did they want to see him about? 'OK. When will that be?' About three weeks from now, knowing them, he thought furiously.

'I can fit you in at two fifteen. Can you make it then?'

Fuck. Harri looked at his watch. 'I'm on my way.'

-

This time he was seen by one of the partners, who cast his eyes over Harri as he came to collect him.

'Well, I can't wheel out my usual phrase,' he said. 'Fat and forty usually makes for one thing. You're forty but look pretty lean to me.'

'What the bloody hell are you going on about?' demanded Harri.

'You've blood sugars of seventy-nine. That's 9.4 per cent in old money. You're diabetic.'

'Diabetic?' Harri had spent the drive to Pembroke worrying about cancer and him leaving Fran to look after the kids. This news was difficult to digest but he wasn't dying. He wanted to hug the GP.

'I'm afraid so. The last time your bloods were taken was five years ago and they were a little on the high side, but nothing to concern yourself about. You've tipped into the diabetic range and we need to get your numbers down as soon as possible.'

'I can change my diet?' asked Harri hopefully. That sounded all right; he'd need to go easy on the takeaways and no more beer.

'I'll be referring you to a nutritional course, certainly, but we need to get you on medication straight away. Have you been feeling tired, thirsty?'

'All of those things. What are you going to give me, insulin?' He'd have to inform occupational health. God, maybe his job was at risk.

'No insulin yet. Let's see what we can do with something different. I'll start you on a low dose of metformin and see how you get on.'

Harri stood, still overwhelmed. Breathe, he told himself. Your children still have a father.

'OK, fine. Will I live a normal life?'

The doctor, he saw, was trying not to smile. 'It's up to you, isn't it? You'll have a surprise when you learn what you can and can't eat. Think carbohydrates.'

'They're good?'

The doctor was shaking his head. While the GP typed in the prescription, Harri cast around for something to fill the silence.

'Do you know Doctor Bowen? She has a practice in St Davids.'

'Gemma?' The GP had his eyes on the screen. 'I know her slightly. Why do you ask?'

'She began her training in a hospital but ended up as a GP.'

'Ended up?' That got his attention. He turned to look at Harri.

'Sorry, I mean, why choose GP after you've been working first in a psychiatric facility and then in an A & E department?'

'You been in a psychiatric unit or A & E recently? They're not jobs for everyone. Becoming a general practitioner requires an additional two years of training on top of your hospital rotation. Any reason for mentioning it?'

'It's nothing. Just musing on something.'

'You're involved in the investigation into Duncan Lyall's murder?'

'I'm heading it up. Why do you ask?'

'I've had a few anxious patients the last few days. I think the community could do with some reassurance there isn't a murderer on the loose.'

But, thought Harri, that's exactly what there was.

32

Superintendent Steph Morris listened to Mallory's account without speaking. Used to Harri's constant interruptions, it was a relief to give her report in her own methodical way. In essence, she had found very little but it was early days and she hoped Steph would take that into consideration when passing judgement.

Everything about Steph was designed to intimidate. She wore a burgundy dress that clung to her figure, which she'd teamed with high-heeled black boots. Since her accident, Mallory couldn't wear anything except trainers and flat lace-ups, but she spent a moment thinking what she might look like in a similar outfit. Toby, she thought, would probably die of embarrassment. She'd had to abandon her shift at the cathedral to meet Steph, citing Toby as the reason. She hoped to God no one called at the flat and discovered she'd left him for the afternoon.

'My priority,' said Mallory, 'is to complete the interviews and construct a reasonable timeline based on the lies in relation to the original statements. If Heledd discovered that one of her former friends had been responsible for Huw ending up at St Non's, it gives us a motive for her death.'

'It's a funny way of going about killing someone, isn't it?' Steph smoothed down her skirt. 'Plying someone with alcohol and leaving them for dead. Hadn't Heledd got a reputation for self-medicating with alcohol? Her tolerance must have been pretty high.'

'Maybe she was on the verge of unearthing something. All six friends have plenty to lose. They were prepared to take a chance.'

'Six? You're including Duncan in this too? His movements check out for the night Heledd died. We've CCTV of him returning to his house and not leaving again.'

'Until I get to the bottom of all six lies, I'm not ruling out anyone.'

'You might as well carry on with your questioning. Ask Jack why *he* didn't mention the scuffle and, more importantly, what it was about. But I don't want you to talk to our MP until you have concrete proof she lied in her original statement.'

'That might be quite hard to do without actually talking to her.'

'Nevertheless, I want you to try. We struck lucky that Eleri agreed to speak to us before Duncan's death. It won't happen again now there's a murder investigation underway. Any idea who might have written the note?'

'No one I've interviewed so far fits the bill but until I was officially on the team, I didn't mention the note. I'm now intending to push it harder but my bet is on Gruffydd Ellis or Bethan Rees. There's a confessional element which fits both their roles.'

'Lean on them if you must. You know, I think my team is going to be relying more and more on civilian investigators and I've read your record. You'd be quite an asset to us. You need, however, to be behind the scenes. I don't want the press focusing on you, thinking we can't do our job, especially given your role in the deaths on Eldey.'

'I solved the case.'

'Eventually.' Steph gave a flicker of a smile. 'Have you got your ID yet?'

'I'm picking it up now. I emailed over my photo this morning.'

'Remember your designated powers. Conducting interviews, taking statements. Anything else, call in support. Think your leg is up to the job?'

'As long as I'm not asked to run after any suspects.'

'You don't have power of arrest so you really don't want to be doing that. What do you think of Harri?'

'Seems a decent sort.'

Steph held her gaze. 'He is.'

—

Neither Gruffydd nor Bethan answered the mobile numbers they'd provided at the time of Huw's death, although it was possible they had been changed. Mallory typed an email to Jack Jones, asking if they could have another Zoom chat, and she called Gemma at the surgery. Gemma rang back within ten minutes. Mallory suspected she'd been waiting for the call since Duncan's death. She asked to be interviewed away from her GP practice and offered to come down to HQ. Mallory was unused to the station and they agreed to meet at a seafood cafe housed in a tiny shack overlooking Porthclais Harbour.

On the way down to the port, Mallory continually looked in her rear-view mirror. If someone could stalk her house then they could also follow her car. Behind her, as far as she could see, there was nothing but empty road. She found the hut perched on the cliff. There were four picnic bench-style tables inside. At the smell of seafood, Mallory realised how hungry she was.

'Do you want anything to eat?' she asked Gemma.

'I'll have a crab sandwich. I'd recommend them.'

'Sounds good.'

While they were waiting for their food, Mallory got her iPad out and brought up Gemma's statement. 'I want to talk to you again about the fact that you failed to mention, in the statement dated 31 December 2011, that you had seen Heledd professionally.'

Mallory saw Gemma's face was pale. 'As I've already told you, Heledd was a patient of mine and I wanted to preserve confidentiality. I'm pretty sure I mentioned more generally that Heledd was suffering from mental health issues.'

'You didn't.'

'But how would it have been relevant? It was Huw who had died.'

'For God's sake.' Mallory wanted to shake the woman. 'The mental state of possible suspects in a child's death is of key importance. You deliberately withheld a key piece of information.'

'But Huw's death was ruled an accident.'

'But you weren't to know that. Something's not right. You're aware that Duncan Lyall is dead. We are hunting a vicious killer. Is it you?'

'Me?' Gemma was outraged. 'How can you even think…'

'Why not? You deliberately lied in 2011, so why not now? What were you doing on the night Duncan died?'

'I was at home on my own. I don't have an alibi but I could never do anything like that. It's been described as a slaughterhouse.'

'When did you last speak to him?'

'About eight years ago we bumped into each other in a supermarket. We said hello and that was it.'

Mallory looked across at Gemma. The doctor's tone had changed as she spoke about Duncan.

'Were you aware that Duncan and Jack had a fight the night when Huw was discovered dead?'

'Oh, that. Tensions were running high, and Duncan would act first and think later.'

'I got the impression,' said Mallory, 'that the two were thick as thieves.'

Gemma's expression hardened. 'You could say that.'

Mallory was trying to grasp at the dynamics of the group and thought back to Joe's comments about Toby's friends. The shifting allegiances were hard to fathom. In frustration, Mallory went on the attack. 'You're nevertheless hiding something and I know for a fact that Heledd had been contacting the people who were at her house on that evening in 2011. So, I'm going to ask you, once again, if Heledd had attempted to contact you before her death.'

Gemma let out a long sigh. 'She did call me at the surgery. She'd not registered with the practice but she was quite insistent with the receptionist that she speak to me. I wasn't entirely sure what state of mind she was in so I thought it best to talk to her.'

Mallory wasn't convinced by Gemma's matter-of-fact tone. 'And how was she?'

Their sandwiches arrived and Gemma busied herself with removing the pepper on the crab meat. 'She was calm. You were right that she wanted to go over again what happened on that New Year's Eve. I have to tell you, I didn't think it was a good idea. I'm all for going over the past if it helps, but in a professional setting.'

'Aren't you a professional?' asked Mallory, pushing her plate away. She could feel on the edge of getting somewhere.

'She wasn't talking to me as a professional. She wanted to know what I remembered from that night and I did my best to oblige. She asked me if there was anything I'd want to change in my statement and I said there wasn't.'

'How did Heledd take it?'

Gemma paused. 'She called me a liar.'

'She did?' Mallory frowned. Heledd had not attempted to contact Jack and had, according to Duncan, appeared to take his reassurances at face value. Why turn on Gemma?

'Do you know why she called you a liar?'

'I have no idea but she said she had proof.'

'Did she say what?'

'I'm afraid not.'

'So, if I told you there was a note that accused all six of you of lying, would you be surprised?'

Gemma's hand twitched, sending her glass of water tumbling to the floor. They both scrambled to pick it up. 'A note? What note?'

'A message was written, accusing all six of you who were in Y Bwthyn that night of lying. "All six of us lied" is the message, so it presumably was written by one of you. I think Heledd discovered the note's existence, although I'm not sure how. Did you write it?'

'Me? Of course not.' Gemma's voice was shrill and the cafe owner looked at them in alarm.

'Did you tell Heledd about it?'

'Tell Heledd of a note I didn't know existed? We're in the realms of fantasy here, especially given the message. I consider my own omission to be a minor thing and I can't imagine Bethan or Gruffydd lying, for example. Have you spoken to them yet?'

'Not yet. It's interesting you mention those two. Does that mean that you can imagine Jack, Duncan and Eleri lying?'

'Of course not. I mean, Eleri's famous now. Lies have a greater impact for her. What does she say about this note?'

'I haven't been able to talk to her yet.'

Mallory called the waitress over and asked her to wrap up her sandwich. Her first thought was that she'd take it home to Toby, and the knot in her stomach tightened when she realised the absurdity of the suggestion. And yet, he would need to be fed while Mallory worked out a plan of action. She desperately wanted to ask Gemma about bulimia, how to get an official diagnosis, for example, but Gemma might be a killer. She turned off her iPad. 'I'm going to see Gruffydd Ellis this afternoon. Are you in touch with him?'

'Not really. We move in different circles now.' Gemma was desperate to leave.

'Who *are* you in touch with? I got the impression you all still talked to each other.'

Gemma stood, wiping her hands in a tissue. 'Whatever gave you that idea? None of them have kept in touch with me.'

33

Gruffydd just wanted to get out of the house. He'd made his statement to a sympathetic uniformed officer with unshed tears in her eyes. He'd wanted to comfort her but he hadn't yet completed his pastoral training and was overwhelmed by the enormity of the tragedy. He'd half-heartedly tried to speak to both Jack and Heledd, but neither wanted his platitudes. Heledd's sister Becca had arrived and taken Heledd away to her house, accompanied by a Family Liaison Officer. Funnily enough, tonight was the first time in a long while Heledd had looked like her old self. The spark that he'd seen when he first met her, which presumably had also attracted Jack, had returned during their brief chat at the party, although it had been clear that Heledd would rather have been home with Huw.

Jack was outside, smoking a cigarette he must have cadged from Gemma, as he'd given up when Huw was born. He'd aged ten years since that evening, his face ashen and lined with despair.

'Mind if I join you?'

Jack shrugged. Gruffydd found his lighter and sparked up, watching the embers drift off towards the sea.

'I'm so sorry, mate.'

Jack didn't answer but continued to smoke furiously.

'Do you know when he left?'

'Of course, I don't fucking know. It could have been any time while Heledd was out. I can assure you he won't have disappeared before then. Heledd always checked to see where he was. He was in bed when she left and by the time she came back, he'd disappeared.'

'Do you think the time he disappeared matters? I mean, that's what the questions I had to answer focused on – what time Huw might have left the house.'

Jack threw his cigarette to the floor. 'They're doing their job properly, that's all. The point is he opened the door and started his walk to St Non's following the sound, according to Heledd and that mad bitch of her sister, of the mermaids.'

Gruffydd braced for the rush of relief which failed to arrive. He thought it mattered very much, and not just to establish the chain of events that evening. In the distance, he saw Duncan coming down the street. He'd probably been to check on Eleri, who could actually look after herself. He joined them and pulled out a bottle of whisky.

'Have some of this, Jack. Good for shock.'

'Haven't you had enough?' asked Gruffydd.

The pair of them turned to him. 'Fuck off, if you haven't anything useful to say,' said Duncan. 'Jack's just lost his son for Chrissake.' He turned to Jack. 'Mate, I'm sorry about earlier. It's none of my business…'

Gruffydd froze. What was none of Duncan's business? He waited for him to elaborate but saw the pair wanted to be alone.

'I'm sorry,' he said. He wasn't needed here, hadn't really been all evening. He'd tagged along like a spare part, making a nuisance of himself. Whatever he wanted to confess, it wouldn't be to these two. He heard the door click behind him and Bethan stepped out, her face pale. She glanced in his direction. 'Do you want to come back to mine?'

Gratefully, he peeled away and followed her down the street, away from Eleri's house, and away from Jack and Duncan, who had turned their backs on him.

'Bethan, there's something I need to tell you.'

34

The Fourth Lie

St Madoc's church was about fifteen miles from St Davids, just off the road to Fishguard. Unlike other places where church property had been sold off, the rectory attached to the church looked to be the original. Mallory hadn't telephoned again, as she wanted to catch Gruffydd unawares but when she knocked on the door, the clatter from the hammer rang around the building. She peered through a window but could only see into a kitchen furnished with drab modern units. A cross nestled between the pot plants, which looked like they needed watering. She could see a light coming from the church, through the window. No stained glass, just thick glass panes reflecting the low sun.

Mallory trudged towards the building, feeling the eyes of someone watching her from the house. She wheeled round and saw a female figure move away from the upstairs window, too quick for her to identify. Mallory turned back towards the church. Unless she was prepared to shout through the letterbox, she was unlikely to get any response from whoever was inside. The knock had been loud enough to wake the dead.

The door to the church was shut but unlocked. Mallory turned the handle and saw a figure sitting in a front pew. He didn't turn as she closed the door to keep out the cold, although it was icy enough inside. She walked to the front and it was only as she neared that he turned to face her, showing no surprise at her presence. His face was pale and his eyes ringed with red, although she saw no discernible tears.

'You've heard about Duncan Lyall?' asked Mallory, sliding into the pew in front of him.

He nodded. 'Bethan called me yesterday evening. I'd missed it on the news, as I was busy with a parishioner yesterday.'

'I'm sorry about your friend.'

Gruffydd laughed. 'He wasn't my friend. He saw me as nothing more than a hanger-on and took great pleasure in mocking my faith. "Saint Gruffydd" was my nickname and that was before I'd decided to train for the priesthood.'

'But you were part of the same group of friends? I mean, that friendship has held, hasn't it? Some of you are loosely in touch with each other, aren't you?'

'Loosely is the right word, as far as I'm concerned.'

'I saw you with Bethan Rees the evening of Heledd Jones's death. Are you and Bethan friends?'

'Sort of. Our paths cross, as we're in the same church circles. Did you know we were engaged for a while?'

'Someone mentioned it to me. Is it all water under the bridge?'

'Of course. I'm married now.'

'Was that your wife up at the rectory?'

Gruffydd glanced up at her. 'She answered the door to you?'

'I saw someone at the window, that was all.'

'She suffers from depression and it's particularly bad in the winter. When the days lengthen, she's a different person.'

'What about your children?'

'Away at school. My wife's family have money and there's a trust fund to educate the kids. Frankly, they're better off out of the house. It gets a bit grim when Mary's feeling low.'

'What does she think of your old group of friends?'

Gruffydd shrugged. 'Difficult to say. They came to our wedding but they're not really part of our social circle anymore, not even Bethan. I'm not sure Mary has an opinion on any of them, except Eleri.'

'What's her opinion of Eleri? Does she like her?'

'I don't think it's a case of liking or not, it's more the fact that she doesn't agree with Eleri's politics. Mary is a Labour Party member, although she doesn't get much chance to participate in politics these days. It was different when she was in Cardiff.'

'Is she happy here?'

'Not really. I've asked for a transfer to a city parish, and I don't mean St Davids. Somewhere livelier might help, especially during the winter months.'

'Did you know I'm now working with the police in relation to the death of Heledd Jones?'

Gruffydd looked to the floor. 'I've heard something about it.'

'When I saw you the day when her body was discovered, were you meeting up with Bethan because you'd heard of the death?'

Gruffydd nodded. 'It was my idea. Bethan didn't want to come out. It was a bitter afternoon, if you remember, and she wasn't happy driving over from Solva, where she lives.'

'I remember. Why did you want to see Bethan?'

'I didn't want to see her.' Gruffydd raised his voice and looked around at the empty church. 'I wanted to talk to my spiritual adviser, Canon Stack. I've known him since I did my discernment training and there's nothing I can't say to him.'

'So how come Bethan was there?'

'She rang me when she heard about Heledd. I told her that I needed to get something off my chest from the night Huw Jones went missing and I was going to talk to Charles, I mean Canon Stack. She said she wanted to come with me.'

'Did she? And why was that?'

He looked her in the face. 'Because she hates the thought of me being happy.'

Mallory frowned. 'Isn't that a little strong?'

Gruffydd drew his collar up to shield himself from the breeze wafting through the church. 'You have to understand that when Huw went missing, it was chaos. There was a mixture of fear, anxiety, terror and panic. But amongst all that, people were thinking – what does this mean for me? I've learnt a lot about human nature in this job and I can tell you this. Whatever happens, people often place themselves at the centre of things.'

'OK. I think I can understand that. So, when you say people looked to see how the tragedy would affect them, you mean some untruths might have been communicated?'

'Something like that.' Gruffydd looked miserable.

'What about people's accounts of that evening? How accurate were they?'

'I can't speak for everyone but I know I was economical with the truth and I've regretted it ever since.'

'Go on.'

Mallory knew that Gruffydd had wormed his way into accompanying Duncan to Y Bwthyn, but she wanted to hear him say that.

'What I never told anyone at the time was that I saw Huw's bed was empty long before he was discovered missing.'

35

The metformin Harri had picked up from the pharmacy on the way to work was still in his desk drawer. He was reluctant to take it, after reading the leaflet in the box, which informed him of the side effects, including nausea and an upset stomach. Perhaps he should wait until he was in bed, although it did say to take the stuff with food. In the end, he put a tablet in his mouth and swallowed it with some fizzy water, waiting for something to happen. After five minutes, it was clear nothing untoward was going to occur and he allowed himself to relax.

Siân came in. 'I got something I want to run by you.'

'Go on?'

'I've been working with the County Lines team, and Zoe in particular.'

'Is Zoe the one young enough to be my daughter?'

'I think that's a bit of an exaggeration. She's twenty-five but I'll admit she looks young. She's great, though. Makes me wish I'd applied for the job that was going a few months back.'

'Oh no,' said Harri.

Siân, he was pleased to see, gave him a gratified smile. 'The thing is, they've been looking at Lyall's Tour buses. What they've been doing is tracking the movement of the coaches alongside the whereabouts of known dealers in the area. The beauty of the racket that they think Lyall has got going is that the timetable for the buses is clear to see on the website. People can pick up the coach along the way so anyone who wants to meet the driver or a passenger knows what time the bus will turn up.'

'Are they getting anywhere with that?'

'Definitely. They've got the registration numbers of all the little coaches and they've been checking ANPR to double-check the buses went where they were timetabled to go. There's no point making arrests if the coach didn't turn up for some reason. In the course of their searches, they've noticed that a coach made a trip around nine p.m. the night Heledd Jones died.'

'Sit down.' Harri gestured at a chair. 'One of the coaches? Do Lyall's Tours do night trips?'

'In the summer, yes, but not at this time of the year. There's nothing on the website so, as far as we're concerned, there's no reason for that coach being on the road whatsoever.'

'They don't think it's drug-related? A bit of moon-lighting, for example.'

'The beauty of the Lyall scheme is that the coaches are going about legitimate business. Why draw attention to yourself by driving a bright yellow bus at night?'

'Where's the coach usually housed?'

'Lyall's have a big depot in Haverfordwest, near Duncan Lyall's property. We can assume he had access to the place, given the offices for Lyall's Tours are attached to the building. We're checking cameras but my guess is it'll all have been wiped. Duncan will have made sure to cover his tracks.'

'Did ANPR pick up the driver?'

'It's pitch-black. All we can say with any certainty is that it's being driven when there's no reason for it to be on the road. We're questioning the other drivers now, to eliminate them, but that'll take some time.'

Harri puffed out his cheeks. 'But you're putting Duncan in the frame, which suggests he's involved in the death of Heledd Jones.'

'He said when we interviewed him together that he dropped Heledd at the station and returned home, which the cameras confirm. However, it's possible he then went to the storage facility to pick up a yellow bus. He could walk to the depot. It's a bit of a hike, maybe half an hour or so, but it's possible. He could have gone on foot to pick up the bus.'

Harri frowned, trying to make sense of it. 'Why would Duncan have killed Heledd? I could swear when we questioned him, he relaxed when we told him we were there about Heledd. He probably thought we were there about his drug racket.'

'Maybe he thought his little plan was watertight. I mean, it's only because of his death that we're looking into the movement of those buses. We'd have never thought to look otherwise. Can I put out the call for dashcam footage? It's possible we might be able to catch sight of the bus nearer to Penterry, where Heledd got off the bus.'

'Go for it. Give away as little as possible but put out the appeal.'

36

'You noticed Huw wasn't in bed and you never said anything?' Mallory kept her tone even, trying to hide her shock at the revelation. Gruffydd had deliberately withheld an important piece of evidence from police and maintained his silence over the years.

'I didn't think anything of it when I went upstairs. When Duncan and I got back from the off-licence, I went to the bathroom and the door next to it was open. I glanced in, nothing more, and it was obviously Huw's room. It was painted blue and there was a poster of Thomas the Tank Engine on the wall. I saw the bed was empty and thought nothing of it. He could easily have been sleeping in Jack and Heledd's room.'

'You never even thought to mention it to Jack?' Mallory couldn't believe it. The friends were drinking in the house while keeping the noise low because Huw was sleeping upstairs. All six knew this and there was no evidence that things had got rowdy. And yet, when Gruffydd passed the room where Huw was supposedly sleeping, he didn't think to mention to Jack that the bed was actually empty.

'I honestly thought nothing of it.' Gruffydd's misery made him pathetic, but it could be an act. Mallory was increasingly aware that every interview she conducted might be with a killer.

'What time was this?'

'I think about ten past five. As I said, I'd just come back with Gruffydd from a booze run.'

'And all the others were there?'

'Not Eleri, or maybe she'd just arrived. She was the last to come and she was making a concerted effort to get us back over to her house.'

'Did no one think of Heledd on her own at the party? You were all so busy enjoying yourselves, did no one think to stay at the party to keep Heledd company?'

'Why lay that on me? I barely knew the woman. If anyone should have been there, it was Jack.'

'If Jack had been at the party none of this would have happened, would it? Duncan wouldn't have left to keep him company, you wouldn't have followed him, desperate to join in.'

'Who says I was desperate?'

'Duncan told his wife that you were impossible to shake off and he never mentioned this to the police.'

Gruffydd swore. 'It's not true. I simply invited myself along to the drinks. I can't believe he said that about me.'

'Why did Duncan hit Jack that evening? I know a fight took place in the time between the discovery of Huw's body and the statements to the police. What was that about?'

Gruffydd glanced up at her. 'I don't know. You're right about the fight but I don't know what it was about. Maybe Jack was taking out on Duncan the fact that we were all there.'

Mallory nearly laughed. Did Gruffydd really expect her to believe that? She felt her mood turn. It had been a long few days and not one of the six friends she'd spoken to had struck her as someone she'd want to spend any time with. Her only sympathy was for Heledd, ignored and patronised by the more socially mobile group. Well, if she were to avenge Heledd then she needed to get to the bottom of why Gruffydd had lied.

'Tell me, when people tried to work out when Huw might have left the house, why didn't you say you'd seen the bed empty at ten past five?'

'I… I don't know. I mean, no one knew I'd gone to the bathroom. I just slipped upstairs and I thought suspicion might fall on me if I said the bed was empty.'

'Suspicion might fall on you? For all you knew Huw might have been out in the night looking for his mother, nothing more sinister than that. I don't get it.'

'You don't remember 2011. I was newly qualified and priests were being accused of paedophile offences. We'd all been warned at theological college to keep ourselves above reproach and I'd fallen at the first hurdle.'

Mallory well remembered her arrest of a London Catholic priest who, thanks to a tip-off from the FBI, had been successfully prosecuted for child sex offences. 'You weren't being accused; you were simply being asked about your movements that evening.'

Gruffydd shook his head. 'I acted in haste and I've regretted it ever since. As soon as the police arrived, I should have said something and I never did. Then my silence became an albatross around my neck. It was too late to say anything and I just had to stick to my story.'

'But you told Bethan. She was with you when you went to see Canon Stack last week, so she presumably knows.'

'I had to tell someone and she was my fiancée at the time.'

'And what did Bethan say when you told her?'

'She told me to stick to my story.'

'Did she?' Mallory let the silence widen. 'Any reason why she might have done that?'

Gruffydd shrugged.

'Do you think she might have told anyone else?'

'I… I don't know. I don't think so. That wouldn't be like Bethan. She likes to keep her little secrets. It gives her a hold over us. I did, however, mention it to Duncan once. I just couldn't keep it in.'

'And what did he say?' asked Mallory.

'He told me to keep shtum. Those were his exact words. He didn't want everything opened up again.'

So, Duncan knew about this lie, which was interesting, but Mallory still couldn't see him writing the message.

'If I told you about a note discovered in the ruins of St Non's that says, "All six of us lied. Six lies killed Huw Jones" would that mean anything to you?'

'What note?' Mallory could see him digesting the news. 'I've no idea what you're talking about. What does it mean about all of us having lied?'

'Exactly what it says. All six of you told a lie. Someone knows about yours, for example.'

'Then Bethan must have written it. It'd be like her to turn it into a game.'

'Do you think she might have told Heledd about it?'

'Yes… maybe. How should I know?'

'What did Heledd say when she contacted you?'

'How do you know—'

'Heledd was trying to work something out and I believe she tried to contact all of you. When did she call?'

'She didn't ring me. She came to the house and Mary let her in. It was last September so Mary was feeling fine and up to talking to callers. I came home from visiting another parish and they were chatting in the living room.'

'What did you think when you saw her there?'

'I was shocked but also reassured. I mean, I'd heard Heledd had been having problems but she looked well.'

'What did she say to you?'

'Mary left us alone to chat and she asked about the night Huw died.' Gruffydd stood. 'I can't sit here any longer. Can we go outside?'

'If you like.' They walked into the icy air. Mallory, glancing up at the rectory, saw that the woman was at the window again.

Gruffydd stood, with his hands in his pockets, his back to his wife. 'She asked me about what I'd said that night. She never mentioned a note but she insisted I go through my account again. In the end, it was easier to tell the truth. I told her about finding Huw's bed empty.'

'How did she take it?'

'Difficult to say. She didn't give much away, and I'm used to reading people's expressions. She wanted to know if I thought any of the others had misled the police and I said I was sure they hadn't.'

'Did she believe you?'

'I'm not sure.'

'Did she give any indication that she thought her life was at risk?' asked Mallory.

'Of course not.'

'Did she say who she was going to talk to next?'

'No. There was no sense of urgency in her questions. It was as if she was trying to unpick a complicated knot. If the note's true, have you uncovered what the other lies were?'

'Yes.' She watched his expression carefully. 'We've discussed one of them already. Duncan conveniently didn't mention the fight with Jack. Neither did Jack, although his lie, I think, was omitting to disclose the fact that a get-together was planned for the evening.'

'And Gemma?'

Was it her imagination or was he holding his breath as he waited for her answer. 'I can't discuss that with you. Can you guess what Eleri and Bethan might have lied about in their statements? I haven't spoken to either woman yet.'

'Eleri.' Gruffydd's lips curled. 'She's a professional liar. You'll never winkle out of her what she's been withholding.'

'That's a little harsh. I get the impression she's done good work as an MP.'

'You won't get anything out of Eleri, that's all I'm saying.'

'What about Bethan?'

'I don't believe Bethan withheld anything. She's too straight-laced for that.'

'I think she did. Can't you guess what it is?'

'No, I can't.' There was an edge of hysteria in his voice. 'You ask her.'

'Oh, believe me, I will.'

37

Harri looked across at Mallory's tired face and wished she'd give herself a break. She'd turned up at his house, freezing cold and with something to get off her chest. Fran had taken one look at her and put the kettle on, making tea in a pot big enough for eight. Harri usually only saw that teapot when it was brought out for funerals. He knew there were problems with Mallory's son and she should be concentrating on that. However, he needed her too. She had the experience he needed but also the tenacity that he admired in all his best officers. It was no surprise Mallory was getting nearer the truth about the six lies. She was pushing against people who'd had years to hone their own version of events but they hadn't bargained on Mallory's persistence.

Everyone in Jack Jones's house had lied. He wasn't surprised. It's what people habitually did, no matter how severe the consequences might be. The biggest revelation, of course, was that they could now narrow down the time when Huw left the house. Between four o'clock, when Heledd left, and ten past five, when Gruffydd saw the empty bed. It was only shaving off twenty minutes, given Heledd returned home at half past the hour to discover her son gone. But still, it narrowed the timeline down, which was what investigators at the time would have been desperate to do. He felt like punching Gruffydd Ellis himself. The problem was, he wasn't sure his lie mattered any longer. He was pretty sure Duncan Lyall had killed Heledd, although he couldn't for the life of him come up with a motive. He'd kept quiet about hitting Jack but there was little to suggest Heledd had been anywhere near unpicking Duncan's lie.

'Good news you're the SIO on the case,' said Mallory. 'Even if you've not been able to nail down the motive for Duncan, have you at least got an idea *how* he killed her?'

'By all accounts – patrons of the pub, the bus driver, a single passenger who saw her leave – Heledd was only tipsy when she left the bus. I think she was walking home; she'd probably mentioned to Duncan that was her plan, and he took the opportunity to draw the coach up beside her and persuaded her to get in. He probably said he had something else to tell her.'

'Which was the focus of her questions.'

'Exactly, so she'd have boarded willingly. I think he probably plied her with more drink.'

'Why did he kill her?' asked Mallory. 'We've no evidence she was near discovering what happened to Huw that night.'

'We need to keep digging, Mallory.'

'And who killed Duncan? One of the remaining five?'

'It's possible, so be careful. I think it's all connected. Huw Jones, Heledd and Duncan. I have personnel looking at Duncan Lyall's business affairs, and any private ones for that matter, but I want you to carry on what you're doing.'

'Private affairs? You think he cheated on his wife?'

'Haven't found any evidence of it yet, which doesn't mean it's not the case. We're still in the golden hours of the investigation. Everything is being followed up. How did you find Steph?' It was the question he'd been dying to ask since the team meeting. Mallory narrowed her eyes. 'Did you see the sign on her desk?'

'I saw it. No confidence issues there.'

Harri smirked.

'You know, I think she's one of your fans.'

'She is?' Harri was surprised, given her usual manner towards him. He'd put off telling Steph about his diagnosis. He'd say he was distracted by the current investigation if it came out, but he didn't want to go through any health check-ups while he was immersed in the case.

'You've four of the six secrets and, as you've pointed out, the most significant piece of information you've learnt is the possible cut-off point when Huw went missing. Go through with me again when each friend was in the house.'

'Jack Jones was there the whole time. On his own for approximately ten minutes, from four p.m., until Duncan and Gruffydd turned up. That gives him just enough time to drive his son to the cliffs at St Non's, deliberately throw him onto the rocks and return to the house. There's absolutely no reason to suggest that this was the case.'

'Then Duncan and Gruffydd turn up around ten past four. We know the arrangement was preplanned with Duncan, and Gruffydd tagged along.'

'Exactly. The three of them are drinking for half an hour or so until first Gemma and then Bethan turn up. Say around twenty to and a quarter to five, although neither woman was looking at the time. They arrived within five minutes of each other. There's no booze left and, at this point, Duncan and Gruffydd go to the off-licence. That leaves Jack, Bethan and Gemma alone in the house, finishing what was left of the bottles of wine filched from Eleri's.'

'Jack was due to go to the party when Heledd got back. She was only going to be there an hour or so. Why not just wait?'

Mallory shrugged. 'Wanted to keep going on the alcohol, I guess. From what we know of Heledd, I seriously doubt they thought she was going to be staying on at the party. You've read the statements, hers in particular. She couldn't wait to get home.'

'Duncan and Gruffydd return from the booze shop. Then what?'

'According to his statement to me, he goes immediately upstairs to use the bathroom, looks into Huw's room and sees that the bed is empty.'

'And he never says anything?'

'He thinks the child could be sleeping in the parents' bed. That's a possibility, I suppose. The fact he never said anything to the police once Huw was known to be missing puts him in a much shakier position. Do you think Duncan and Gruffydd might have taken Huw?'

Harri shook his head. 'The problem is the shop is just around the corner and the cashier not only remembered serving them, but they were also filmed on camera.'

'What about the others left in the house?'

Harri picked up his drink. 'They didn't have time either. All this information fed into the original investigation. No one except Jack Jones actually had time to take the child down to St Non's and even that's pushing it. And Eleri turns up at five past five?'

'Exactly. She wants to know why all her friends aren't at *her* party. Twenty-five minutes later, Heledd comes home and finds Huw is missing. The sad thing is if, say, Huw left the house at five, he was probably still making his way to St Non's while the search took place around Y Bwthyn. By the time Heledd guessed about St Non's, it was too late.'

'What about another scenario? Everyone's alibied or alibiing each other. A search takes place for Huw, and it extends to the outside and eventually the nearby streets. Say Huw's hiding under the bed and he's discovered by someone who then takes him down to the cliffs.'

Mallory shook her head. 'I'm not sure. Huw was discovered at seven twenty and I can tell you everyone was looking for someone carrying a child. Unless, of course, he was bundled into a car. That's a possibility, although I assume the original investigation looked at people's movements.'

'You need to keep going with this, Mallory. You're getting there. I'll keep you updated on what's happening with the Duncan Lyall investigation.'

'And Heledd Jones?'

'The same. I've asked the coroner for a second autopsy, which is taking place tomorrow.'

'A second autopsy? What are you hoping to find?'

'Something to conclusively link Duncan to Heledd's death. Siân will be in attendance, along with the original pathologist, who'll be explaining his findings to the second expert.'

'Make sure you keep in touch. I'm meeting Bethan tomorrow but what I really want to know is what Eleri Tew's secret is.'

'Unfortunately, Eleri Tew is out of bounds,' said Harri.

'Oh, come on.'

'Orders from the top. You can't see her. Find out Bethan's secret but leave our MP alone.'

Mallory took it surprisingly well. She leant back on his sofa, resting her tea on her stomach. Harri wondered if she'd kept in touch with that doctor she'd seemed to get close to when they'd met on Eldey. St Davids was bloody hard to get to, and hadn't the chap been from somewhere in England? Not so easy to keep in touch, he guessed.

'So,' she said, 'we know four of the secrets but we don't know who knew them or, in fact, all six of them to cause them to write the note. If we go through them in the order I discovered them: Duncan knew that Jack had lied about the preplanning of their get-together; he also knew Gruffydd's lie and, obviously, his own. I can't find any evidence he knew of Gemma's lie.'

'And yet, you know, while we unpick his affairs, I can't shake the feeling he liked to be in the centre of things. I'm not ruling him out as the writer of the note yet.'

'Well, all right,' said Mallory. 'Jack obviously knows of his own lie, and he knows Duncan hit him and didn't mention it in his statement, otherwise he'd have been quizzed about it. We assume he didn't know Gruffydd had spotted Huw's empty bed but I wonder if he guessed Gemma had seen his wife on a professional basis. I mean, it's a small community. He must have wondered.'

'There's no mention of Heledd's mental health in his statement either, is there?'

Harri watched Mallory frown. 'No. No, there isn't. That's odd, too, isn't it? I need to think about that some more. One thing's for sure, though. He's a lawyer and he knows the value of written evidence. There's no way he wrote the note.'

'And,' said Harri, leaning forward to refill Mallory's cup, 'we've no evidence Heledd tried to contact him, although we think she got in touch with all the others. Think he's lying?'

'It's a possibility. I've emailed him to ask for a Zoom meeting but heard nothing. He was quick to reply the first time we spoke.'

'Get onto IT,' said Harri, 'and ask for your work email address as soon as possible. Then contact Jack again and tell him you're acting in an official capacity. Make that clear to him. But you're right about him not writing the note. Not his style. Gruffydd definitely denied writing it?'

'He did and maybe he's lying to me, but he seemed to want to get everything off his chest. I was his confessor, as it were.' Mallory snorted. 'First time for everything.'

'Bethan's a possibility and I don't like the fact she told Gruffydd to keep quiet about his secret. It suggests a relationship weighted in her favour. Did you meet Gruffydd's wife?'

'She seems to be a bit of a recluse. Not everyone takes to country living.' Mallory groaned and ran her fingers through her hair. 'You know what, I'm going to push Bethan a bit harder than the others. Why not? I've nothing to lose. I'm officially on the team and the news of a note is evidence, even if we don't physically have it.'

As she picked up her mug, Harri saw her hand was trembling.

'How's Toby?' he asked her.

'I dropped in after seeing Gruffydd. He was out for a run and I waited for him to come back. I cooked him macaroni cheese for dinner. I mean, it used to be his favourite dish but I'm all at sea. One positive is that I spoke to Joe, his father, and he's emailed me a list of adolescent counsellors in the area. I'm going to try to get Toby in to see one as soon as possible. Joe's also decided to drive over here and to talk to Toby.'

'Do you think that's a good idea?'

'I don't know but I can't deal with this all by myself.'

Harri smiled. 'You know, the first thing about having children is that you never really know them, right? Maybe counselling is the right route to go down. It might bring things to light, although I suspect bulimia is more complex than cause and effect. You know, you can always call a halt to this contract now, if that would make life easier.'

'It would not. There's two of us in that small flat, circling each other like caged tigers. I'm only part-time at the cathedral. I need to get out. Only...'

'What?'

'My neighbour thinks someone's been hanging round the flat. I've not spotted anyone but I made a big show of shutting my front door and getting into the car today. If someone was watching they'll know I'm not there but I can't live like that.'

Harri picked up his phone. 'I can send a patrol car for the next night or so. I don't like the idea of you being watched. For God's sake, be careful.'

38

Bethan had to fall back on all her reserves to make sure she kept her cool. She took Gruffydd into her house at the bottom of the hill, with its view over the cathedral. She rented it for a song from the diocese but they'd only sign yearly lets, which meant she had no security of tenure. One year, they'd simply ask her to leave for a tenant they felt more deserving and that would be that. Gruffydd didn't realise how lucky he was. He was in his final year of training and he'd soon have a parish, along with somewhere to live. As his girlfriend, there'd be no overnight stays, unless they formalised their arrangement, but Gruffydd had said he needed to get settled first, before he even thought of marriage. Which left her alone in this draughty house.

At one point, it had been her who had wanted to enter the priesthood. Her parish vicar had been hesitant to support her recommendation, mumbling something about compassion and humility. She supposed that meant she had none, which was a bit rich coming from him. In the end, she'd withdrawn her application. Her parents weren't keen and it was their money she'd need to fund herself through college. Instead, she'd taken a job at the cathedral as a lay helper, which gave her some satisfaction that she was doing good.

It had been excruciating to walk through the town with Gruffydd. The place was in shock and people were talking to each other on doorsteps. It was still only eleven o'clock and she'd have to endure the sound of 2012 being rung in. She'd called the Dean's office but had got through to the answerphone. She supposed it was too much to expect a death toll but it was what she wanted to hear. A sound to mourn Huw's passing.

She'd never forget the look on Heledd's face. She'd known there was something terribly wrong as soon as she'd stumbled into the room. A mother's instinct, Bethan supposed. She could hardly remember the boy, had paid little attention to him, but now she felt the hollowness of the loss.

While he was nursing his hot chocolate, Gruffydd told her about the empty bed. He'd wanted to confess on the way home but there were too many people around, so she'd made him wait until they were alone in the house. She couldn't believe he'd been so stupid as to keep quiet about it to the police. He'd never been good in a crisis and now he'd dug a hole for himself. He could hardly go back to the investigative team and say, oh by the way, I've remembered that I passed Huw's empty bed at ten past five. Fool. She'd told him to stick to his story and no one would be any the wiser.

She had a feeling she'd have to keep a close eye on Gruffydd. It was of the utmost importance that they all supported each other's accounts and most of the group could look after themselves. As could she. The night had held its own traumas for her but she was determined to put it behind her. She was pretty sure no one would comment on her own lie, if they ever discovered it. That's what friends were for. To cover your back, whatever the cost.

39

The Fifth Lie

Bethan Rees lived in a daffodil-yellow house on the main road going through Solva, a town to the east of St Davids. It reportedly had a picturesque harbour that Mallory had yet to visit, saving it for the summer season, when she could make a trip with Toby. Mallory still hadn't got used to the multicoloured houses that lined some of the villages in Pembrokeshire. They were a cheering sight in the depths of winter, although they must need a regular coat of paint in the harsh elements. She passed the house twice, as she looked for somewhere to park, and in the end she left the car in a public space with what she hoped was enough time on the ticket.

Bethan answered the door in a long white towelling dressing gown, pulling the belt tighter when she saw Mallory on the doorstep.

'I thought it was the postwoman. She usually calls around this time. I'm expecting a parcel.'

'Can I come in?'

Bethan hesitated. 'Is it official business? I mean, is it to do with the cathedral?'

Mallory shook her head. 'It's police business.'

Bethan stepped back and let Mallory in, shutting the door and putting the chain on. 'Come into the lounge.'

It was more cell than living space. The yellow of the exterior walls was in stark contrast to how Bethan had decorated the inside of her home. Two pale grey sofas on pine legs were set at angles against the wall and a small TV set sat on a chest of drawers in the corner. That was it. No paintings, ornaments or evidence of books and magazines. Bethan saw her taking in the room and gave a thin smile.

'I went on a course a few years ago that recommended an ascetic lifestyle and I've tried to emulate it. You should try it.'

Mallory thought of her son in front of his fifty-eight-inch TV and winced. 'I get by on little but there are others in my life to consider.'

'Of course. I'm aware of the privilege of being single.' Bethan indicated the sofa for Mallory to sit down.

Privilege? wondered Mallory. It was an odd turn of phrase. Since she'd been single, she'd experienced loneliness, uncertainty and a feeling of life slipping away. Maybe it was a privilege if you craved solitude, but surely even someone as composed as Bethan must occasionally miss someone to share her life with.

'You like the single life?' asked Mallory.

'I do. You?'

'I suppose I do. I have a son, though. I think I mentioned him in my interview, so I have dependents.'

Bethan gave a half-smile. 'You know we had a meeting about you the other evening? There are some people in the chapter a little concerned that we've employed a member of staff who's also working for the police.'

'I'm sure chapter members are aware I can't live off the wages of a job that pays me for eighteen hours of work a week. Or do they need a lesson in the cost of living?' Mallory shrugged off her coat. Bethan might think she was embracing the ascetic lifestyle but the room was a couple of degrees warmer than her own flat.

'It is, of course, entirely up to you what you do in the time you're not employed by us.'

'Entirely up to me,' agreed Mallory, pulling out her reporter's pad. 'And as one of the interviewers, you knew my police background anyway, didn't you?'

Bethan didn't reply, keeping the smile on her face.

'I'm sure you've heard about the murder of Duncan Lyall. We're linking it to the recent death of Heledd Jones.'

'I hadn't heard that.' Bethan's voice was sharp. 'Can I ask why this is the case?'

'Mr Lyall died within a week of Heledd and he was one of the last people to see her alive. We're investigating a possible connection between the two cases. It's a major line of inquiry.' Along with many others, thought Mallory.

'I heard that Heledd died of hypothermia.'

'One possibility is that Heledd lay down in the field and died. Another scenario is that someone got her sufficiently intoxicated to render her virtually unconscious and then left her to die.'

'Duncan?'

'He said in his statement that he drove her to the train station and left her there.'

'Then it suggests someone else was involved. The Crosses own that land, don't they? Did you know Catrin is related to Eleri Tew?'

'We did.' Mallory didn't mention that they'd had to work it out for themselves, as neither Catrin nor Eleri had been forthcoming with the information. The fact that Bethan was prepared to drop her friend in it was illuminating and suggested a fissure in that relationship.

'My main focus,' said Mallory, 'is to look again at the events surrounding the death of Huw Jones to see if it had any bearing on Heledd's death. It's possible that all three deaths are in some way connected.'

'This was a long time ago.'

'A decade or so. It's not that long, especially when you've lost a child.'

Bethan flushed. 'None of us were kind enough to Heledd, I don't think. We tried but once Huw's body had been found, she sort of shut down. I do feel guilty about that.'

'I've not come here to judge you about what you did or didn't do in relation to your friendship with Heledd. I want to ask you about your actual statement on the night.'

'OK.' Bethan wasn't as wary as Mallory had expected, suggesting one of the others had tipped her off about her line of investigation. Gruffydd had probably been on the phone the minute Mallory left St. Madoc's.

'We have evidence that there are inconsistencies in relation to all six statements made by people at the house when Huw went missing. I'd like to go over your statement again.'

Bethan let out an exaggerated sigh. 'I don't think there's any need for that. I stand by the account I gave to the police the evening Huw died.'

'We'll come to that in a moment. During my interview with Gruffydd Ellis, he told me you'd advised him not to correct his statement, when in fact he'd noticed Huw's empty bed.'

'For God's sake. Once I discovered that Gruffydd had been foolish enough to lie to the police, Huw had already been found dead. What good would it have done to ruin Gruffydd's career by telling them he'd lied to them?'

'Establishing a timeline for events is one of the most important elements of a criminal investigation. It would have been crucial to know at what time Huw had definitely disappeared.'

Bethan shrugged, unconcerned about procedure or the moral implications of what she'd done, a complete contrast to Gruffydd Ellis.

'You were Gruffydd's girlfriend at the time, I believe,' said Mallory.

'I was but even if we'd been just friends, I'd have advised him to think carefully about what he said. His career would have been over if he'd revealed he lied in his initial statement.'

'I don't think he ever recovered from the guilt. Hadn't you thought of that?'

'I can't be held responsible for people's consciences. Gruffydd came to me for help and I gave him whatever advice I could. Go away, Mallory, I can't help you.'

'I will go, but after I've been through your statement.' Mallory pulled out her iPad and brought up Bethan's account of the evening.

'It says you were at the party at Eleri Tew's house from 3:30 p.m. You and Gruffydd arrived together – you were both living in St Davids at the time, although in separate houses.'

Bethan took a deep breath. 'Yes.'

'At some point – you estimated around quarter to five – you noticed that Gruffydd and Duncan were no longer at the party and guessed they were at Jack Jones's house.'

'It made sense. As far as those two were concerned, it wasn't a party unless Jack was there.'

'You went across the road. Was the door ajar?'

'I don't think so but it was unlocked. I think I turned the handle and went in.'

'You didn't find that surprising?'

'Not at all. People left their front doors unlocked even a decade or so ago.'

'Even with a small child in the house?'

'Why not? We thought he was safely in bed. I didn't know much about children, I assumed he'd be in some kind of cot.'

'At three years of age?'

Bethan shrugged, leaving Mallory furious. During her interviews with the other suspects, she'd kept her temper. There was something about Bethan's casual aloofness that implied the tragedy and grief experienced by Heledd were nothing to do with her.

'Go on,' said Mallory. 'You walked into the front living room and… what?'

'Four of them were in there. Jack, of course, Duncan, Gruffydd and Gemma. I was surprised to see Gemma. She'd made no indication that she was intending to go over. I thought she was still at Eleri's house.'

'Why do you think she was there?'

'She probably saw Duncan and Gruffydd leaving the party and decided to join them.'

'It's more or less what she put in her statement.'

'There we are, then.'

'Where was Eleri at this time?'

'At her own party. She came over about fifteen minutes later, looking furious, and demanded we return to her house. She hadn't minded Duncan coming over to keep Jack company but she wasn't happy when she realised that there was another gathering going on, where she'd rather be.'

'You think she'd rather have been at Y Bwthyn?'

'Of course. It was just screaming kids and people you had to invite, over at her house. Things were likely to improve later in the evening. Jack's house was where it was at.'

'Jack and Heledd's house.'

'Yes, of course.'

Mallory paused, feeling a trickle of sweat run down her back. Why did Bethan leave the house so warm? 'Did Heledd try to contact you in the last few months?'

'She left a number of messages on my answerphone. Once last year, then just after Christmas.'

'Did you ring her back?'

'No, I didn't. She sounded fine, to be honest, sort of calm and collected, but she said she wanted to talk to me about the night Huw disappeared, and I wasn't going to have that. I wanted to put that night firmly behind me.'

'You definitely didn't see her?'

'I definitely didn't.'

Mallory wasn't sure she believed her. Furthermore, she worried that the trickle of sweat down her back was also the result of fear. Because Bethan's implacable view of the world was frightening in its own way. Anyone who threatened that would be ignored, dismissed or perhaps worse. It wasn't a stretch to imagine it was Bethan who had stood watching her flat. Mallory looked down at her iPad.

'I need to know what part of your statement was incorrect or whether you have deliberately omitted something.'

Bethan flushed but kept her eyes on Mallory. 'I have nothing to add.'

'Are you sure about that?'

'Absolutely.'

'Would you know, then, the meaning of the following message: "All six of us lied. Six lies killed Huw Jones."'

Mallory didn't get the reaction she was expecting. Bethan stared at her, stupefied. 'What... where... who the hell has been telling you this?'

'A note was written, containing that message,' said Mallory, feeling some of her certainties slip away. 'Were you the one who wrote it?'

'Me? I've no idea what you're talking about. What do they mean that we all lied?'

'That's what I'm asking you.'

'Does Gruffydd know about the note?'

'I asked him and he said he wasn't the writer.'

'It wasn't me either. He never mentioned a note when I spoke to him.' She looked nonplussed that Gruffydd had withheld the information from her. 'What lies did the others tell?'

'I don't want to talk about them. I'm asking you about what you withheld from the police.'

'Bastard.'

'Excuse me?'

Bethan stood, striding around the small living room. 'After everything I've done for that bastard, he lets you spring this on me. He was always oblivious to me, even when we were engaged.'

'Meaning?'

'Meaning I've covered for him for too long. It's no surprise his marriage is a disaster. Gruffydd, let's say, prefers the company of men.'

'He's gay?'

Bethan flinched. 'I don't know if he's actually gay. Maybe bisexual or, based on my experience, asexual. I don't know. The funny thing is there are plenty of gay priests. I'm not pretending there aren't issues around tolerance in some sections of the congregation, but there are plenty of homosexual men in the priesthood. Why bother to hide it?'

'And how did you work this out?'

'Initially, I thought he was shy. I wasn't much more experienced than him but I was definitely keener. Then I noticed that his attachment to Jack and Duncan was definitely a little intense.'

'Jack *and* Duncan?' Mallory asked.

'More Duncan than Jack, I'd say, if pushed. I mean, they went around as a pair anyway so it's difficult to separate them, but Gruffydd was more interested in them than me.'

Mallory frowned. Despite Bethan's claims, she wasn't coming across as very experienced. Gruffydd had been at an age when male friendships and validation were important. Should she trust Bethan's reading of a sexual attachment? Perhaps it didn't matter. Bethan had believed it, which was important. 'What's this got to do with that New Year's Eve? Is that the reason you went over to the house? To check what Gruffydd was up to?'

Bethan studied her fingernails. Mallory saw they were inflamed at the cuticles where she'd picked at the skin. 'I was wild with jealousy. I stormed over there and when I saw that Gemma was in the living room, I calmed down a bit. I mean, it was just a group of us sneaking off from the main party, wasn't it? Then Duncan said he was going to get some more booze. He was always the one with more money than any of us in those days, and Gruffydd jumped up and said he'd help to carry it. Off they went. I was furious with the pair so, after a minute or so, I followed them.'

Mallory stopped writing. 'You followed them? There's no mention of that in your statement.'

'Why mention it? Gemma was with Jack, and I followed Duncan and Gruffydd to the off-licence. It didn't add anything to our statements, because at no point was anyone alone with Huw, assuming he was still in the house by then. I didn't want Gruffydd to know I'd been creeping after him. Or Duncan, for that matter. Duncan always had a hard edge to him and he'd have loved to have something over me.'

'Then who did you tell?'

'No one.'

'I'm sorry, Bethan, but you must have told someone because the author of that note knows you lied in your statement.'

'I tell you, no one knows about this. I'm only telling you now because it bears no relation to any crime. How can it? As I said, everyone is accounted for.'

Mallory shook her head, still piecing together the impact of what Bethan had said. She thought it mattered very much but it was interesting that whoever knew of Bethan's secret had kept it to themselves. Bethan had spent the decade thinking she'd got away with it and yet, there were people in the house who had known her lie. Jack and Gemma, certainly, and also possibly Eleri. She had to find a way to get to Eleri.

Mallory looked up and saw that Bethan had crossed to the window. 'What is it?'

'Nothing, probably. I can't get rid of the sense I'm being watched.'

Mallory stood and joined Bethan looking out onto the street. 'Have you actually spotted someone watching you?'

Bethan scratched her neck. 'Not here. Maybe at the cathedral. I'm not sure.'

'Do you feel it now?'

Bethan sighed. 'Maybe not.'

Mallory got out her notepad and scribbled her number on one of the sheets. 'Call me if you see anyone you don't like the look of. Promise?'

Bethan nodded.

40

Harri arrived at Fforest Country House Hotel, wishing he'd stopped to change his clothes. The call from Gavin Lavine at lunchtime had been a surprise. He'd thought the stonemason would be back in London, but it seemed he'd decided to make a holiday of his trip to West Wales. Fair enough, it was a long way to drive, but what he couldn't fathom was why the guy wanted to speak to him. He and Mallory had appeared to hit it off and she was the one leading on the line of inquiry in relation to the message he'd discovered at St Non's.

Stonemasonry clearly paid better than police work. The rooms at Fforest cost a couple of hundred quid a night and Gavin had already been here for nearly a week. Perhaps after working in the open air, you preferred your creature comforts. Harri's grandfather, Dafydd, had been a stonemason, but nothing on as grand a scale as cathedral work. Just houses in the village and Harri always felt a swelling of pride whenever he passed the row of terraces with the initials D. E. carved high into the centre.

Gavin was waiting for him in the bar and Harri was relieved to see he was also casually dressed. Harri ordered himself a Diet Coke and bought another whisky for Gavin. They took their drinks over to a table and sat down.

'I'm surprised you didn't call Mallory,' said Harri. 'She thought highly of your account of the note.'

'I tried her three times and she's not answering. I need to talk to someone urgently, as I'm heading back to London. I've been thinking over and over about the note left at St Non's.'

'Do you have more information?'

'I don't know how relevant it is. I've been talking to my wife about the whole thing. She joined me on Wednesday after I told her how lovely it is here. It was good to come back and exorcise some old ghosts.'

'You've not been to Pembrokeshire since the accident?'

'Haven't had any desire to. Now I'm here, I realise what a beautiful part of the world it is. The thing is, today I was talking about the note I found and how much it must have made an impression on me at the time. Apparently, when I was taken to Haverfordwest hospital, I was raving. Talking in a stream of consciousness, according to Rachel, my wife. And I kept mentioning the note and Huw Jones.'

'When was this? In the ambulance, at A & E admissions, on the ward?'

'I never got to a ward. I was in A & E for thirty-six hours and then transferred to London to a specialist brain unit. I don't know about the ambulance, as Rachel wasn't there then. She was called down to the hospital by cathedral staff. All this happened while I was in A & E.'

'Is your wife available now?'

'You think it important?'

'I do. Give her a call, would you?'

Rachel Lavine was a tall blonde woman, whose navy fitted dress was more suited to the decor of the hotel. She grabbed her husband's hand as she sat down. 'It's been quite stressful reliving that accident.'

'Gavin tells me you were in the hospital with him when he was talking about the note. How lucid was he?'

'Not lucid at all. He had a bleed on the brain; doctors gave him pain relief until he could have a CT scan and lumbar puncture, but nothing else. It was while we were waiting for these that he kept talking about a note and Huw Jones.'

'Did he say what was in the message?'

'He kept shouting "all six lied" but I didn't really know what he was talking about. It was the note that seemed to have had more of an effect on him, rather than its contents. He grabbed me and said, "Go to St Non's and look behind the cross." I thought he was raving, to be honest. I never actually thought there was a note.'

'You've not discussed it since the accident?'

'Of course we've discussed it. We've occasionally wondered if the note would still be there but I didn't tell Gavin that he was shouting about it in hospital, until today. Being here seems to have revived some old traumas.'

'And he mentioned Huw Jones?'

Rachel screwed up her eyes. 'I *think* he did. The problem is I know the message from later conversations. He was shouting about lies and St Non's and a note. He might have mentioned Huw Jones but it wouldn't have meant anything to me.'

Harri sat back in his chair. It probably didn't make any difference if the boy's name had been mentioned. St Non's, reference to all six lying and a letter behind the cross would have been enough. And he had a pretty good idea which of the suspects would have been in an A & E department.

41

It was a dark night, the waning moon high in the distant horizon and only a smattering of stars in the cloudy sky. Toby had retreated to his room, which was a worry. Mallory preferred it when he was stuck in front of the television. She didn't like shut doors and silences; when she'd knocked to check he was OK, he'd told her he was trying to sleep.

For the first time since her divorce, she missed Joe. Perhaps there was stuff Toby wanted to talk about that only a father would understand. At least if Joe were here, she would have someone to consult with. Harri had told her that his daughter Ellie went through difficult times but it didn't sound the same at all. Once more, Mallory was aware of her deep inadequacy as a mother.

She looked at her watch. It was only five o'clock and the evening stretched in front of her. She needed to do something. Anything.

'I'm going out for a walk,' she shouted to Toby and received no answer.

Getting outside was a relief. The thaw had washed away some of the dirt of winter and, for the first time this year, it felt like spring might be coming soon. Perhaps she should take Toby on a hunt for the first snowdrops, as they had done when he was a child. A small thing to do, but reconnecting with nature might provide some solace for both of them. She automatically looked across the road before setting off, but there was no one in sight.

Mallory found herself on the path towards Y Bwthyn. She'd not paid the place much attention, given the house had been sold on soon after Huw's death. The tall narrow building was in darkness and she spotted a key safe to the right of the door, suggesting its use as a holiday cottage. As she was about to turn away, a light came on in the hallway and a tall shadow passed through to the front room. On impulse, Mallory opened the gate and knocked on the front door.

The man who opened it had the leanness of an extreme athlete. His face sported a red, mottled texture usually associated with those who spend time out of doors. He was holding a plateful of toast.

Mallory got out her ID and showed it to the man. 'I'm really sorry to be disturbing you on a cold night but I'm working with Dyfed Powys police. A little boy went missing from this house in 2011 and I just wanted to have a quick look at the layout of the rooms, if you're OK with that. It'll take ten minutes maximum.'

'Well… sure. Can I take a look at your ID again?'

She handed it to him. 'I have a number to call for the Detective Inspector if you'd like to confirm everything is legit.'

He looked her up and down and decided she was unlikely to be a thief. 'Come on in. I'm Pete, by the way. It's not about that little boy who died, is it? When did you say it was?'

'In 2011. He walked from this house to St Non's and died on the cliffs there.'

'I know St Non's. It's quite a landmark on the coastal path.'

'To be honest, I'm having a little difficulty believing he made it all the way down there by himself, but that's what the evidence appears to suggest. It's a long way for a three-year-old to go.'

'You know, I did something similar when I was a child, in Cumbria. Just took myself off for a walk one day. The mountains have always been a draw for me. Maybe the sea had the same attraction.'

'His mother used to tell him stories of mermaids.'

'There you are. We all need our stories. Perhaps he even found them.'

'I really hope so too. Perhaps I could start with the front living room, where the boy's father was sitting with his friends.'

'Sure. It's here.' He pushed open a door to the right, leading on to a box-shaped room with an unlit wood-burning stove.

'I thought you'd have that on,' said Mallory, feeling her leg seize up in the cold.

'I've just got in. I cycled to Fishguard and back, and I'm refuelling before I settle down for the evening. Where was the boy last seen in the house?'

'He was in an upstairs bedroom and the theory is that he let himself out and walked into the night without anyone in this room noticing.'

Pete pulled the living room door open as far back as it would go. It looked original to the cottage. 'Unless you're standing at the entrance, you have no view of the stairs.'

Mallory nodded. 'Agreed, which tallies with the father's statement. Can I just take a look at the back door?'

'Sure, but I think the kitchen has been extended.'

Pete placed his toast next to a copy of the *Western Mail*. Mallory saw that the room had been added on to the original layout of the house.

'That's fine.'

Pete switched on a light that illuminated the back garden, enclosed by three high stone walls. 'There's no side passage.'

'Could I take a look upstairs? The boy was sleeping in the small room overlooking the back garden.'

'Go on up. It's next to the bathroom. I'll make you a cup of tea. It looks like you need it.'

'I'm all right, thanks, but go ahead if you fancy it. I won't be a minute.' Mallory was already up the stairs, sticking her head into each of the bedrooms, which were sparsely furnished, reminding her a little of Bethan's house. The owners of this holiday cottage weren't going for country chic. The small room contained a single bed covered in a checked duvet. Nothing to see here and it confirmed, once more, that Huw could easily have slipped down the stairs and out into the night. But he must have been sure his mother wasn't in the house.

Mallory stopped trying to get into the mind of a fractious three-year-old. He'd got up after an afternoon sleep and possibly looked for Heledd upstairs. Finding the rooms empty, he went downstairs, probably hearing noises from the living room. There was initially just Jack, then Jack, Duncan and Gruffydd, and then various configurations until the end, when all six were in the room. Despite them keeping their voices low, there would have been plenty of noise for him to gravitate to. However, if Gruffydd's revised statement was to be believed, Huw had gone before Eleri arrived. Presumably, Huw came down the stairs and made his way towards the living room and then… what? How about a scenario where Huw stopped at the entrance and refused to go in, preferring the siren of the cliffs? Mallory had not been able to find a motive or opportunity which meant one of the six removed Huw from the house, so she had to find why the six had deliberately concocted lies – some alone, others with the connivance of their friends. So, what did Huw see?

–

From Y Bwthyn, Mallory tried to put herself in the mind of Huw who, she believed, had seen something in the living room and gone to look for his mother. Saying goodbye to Pete, at the gate, she hesitated. Left or right? Heledd had been at Eleri's house to the left but Huw had been found at St Non's, in the opposite direction. Mallory turned right. In neither Heledd's nor Jack's statements, for what they were worth, was there any mention that Huw knew there was a party going on across the road. This, she thought, she could probably take at face value. Huw had gone into the night to look for his mother and the mermaids. Heledd and Huw had told stories to each other. Heledd had a vivid imagination and she'd made up a story about St Non's, where you could talk to the mermaids. His mother wasn't in the house so the natural place to look for her was at the end of their favourite walk.

Once she'd passed the last house at the edge of the town, the light disappeared and she was left to pick her way down the dark road, wishing she'd brought her torch with her. It was impossible not to think of a little boy stumbling down this same street looking for his mother, or maybe Heledd's story held true and he had been attracted to the sound of the sirens luring him to their company. She ploughed on, not sure what she was expecting to find. It was impossible not to think of her own son, as lost as Huw had been in 2011. She wondered what place Toby drew comfort from and whether she was to blame for failing to enchant him with an imaginary world, as Heledd had with Huw. She and Toby had read books together when he was a child but Mallory was no storyteller.

The dark held no demons for Mallory but she became aware of a shift in the night's air. The swish of fresh, bitter wind and the thump of waves became overlaid with another sound. A stealthy shuffle of someone behind her. Mallory stopped and looked round but could see no one. She had passed a bend and it was possible she was being followed. Her training kicked in and she walked the other way, retracing her steps, reaching for her door key to use as a weapon.

As she passed the bend, she braced herself. There was no one, just the empty road she had come along. She waited for a minute, still sensing danger but unable to pinpoint its origins. Perhaps someone was in the fields. She thought of Toby in the flat, finding some comfort with her away from London. She'd be no use to him lying dead on a cliff.

With a sigh, she turned her back on the sound of the sea and focused on the lights in the distance. It was a mistake, as she heard the rustle of someone coming up *behind* her. Mallory's heart leapt in her chest and she wheeled round to see a figure dressed in black coming towards her. She waited for them to catch up with her. Running was pointless. Her leg was her weakest point and she wouldn't be able to get far. She would not be attacked from behind but face her foe.

She grasped her keys tighter, so that the back-door one was jutting out between her third and fourth fingers. It had a serrated edge which she could use as a weapon. When the figure was upon her, Mallory saw with horror that they were wearing a plain mask, reminding her of the jack-o'-lantern she used to carve as a child out of swedes. She saw the hand raised and the glint of a hammer head bearing down on her. Mallory lunged at her attacker, using the key to score a line down their face. The metal from the weapon glanced off her temple but her assailant was also wounded, dropping the hammer in shock.

They scrambled for it. If her attacker got hold of the weapon once more, Mallory knew it would be all over for her. She'd never outrun them. She bent down and got to the hammer first, picking it up and hurling it over the high hedge into the field. Her assailant took the opportunity to flee, not towards the town but towards St Non's and the coastal path that could take them to safety.

–

Back home, Mallory sat at the table in the living room, nursing her agonising head. When she got to her front door, she realised she'd dropped her keys during the assault and she needed to bang on Toby's window to wake him up. Unlike when her leg was injured, which Toby wilfully ignored as she limped alongside him, he seemed concerned about the injury to her face. When she looked up, he was standing over her with a grubby flannel in his hand.

'Hold this over your face, Mum. It'll reduce the swelling.'

She took the flannel off him and had to admit the coolness gave her aching head some relief.

'Who did this to you?'

'I don't know. Someone, I suspect, who thinks I'm getting too close to them. Don't worry, I'm waiting for the police to arrive. There's a hammer in a field I want them to find.'

'A hammer? Fucking hell, Mum. I heard what happened to that coach guy. You could have been killed.'

Toby burst into tears, noisy sobs that convulsed his body. Mallory, aware she was spreading blood over her son as well as disturbing forensic evidence, pulled him to her.

'It'll be all right. I promise.' She didn't specify what would be OK. She didn't actually know but it felt important to say it.

After a minute, he pulled away. 'What does Harri say?'

Mallory examined the scarlet-smeared flannel. 'Why do you ask?'

'Does he know you're injured? That someone attacked you?'

'Well...'

'You mean you've not told him?'

'It's Sunday night. I'll call him once the patrol car has been here. Go play a game. I need to look up some things before the police arrive.'

'I'm tired of the game, to be honest. Do you want to watch a film once they've gone? You're supposed to stay awake after head injuries.'

Mallory was pretty sure they'd take one look at her and call an ambulance, which was the last thing she wanted. She needed to clean herself up.

'Sure, give me a chance to bag up my clothes while you choose a movie. Nothing too gory, please, and preferably one where the women do something more than scream.'

He shot her an offended look but fired up Netflix and began to browse through the recommendations. Mallory retreated to the bathroom, stripped off her clothes and took a shower. She'd get in trouble for doing so but it was more important she present a reasonably uninjured figure to the police when they arrived. There was something she wanted to check out first.

In her dressing gown, Mallory grabbed her laptop and put St Non's into the search engine. It was no coincidence she'd been attacked near the ruined chapel. It was the place where Huw had died and where the note had been placed. She'd forgotten the importance of geographic forensics in an investigation, when location was scrutinised for clues to a crime. It would be currently happening in relation to Duncan's murder but she should have given it the same focus when looking at Huw's death. She needed to find a link between St Non's and one of the six friends. She began with Jack and Duncan. Jack had no hits in relation to the tourist spot but she did find a picture of him and his wife, the French Marie-Axelle. She had glossy black hair and looked effortlessly glamorous. With Duncan, she found a hit, but it was a fluff piece in relation to one of the tours which stopped at St Non's and gave no indication that Duncan had any particular affinity with the ruins.

The other members drew a similar blank. While she was on Eleri's profile, she noticed a disclaimer at the bottom of the search engine.

'Toby – what does this mean? "Some results may have been removed under data protection law in Europe." It's at the bottom of the page I'm looking at.'

'It's there on most pages. If you're worried about your privacy, you can ask for data to be removed.'

'You can?' Mallory shut her laptop. 'Then that's no use to me.'

'That's just with Google, though. Try another search engine that doesn't track your searches.'

'Really?'

Toby came over and took the laptop off her. 'It'll be quicker if I do it. Look.' He typed in a web address that came up with a duck icon in the centre. 'Right, who do you want to look for?'

'Search for Eleri Tew and St Non's Chapel.'

'Hold on.'

Mallory leant over his shoulder as a list of websites came up. Her head was beginning to ache again and, if it didn't subside, she'd be taking a trip to A & E in the morning. 'What's that one?' She could see Eleri standing outside, next to the sea.

Toby opened up the website while Mallory leant in closer to read the text.

'Well, fuck me.' When she looked down, she saw Toby was laughing.

42

Harri switched on the TV, which was unusual for him when he had the house to himself. He liked the silence, which he got precious little of at home. Sunday night, though, and the two kids were out, Ellie sleeping over at a friend's and Ben getting in at God knows what time. Fran was upstairs in her room with a headache. She was listening to a true crime podcast with the lights dimmed and had told him to fend for himself for dinner. Harri's hand crept towards the pile of takeout menus and paused. He would have a follow-up blood test in a month to see if his medication was working. He might at least try to cut down a bit on the takeaways. He would look in the fridge once he'd finished this bottle of beer and had a scan of the news.

Duncan Lyall's death was still in the headlines, although there was a clip of the tour buses continuing to ply their trade, which was a good thing. While it was business as usual for them, they would have been surprised to learn of a few extra passengers who had booked at the last minute this week and were keeping a very close eye on the buses' movements. Bored with the news, Harri flicked channels until he settled on one showing a programme on the history of the Welsh woollen trade. He half-expected Becca's face to pop up on screen. He'd been impressed by her business at the old mill, keeping Welsh traditions alive, but the programme was focusing on the north of the country. Typical. Bored, Harri scrolled through his phone but there were no messages from Mallory or other members of his team. A quiet Sunday night.

His phone rang and he picked it up, glad to see the number that flashed on his screen.

'Hello, Mallory.'

'Actually, it's Toby.'

Harri sat up. 'Is she all right?'

'Mum's just out of the shower and she doesn't know I'm using her phone.'

Harri relaxed a fraction. 'What's the matter?'

'The thing is, someone hit her over the head tonight. She was out and she came back bleeding.'

'Out where?'

'She wouldn't tell me but she didn't take the car so it must have been local. She's called the police, because the weapon is lying in a field.'

'What weapon?' Harri caught his breath.

'A hammer.'

'Jesus.' Harri looked at his watch, wondering if he should make the journey up there himself. They already had the weapon that killed Duncan Lyall but forensically it had drawn a blank. It was too much of a coincidence that Mallory had been attacked with a similar bludgeon.

'Toby, can you call Mallory an ambulance? Head injuries should be checked out.'

'She won't go to hospital.'

Harri wondered about the dynamic between mother and son. He suspected Toby's as yet undiagnosed eating issue was constantly on Mallory's mind but they didn't seem to have had a proper conversation about it. Now, the roles were reversed.

'Did she see her attacker?'

'She said they were wearing a mask but she doesn't really want to talk about it.'

'A mask? Like a balaclava?'

'Uh… I'm not sure. How's Ellie?'

Harri smiled. 'She's fine. Maybe you want to come down with Mallory sometime and have lunch with us.'

'Um… great.'

'Would you go and get your mum now so I can have a chat with her?'

'OK.' The phone went silent, although Harri could hear Mallory berating Toby in the background before she picked up the phone.

'Bloody kids. I can't leave my phone for five minutes before they're unlocking it.'

'What's your passcode? Please don't tell me it's 123456.'

'It's 999, twice,' he heard Toby shout in the background.

'For God's sake, Mallory, change your password to something harder to crack. What's all this about you getting attacked this evening? Where were you?'

'On the road out to St Non's but I'm all right. Listen, it's the weekend so do you think Eleri will be at her constituency home?'

'Probably, why?'

'I've found a connection to St Non's. There's a newspaper article where she talks about her affinity with the place. I think she left the note.'

'Eleri? No chance.'

'I'm sorry but you need to trust me on this. Give me her mobile number, would you?'

'She's out of bounds. I've told you, and I'm pretty sure Steph did too.'

'I need that number, Harri.'

'Don't you think it's dangerous to contact her? If she has an affinity with St Non's, how do you know it wasn't her who attacked you?'

'Eleri is slight. This was someone hefty, although male or female, I couldn't tell you.'

'Her husband, then.'

'I need to speak to Eleri, please, Harri. It could crack the case.'

'I've got something that you might want to hear. I had a drink with Gavin Lavine this afternoon. According to his wife, he was talking about the note after his accident. He was in A & E, and telling everyone who would listen that there was a note in St Non's with a message that all six lied.'

'Which leads us to Gemma Bowen.'

'Exactly. So, leave Eleri—'

'I think Eleri wrote the note and Gemma discovered its existence. It's the only thing that makes sense – two different people were involved. I want to interview Gemma under arrest.'

'Arrest for what?'

Mallory sighed down the phone. 'I don't know. I can't link Gemma with Heledd's death. I still need to speak to Eleri and find out what she lied about. Please, give me her number.'

Sometimes, Harri reflected, it was easier just to give in. After cutting the call, he picked up a leaflet for the local Indian takeaway and dialled in the order. It was Sunday night after all.

43

Eleri was alone with the detritus of her party. The blue lights twinkled in the garden, their cheeriness an outrage, given the events of the evening. One of the teenagers had brought party string in a can and sprayed the living room a rainbow of garish colours. The kids had loved it but it was their piercing screams that had led her to scurry over the road to drag her friends back to the party. Eleri didn't think she'd ever forget Heledd's face when she'd pushed open the door of the sitting room. She stood there like a phantom, her eyes pleading with them for Huw to be in the room hiding, perhaps, behind the sofa. Huw had probably been still alive then, his little legs hurrying towards St Non's. Eleri closed her eyes. Why there of all places? She knew the answer, of course. Huw had felt the same emotion that she'd experienced since she was a child. The sense of awe and wonder at the most sacred of spots. Tourists flocked to the cathedral but it was St Non's that held the wonder of their ancestors.

Eleri tore off a bin liner and began to clear up. Paper plates and plastic cups were dumped into the bag, along with food. No one would feel like eating canapés after the shock of the evening. A few of the guests had tried to linger, going over and over again what had happened, but

Eleri had thrown them out. She wasn't interested in idle chit-chat while she shivered in shock. For the first hour or so she had been numb. She had no interest in children but Huw had been a charming boy and his death a dreadful tragedy.

The problem was she had to start thinking about the impact of what had happened on her own career. The press would soon be sniffing around for an angle of interest. She, as leader of the council, was a good story on which to base an article, so she'd have to face that. But, thank God, she'd only been in Y Bwthyn twenty or so minutes before Heledd came storming into the room. Huw, she was pretty sure, had already gone by then. She would brazen it out and emphasise her presence at her own house when Huw had disappeared.

The first thing to do was dump Duncan. She'd let that relationship continue long after he had outlived his usefulness. Any contacts he had as the son of a prominent businessman had been identified and exploited. She needed a period on her own to make the next push in her career. She'd also need to start distancing herself from her friends, whose allegiances were now under scrutiny. She had little in common with Gemma and Bethan, but guessed both of them would have their own reasons for modifying their accounts of the evening. Gruffydd, she neither knew nor cared about but his expression of absolute misery suggested something had gone on that night that he was desperately trying to cover up. It seemed, perhaps, he was in the same boat as her, so she might have a little word with Bethan. There was no point talking to Gruffydd, who was a little leaky in his current state.

Jack, Huw's father, could look after himself. She felt sorry for him in the way she also felt sorry for Heledd.

They were grieving parents and she would let them be, but Jack also had his own secrets, she was sure. Eleri tied a knot in the first bag and threw it into the back garden. She'd ask her niece Catrin to come over tomorrow to help her take everything to the rubbish facility. The girl was perpetually short of money and would appreciate the tenner she'd give her.

Opening another sack, her hand hovered over a set of bricks left behind by one of the toddlers. Worrying about her career was a travesty in the midst of such a tragic death and yet, she couldn't change her personality, in the same way that none of her friends could alter theirs. They would all be shaping their accounts of this evening to minimise the impact to their own reputations. The thought gave her little comfort.

44

The Sixth Lie

Eleri stood by the cliff at St Non's, staring out at the sea. It was a calm day: freezing cold but without the bitter wind that Mallory had come to associate with the peninsula. If she closed her eyes and ignored the chill in her bones, it might be a summer's day and Toby a child again, with his bucket and spade on the beach below.

Eleri had watched Mallory approach with none of the trepidation she'd seen on the face of the other suspects. Eleri knew her place in the world and wasn't afraid of it being taken from her. This meant she was either a benign figure or very dangerous and Mallory couldn't yet discern which. Meeting her in person also confirmed that she definitely wasn't her attacker.

'I always come here when I can.' She spoke to the sea as Mallory reached her, trying not to show how tiring the walk had been. 'I like the silence and the sense of peace. Can you feel it?'

Exhausted, Mallory sat on the low wall near the well. Friend or foe, she needed to rest. There was only so much tension your body could take and she'd reached the limit of hers. Her head was pounding but she'd put off the trip to the hospital. Eleri had answered her mobile promptly and agreed to a meeting. She would have been well within her rights to refuse but, perhaps, curiosity had got the better of her.

'It was you who wrote the note. I realise that now. Of all the friends, it was only someone like you who would know all the lies that were told that evening.'

Eleri smiled. 'I've always liked to be in the centre of events. I'm not a natural confidante, people don't trust me well enough for that, but I have a knack for working out the order of things.'

'When did you realise that everyone who gave a statement that evening had lied to the investigative team?'

Eleri turned, her blue eyes holding Mallory's. Her eyelashes were caked in mascara and stood in spikes on her face. Her foundation was thick but not contoured. Eleri liked makeup but stuck to her routine from a decade earlier. It reinforced Mallory's view that she was a woman who preferred her own way of doing things.

'I realised straight away. Have you ever been in a close group of friends?'

Mallory shuffled her feet to get some circulation back to her toes. 'Not really. Not like yours, certainly. I've wondered who the leader of the group was. I know Harri, DI Evans, thinks it was Duncan.'

'It doesn't work like that. Duncan certainly had the most forceful personality but there was an element of him that only looked out for himself. You can't lead with that kind of personality.'

'You, then?'

Eleri shook her head. 'Not me. There are a number of forceful personalities in our group. Maybe looking for one leader isn't helpful.'

'Let's start with the lies, then. Jack had planned that Duncan would come round. When did you learn of this?'

'Straight away. Duncan and I were seeing each other on and off back then. Just casual, as you are in your twenties. Duncan was never going to be a politician's spouse, that much I was sure of. He told me he was going to slip over to keep Jack company, which was fine by me. As I said, everything was casual.'

'And when he didn't mention it to the police?'

'He should have been upfront. I didn't realise what Jack had done until Duncan told me and I wasn't going to make an issue of it. Jack was a grieving father and all our accounts were given under great stress. Of all the lies, I think Jack's was the most forgivable.'

'But isn't calling it a lie a bit strong?'

'Maybe.'

'The second lie involves Gemma Bowen.'

Eleri frowned. 'Second lie?'

'Sorry, I've mentally given each lie a number based on the order I've been speaking to people. Gemma Bowen said she'd seen Heledd in a professional capacity during her training. Why would she not mention that?'

Eleri kept quiet, her gaze back on the sea. 'I think you'll have to ask her why. Gemma and I spoke a few weeks after the tragedy and she told me about seeing Heledd at Larch House. I asked her if she'd mentioned it to the police and she said no. Not an omission: a deliberate decision to withhold information.'

Jesus, thought Mallory, you could tell Eleri was a politician. She wasn't getting anywhere with this conversation. 'What about the fight between Jack and Duncan? Why did Duncan keep quiet about it?'

Eleri walked over to Mallory and sat down, shivering in the cold. 'I didn't find out about that until two years after Huw's death. Duncan and I went out for a drink together and things turned… well… intimate. I wasn't married but I think Duncan had met Lizzie.'

'Think?' asked Mallory.

'Well, OK, they were seeing each other but definitely not engaged. Afterwards, in bed, we got talking about that night. I've never really properly spoken about the evening, as I've been trying to keep my powder dry for my political career. It was at that point he told me how much he regretted hitting Jack.'

'But what was the fight about?' asked Mallory.

'I don't know but I can guess. Again, you need to speak to Gemma.'

'Gemma. Is she the one this all hinges on?'

'Probably, but it's never just one person, is it? It was Duncan who also told me about Gruffydd's lie. He couldn't keep it to himself, even though Bethan had told him not to tell anyone. Duncan was a little like me. He liked to wheedle secrets out of people.'

'Bethan was convinced he hadn't told anyone.'

'Poor Bethan.' Eleri regarded her suede boots. 'I presume you've worked out her lie.'

Mallory nodded.

'You know, jealousy's a killer in any relationship. I certainly don't allow it to flourish in mine. Gruffydd could have gone to the shop with any of us and she still would have followed. So which lie am I?'

'You're the final one. The sixth lie. I only managed to speak to Bethan the other day but I think her lie was perhaps the most significant. By deliberately withholding the fact she'd left the house and followed Duncan and Gruffydd to the off-licence, she throws into doubt the others' statements.'

Eleri pursed her lips. 'There we are, then. You know, it was Duncan who spotted Bethan lurking in the shadows, which was pretty impressive given how drunk he was. I didn't realise she hadn't given that information to the police until much later. By then it had become clear that all of us, in our own way, hadn't told the truth that evening.'

'How do you feel about Duncan's death?'

'Tired. That's how I feel. I also want to help as much as I'm able to. All the deaths are connected, aren't they?'

Mallory pulled up the zip of her coat. 'I think so. When I spoke to Bethan, she hinted that there might have been some kind of attraction between Gruffydd and Duncan. She was convinced that some kind of intrigue was going on.'

'Was she?' Eleri's eyes flickered. 'She's barking up the wrong tree on that one, I think.'

'Would you care to elaborate?'

Eleri shook her head. 'When did you realise it was me who wrote the note?'

'My son showed me how to bypass the Google search engine. It's a whole new world for me, but your interview is there for all to see if you know where to look.'

Eleri smiled. 'You know, I never thought of that. I've used the European data protection law to have all references to me and St Non's removed from the internet, citing privacy concerns. I thought that'd be enough.'

'It's a single article, from before you were selected as parliamentary candidate.'

Eleri shrugged. 'I don't remember. How old's your son?'

'Fifteen. Why do you ask?'

'Just younger than Huw would have been.'

'I know. You never had any yourself?'

Eleri looked back out to sea. 'No, but it's not the reason behind the note. I can see you're dying to ask me why I wrote the message.' She shivered. 'You know, I can't stand this cold. Can we go to the car?'

Mallory joined her, trudging to Eleri's white Range Rover.

'It was something primaeval to do. After the night with Duncan, I discovered I was pregnant. I wasn't sure what to do. A baby wasn't part of my plans, and Duncan and I would never have made a decent couple. Have you met his wife?'

Mallory nodded.

'Lizzie is more, let's say, amenable than I am. Also, I needed a partner without Duncan's dubious reputation. He was still drinking then.'

Mallory wondered how much Eleri knew or had guessed about Duncan's bus company.

'What happened to the baby?'

'I lost it, I'm afraid. I don't know if it was a curse or a blessing but it laid me very low. For a while, everyone I met had a baby in their arms, and I started to think about Heledd and Huw.'

'Did you get in touch with her?'

They'd reached the car and they slid into the front seats. The interior smelt of leather and Eleri's citrus perfume.

'Heledd didn't need my sympathy, which didn't mean I wasn't sorry for her. The funny thing is I met a genuinely religious person. I'd never had much truck with either Gruffydd's or Bethan's form of religion. Gruffydd is all smells and bells, and Bethan holier-than-thou. I met one of the chaplains at the Commons and told him what had happened to me and how guilty I felt about that night.

It was he who suggested writing the note. A form of penance.'

'When did you write it?'

'May 2015.'

'But that's only a month or so before it was found.'

'I hoped it would fade with time, and that would be that. I didn't realise wrapping it in a plastic bag would preserve it for posterity.'

'When did you discover the note had been found?'

'When Heledd called to say she had new evidence she wanted to discuss, she mentioned a note. At that point I realised it had been found. I came down to St Non's and saw that it wasn't there any longer.'

'You never mentioned any of this in your interview with DI Evans.'

'I gave the bare facts. No lie. I'll amend my statement if you wish. I've no idea how Heledd got hold of that note.'

'There's a possibility that the person who originally found your note, Gavin Lavine, and Gemma were in the same hospital the night he had his accident. The A & E department will have been busy and Gavin says he was delirious. Gemma might have told Heledd about the note.'

'When, though? When did Heledd learn of the note?'

'Six months ago.'

'Six months ago? You said the note was found just after I wrote it. Why wait that long before giving it to Heledd?'

'That's what I need to ask her.' Eleri was silent. Mallory could hear a phone vibrating in the bag on the back seat. 'I think someone's trying to get in contact with you.'

'I don't get a moment's peace. It'll be my husband, who's worried about me. There have been some nasty instances recently.'

'Nasty in what way?'

'Trolls, mainly on social media. It's usually par for the course but my diary secretary tells me she's been getting odd calls too. Someone trying to book appointments at my Friday afternoon surgery and insisting on a one-to-one meeting.'

'Do you do those?'

Eleri pulled down the sun visor to check her makeup in the mirror. 'Not anymore. It's left my husband jittery, so he's accompanying me to my surgeries at the moment. I still look forward to coming home. My family have been here for generations. You lose part of yourself when you leave your ancestors' turf. Here is the only place I can be myself. Do you think it a coincidence that Heledd's body was found in my niece's field?'

'It might be. It's just a field, after all, near Heledd's cottage.'

'Bit of a coincidence, though, isn't it? I think someone is having – or should I say *was* having – a laugh at my expense. Do you think Duncan had a hand in Heledd's death?'

Mallory hesitated. 'It's possible. What do you think?'

'He's certainly capable of it. What about suspects for his murder?'

'I don't know.' Mallory touched her sore head, convinced her attacker was the same person who had killed Duncan.

'I need to ask you what your lie was that evening. What is the sixth lie?'

Eleri turned to her, back in politician mode. 'I can't tell you. I'm sorry, I'll admit to writing the note but there are other people involved. I will tell you that my account was essentially truthful. I arrived at Y Bwthyn twenty-five minutes before Heledd got back. I was literally in and out of that house.'

'I'll find out what you know.'

'Be careful.' Eleri reached out an arm. 'There's more at play than you think.'

45

'So, what the bloody hell is the sixth lie? I don't want the flimflam, just give me what Eleri knows that we don't.'

Offended, Mallory resisted the temptation to throw the phone into the sea. 'She wouldn't tell me. She admitted to writing the note, which is one mystery solved.'

'Mystery solved? This isn't a game of Guess Who? I've got the killing of Duncan Lyall to solve. Do you think I should arrest her?'

'What for? She's got an alibi for Duncan's death, hasn't she? She was at a dinner in the House of Commons so she's off the hook. What will you charge her with?'

'Withholding information in relation to the death of Huw Jones. She wrote the note, which makes her culpable in relation to all six lies. That'll be enough to ruin her political career.'

'Well, you've changed your tune. Only last night you were telling me to stay away from her.'

Mallory was fuming. Eleri was doing what politicians did the world over. She was protecting her own position to insulate her career from an event that had occurred in the past. Mallory believed her when she said she only entered the house for the final twenty-five minutes before Heledd returned home. Her involvement in 2011 was marginal but had overshadowed her time in politics, and Mallory thought, on balance, these years had been a force for good.

'She's not going to tell me what she knows but one thing I picked up from our conversation is that Duncan's death is connected to all this.'

'How?'

'If I knew that, do you think I'd be standing here?' Mallory shouted at Harri as a dog walker did an about-turn at the sound of her anger. Mallory couldn't really blame them, as she wouldn't want to encounter someone like herself in such an isolated place.

From her car, Mallory tried Gemma Bowen's practice. A harried receptionist told her the GP was currently out of the surgery. Mallory picked up a hesitant note in the woman's voice.

'It's Mallory Dawson from Dyfed Powys police. I do need to speak to Doctor Bowen as soon as possible.'

'Is anything the matter? We can't get in touch with Gemma and we've been trying all morning. We've had to move patients to other GPs so there's a terrible backlog.'

'Is she not answering her mobile?'

'It's switched off, which is unusual. She prefers to leave it on silent so she knows who's been trying to contact her. We're worried she might have been in a car accident, given the state of the roads.'

'I can check to see if there have been any reports but I think I might have heard if that was the case.' Mallory looked at her watch. 'It's eleven now. What time was her first appointment?'

'Eight thirty. We thought she was just late but at nine fifteen we began to reallocate her patients. We're just about to cancel her afternoon appointments, as we're at bursting point. People will just turn up anyway if we can't get hold of them.'

'Have you any idea where she might be?'

'She's not at home. I got a colleague to go round her house and her cleaner answered the door. She said Gemma had already left that morning, before she arrived.'

'She's definitely not there?'

'Definitely not. I got her to check each room in case she'd fallen ill.' The receptionist fell silent. 'Do you think she's OK?'

'I think you should call the police and report her missing. Tell them she was a witness to the death of Huw Jones in 2011 and it might be relevant to a current murder inquiry. I'll make some enquiries this side.'

Mallory cut the call and looked at her watch. Damn. She had to get to work for midday, which gave her precious little time to undertake any investigating. It was a joke, trying to hold down two jobs at once. Either she was a shop assistant or she was a civilian investigator. Actually, come to think of it, she was also a mother to a troubled son. She tried Toby's mobile but he didn't answer it. He was probably still in bed. She left a message.

'Toby, I'm going to work. Come down and meet me, and I'll buy you lunch. It'll be good to get out.'

Mallory looked up at the sky and cursed. Slate grey clouds were gathering, threatening snow, and the last thing she wanted was to be stuck while Gemma was worryingly missing. She wondered whether to ring Harri but his attitude had infuriated her. Instead, she rang Siân and told her what the receptionist had said.

'I think I'll take a drive to the house anyway. If the cleaner's still there, she can let me have a look. Think she might be in trouble?'

'Gemma's a catalyst for everything that happened. She discovered the note's existence from Gavin but for some reason, she kept it to herself. I need to discover why she decided to share it with Heledd around July last year.'

'Think she might be in danger or a danger to others?'

'I don't know.'

46

The problem with civilian investigators, thought Harri, especially when they were ex-force, was that they conveniently forgot there were procedures they needed to follow. In Mallory's shoes, he'd have had Eleri Tew down at the station being interviewed by his DCs Siân and Freddie, who wouldn't have been as forgiving as Mallory. Never mind Steph wanting to keep a lid on adverse publicity. What the community wanted was the killer caught quickly and stability returning as soon as possible. Mallory was an outsider, which gave her certain advantages but she failed to see how the death of Huw Jones ten years earlier was as important to the people of Pembrokeshire as Duncan Lyall's murder only days earlier.

He picked up a report from the County Lines liaison officer. The conclusions were unambiguous. Lyall's coaches were being used to ferry small amounts of Class A drugs to various tourist destinations. The drugs were then passed around rural communities by a network of contacts, most of whom were of school age. Toby had been on the right track when he'd noticed unusual activity on one of the yellow coaches. What no one could understand was why Duncan Lyall was dead, and the report could find no convincing reason why he might have been murdered. The suggestion was that he had masterminded the operation but everyone was happy with the deal, especially the contact who imported the drugs via the port of Milford Haven. For the moment, the network was being monitored alongside French colleagues, with a view to identifying the operation on the Continent. It had been decided that rounding up the drivers and passengers involved in the distribution of narcotics around Pembrokeshire would simply create a gap for others to fill. There were bigger fish to catch.

Harri put down the report. It felt like a dead end. Pembrokeshire wasn't Miami, although maybe he'd watched too much 1980s TV and Miami wasn't like that either. The point was, the operation was relatively small and the ferocity of the attack still needed to be accounted for. The investigator who'd looked into the legitimate arm of the Lyall operation had been unable to unpick anything more sinister than the odd driver who shouldn't be behind the wheel of a coach. One had been caught masturbating in a lay-by to porn on his phone and had been sacked. He'd been interviewed and eliminated as a suspect, apparently bearing his ex-boss no ill will. Others had been reprimanded for fiddling expenses and mileage but had been kept on as employees. No reason for them to hold a grudge.

A team of detectives was trying to unpick other interests but Harri was now linking Duncan's death to that of Heledd Jones. All five remaining friends had been contacted to rule them out as suspects. Eleri had been at a dinner in the House of Commons, and Jack and Gruffydd at home with their wives. Gemma and Bethan had also been at home, but without a partner to support their alibi. There was nothing, however, to suggest either of them had been at Duncan's house that evening.

Siân rang him, her voice tinny from the hands-free mic. 'Mallory just called. Gemma Bowen hasn't turned up for work today. I'm going to the house now.'

Harri swore. 'For God's sake, be careful. Where's Freddie?'

'Day off. Look, there's a cleaner in the house so it doesn't sound like she'll be there but I might be able to find some clues to her whereabouts.'

'I'm coming up with you. Wait for me before you go into the house.'

'Seriously, boss, Mallory doesn't think she's there.'

'Mallory your pal now?' asked Harri, annoyed the two had spoken without involving him, but he realised he was talking into thin air.

He grabbed his coat, trying to remember if he'd taken his medication that morning. Pretty sure he'd skipped a dose. He bought a croissant from the canteen, which he ate while walking to the car before swallowing a tablet.

As he drove towards St Davids, he again thought of Gemma nursing the secret of a note behind St Non's Cross. He wondered if it was she or Heledd who'd retrieved the physical evidence. He suspected Gemma must have looked for the note when she first discovered its existence. Gavin's message had been dramatic enough but Gemma would have wanted to check that what he was saying was true. She would have gone to St Non's, found the note and then, what? Put it back, he guessed, and told Heledd where it was last year. Another scenario was that she'd taken the note and given it directly to Heledd. Harri didn't suppose it mattered, more important was her impetus for passing the message to Heledd. She probably didn't even care who the author of the message was, as long as Heledd received and understood the meaning of the note. Motive, though. The issue with this case was why people acted as they did. He wasn't surprised the group of friends had covered up for each other, but he had less insight into why relationships had begun to fracture.

It continued to worry at him as he drove to St Davids. July last year had been a hot summer, too hot at one point to do anything other than sit in an air-conditioned office. The team had been lethargic and crimes had mainly been a result of drinking too much in the sun. Harri frowned, trying to remember why that had currency for him. Why did a hot summer ring a bell? He emptied his mind and tried to recall the reference. Hot summer. And it came to him.

47

The shop was busy for the first hour of Mallory's shift. A coachload of tourists from Weston-super-Mare migrated from the warm refectory to look for souvenirs until their anxious driver, taking a look at the clouds, marshalled them onto the bus. Mallory had received no reply to her message to Toby so she sent it again, both on WhatsApp and via text. She decided that if he didn't answer within the hour, she was going to close the shop and return to the flat to check on him. She wasn't officially allowed her phone while working on the till but she kept it in her back pocket, waiting not only for Toby's reply, but also a call from Siân to say what she'd found in Gemma's house. The anticipation was excruciating. The departure of the coach had emptied the shop, leaving her alone with her imagination. She straightened the books and rearranged the scarves for sale then retreated behind the counter with a copy of the *Mabinogion*. If she was going to stay here, it was about time she immersed herself in Welsh myths.

The silence inside the building was restful, although the wind was beginning to pick up. She started reading the story of Pwyll, Prince of Dyfed, while shuffling from leg to leg to keep her feet warm. She was disturbed by a sharp cry and she heard footsteps on the stone floor coming towards the shop. The door opened and a woman in her sixties came in, panting with the exertion.

'Can you help me? I think there's someone up on the roof of the tower. I spotted them when I was crossing the grass and they're behaving really oddly. They're sort of just standing there, which is ridiculous in this weather.'

Mallory signed off the till and locked the shop, following the woman out into the cold air.

'Look.'

Mallory followed the woman's gaze upwards to the roof of the square tower. A figure stood, just discernible amid the sleet that was beginning to fall. It reminded her of an Antony Gormley statue. The absolute stillness and focus on a point in the distance was chilling.

'Do you have a security guard?' asked the woman.

Mallory almost laughed. There was her, a volunteer or two and, possibly, if she was lucky, a member of the cathedral chapter.

'Leave it with me, I'll go and find out what the problem is.'

Mallory was unsure how the figure had got up onto the roof but there must be an access door to the tower somewhere. She ran down the south aisle, looking for an entrance that would take her up onto the roof. She ran into Bethan Rees, who was walking from the choir.

'You'll never guess who I've just seen in the corridor by the refectory. I mean, what's he doing here? My God, what's the matter with your head?'

Mallory touched the spot where her hair was matted onto her scalp. She thought she'd cleaned it in the shower but the wound had begun to seep again. 'Bethan, I need some help. There's someone up on the roof of the tower. How do I get up there?'

'Who? Who's on the roof?'

'I won't be sure until I look but I have an idea it might be Gemma. Can you get me up there?'

'Gemma? Come with me.' Bethan guided her over to a door, pulling it open. 'It's a long climb. Let me go up with you. If it's Gemma, she'll need to speak to someone.'

Mallory pushed past Bethan. 'Let me go. Ring the police and say it's an emergency. Even if I get onto the roof, it doesn't mean I'll be able to reach her. Get help as soon as you can.'

'Do you think that's why I saw—'

Mallory didn't hear the rest of Bethan's words. She texted Harri, as she climbed the stone steps, to tell him what she was doing. She knew if she spoke to him, he'd tell her to wait for backup. Any decent cop would have done the same but time wasn't on her side. Mallory inhaled the smell of centuries of damp and dust as she puffed up the steps. The climb was exhausting and by the time she got to the top, she thought she was going to vomit.

The wind ripped through the parapet as she wrenched open the door. As sleet hit stone, the going was treacherous. Mallory inched along the ledge, holding on to the wall when she could get a grip. She thought of Gavin working on the exterior and suffering such a catastrophic head injury. She wasn't sure she could cope with another bang to her own head.

'Hello!'

The snow was sticking on her eyelashes and she tried to rub them clear, leaving her vision blurred.

'Gemma?'

Mallory pushed onwards, praying Harri had received her message. She remembered Gemma's height and realised it could be her she'd met on the road to St Non's. The hammer had been found in the field where Mallory had thrown it. A common DIY tool with nothing to suggest who had owned it, although forensic tests were already underway to see if DNA or other evidence could be identified. If Gemma was the killer, another hammer could easily be procured.

The figure turned, as Mallory neared, and pulled down the hood of their coat. Gemma Bowen, towering over Mallory, stepped forward, her face impassive.

'How did you know I'd be here?'

'I didn't. You were spotted from below. Did you choose here deliberately to attract my attention?'

'You?' Scorn dripped from Gemma. 'I'm meeting someone here.'

'Who are you meeting here on the roof?' The woman had clearly had a catastrophic breakdown. No one would plan an assignation on the roof of a cathedral, unless they were seriously deranged. Mallory quickly looked round, unwilling to take her eyes off Gemma even for a second.

'It's a special place for us. We used to sneak in as teenagers, as my aunt was a volunteer here. I got hold of her keys one day and got a duplicate set cut. This was our romantic place.'

Mallory's teeth were chattering from terror as much as the cold. She'd been wrong to be so casual about ascending onto the roof without support. She could sense danger again, even if Gemma's anger wasn't obviously directed at her.

'Who are you waiting for?' Mallory glanced over the parapet and saw Bethan, in the centre of the lawn, calling for help on her phone. Was it Bethan that Gemma expected? She'd spent time considering the dynamics of the group, and some friends had been closer than others. Eleri and Duncan, for example, or Gruffydd and Bethan.

Gemma had given the impression she was essentially more independent. In the distance, she saw a familiar figure hurrying down the slope. Toby. Mallory's stomach somersaulted.

'Stay away. Go back to the flat,' she hollered at him. He stopped for a moment and saw her gesticulating at him, then he continued to run towards the cathedral entrance, making fast progress.

Shit. Turning back, she saw that Gemma was looking beyond her, so Mallory spun round. The door to the roof opened and a figure emerged. It was a man, lean of build, and someone Mallory had not met during her investigations. A stranger? Mallory stepped forward until she could see his face.

'Jack?'

His expression was grim. 'Leave Gemma alone.'

'I have every intention of doing so, I just need to get her to come into the warmth. She'll feel better there.'

'No need for her to feel better. She stays out here.'

Confused, Mallory looked between the two. 'But… what's your role here?'

'Leave us,' said Gemma. 'This is between me and Jack.'

Mallory folded her arms. 'I'm staying here. What the hell's going on?'

'Gemma has been playing games and I've come to put a stop to things.'

'Jack, I—' Gemma pushed past Mallory, her arms reaching towards him.

He slapped them away. 'Don't "Jack" me. Hadn't Heledd suffered enough? You had to involve her in this, didn't you?'

'Look.' Mallory stepped between the two. 'Why don't we get off the roof and go downstairs to chat about this?'

Jack took her by surprise, yanking her away from Gemma. 'I have no argument with you. Go downstairs and leave us. I'm going to put a stop to this once and for all.'

'I hate you,' shrieked Gemma. 'Isn't it enough that I stuck by you all these years?'

The penny finally dropped. 'You were together? A couple?'

Jack's face was puce with fury. 'We were *not* a couple.'

'That's right. You've not been able to keep away from me and now you've dropped me like I'm an embarrassment.'

'You are.' A gust of wind swept under their feet, thrusting Gemma towards Jack. He roughly shoved her away and she landed, sprawled, on the icy floor.

'Now, hold on.' Mallory grabbed Jack and he turned on her in fury, pulling her off her feet. She struggled, jamming her hand against Jack's stomach but she was no match for his strength. She remembered the weights displayed prominently in the background of his computer screen. He had her in the air and Mallory saw the steep drop below her.

'What the hell are you doing?' she screamed at him.

Christ, if she went over the ledge, she'd never survive a fall from this height. It wasn't a sheer drop. She would bounce off the buttress, which was even worse. Suicides usually lost limbs when they hit protuberances on the way down. She managed to get her mouth around one of his forearms where the sleeve of his coat had ridden up and she bit down hard. He yelped but his grip remained strong.

'Leave my mother alone.' Toby came rushing through the door, a ball of fury. In his hand he had what looked like a gold stake, which he brandished at Jack. Mallory panicked.

'For God's sake, stay away, Toby. Get help.'

She was terrified to look down and tried to jam her hand under Jack's chin. She saw out of the corner of her eye Toby launch himself at Jack, throwing the three of them to the floor. She heard a cry of horror below but they were hidden from onlookers. Where the hell was Gemma? Jack had managed to get hold of Mallory's hair and was slamming her cheek into the stone. More agony after her attack the previous evening.

Just when she thought her brain was going to explode, she felt Jack's grip loosen and she was able to shake herself free. Trying to work out what had happened, she scrambled to her feet and saw Jack's head covered in blood.

'Have I killed him, Mum?'

Mallory turned her head. 'I fucking well hope so.' Jack groaned in pain. 'He's alive. Don't you worry about it, Tobe.' She lowered her voice. 'What did you hit him with?'

'A candlestick. I got it from the altar.'

Mallory, in her hysteria, wanted to laugh. 'Give it to me.' Toby was wearing his running gloves, although someone may have spotted him take the candlestick. She placed her own hands around the metal and put her prints near the base.

She pulled Toby close and whispered in his ear. 'If anyone asks, I took the candlestick from you when we fell down.'

'I can see the police,' he said. Mallory looked over the edge and saw the flashing lights at the top of the hill, and a swarm of police rushing across the cathedral green.

'Better late than never.' She glanced across at Gemma. 'No!'

Gemma had one leg across the parapet and was levering herself to sit on the edge of the sheer drop. Toby moved forward but Mallory grabbed him. 'Don't touch her. She'll have you over the side too. Go downstairs and ring for an ambulance. Please.'

'I'm not leaving you, Mum.'

Gemma turned to them. 'Lucky you. I'd have liked children but after what happened with Huw, it was never going to happen.'

'Please, Gemma, stay.' Mallory moved forward, aware of Toby just behind her.

'I can't. I'm sorry. I thought the note was a way of telling Heledd what happened that night. You see, I wanted her to work it out for herself.'

'Why not just tell her about you and Jack? It would have given her some closure. That's why Huw left the house, wasn't it? He saw you and Jack together and went looking for his mother. Why not just tell Heledd that?'

'Because we were all liars. I wanted her to see that.'

Mallory inched forward a little more. 'Did you know Eleri was the writer of the letter?'

Gemma shrugged. 'Who cares?'

With a flash, she was gone.

48

Harri pulled off his seatbelt before Siân had come to a stop.

'You'll get yourself in trouble if you keep doing that. Just wait.'

But Harri was already out of the car. His heart was pounding due to the new medication. It had worked a treat with some of his symptoms but he had a perpetual pain in his chest he couldn't shake. There was a bank of uniformed officers in front of him and all were rushing towards a figure lying on the ground. For a heart-stopping moment, he thought it was Mallory, until his gaze swept upwards towards the parapet and he saw her with her arms around Toby.

'It's Doctor Bowen,' shouted Siân, who had sped past him.

He pushed past the crowd gathering around Gemma and ran towards the cathedral entrance. He was unfamiliar with the place and shouted at a woman wearing a lanyard, who was trying to make a call on her mobile phone.

'How do I get up on the roof?' He didn't know the name of the damn place but fortunately the volunteer got it straight away. 'Take the door on the right.'

He followed the woman's directions, huffing up the stairs, until he met Mallory, who was holding onto her son in the narrow stairwell.

'Let me get Toby down. Jack is lying on the floor and he needs the attention of one of the paramedics.'

'Go down and get an officer to call for one. I'll check on Jack now. What happened?'

'He attacked me and I managed to hit him over the head.' She tightened her grip on Toby.

'He's not dead, is he?' Toby didn't sound much sorry and for the first time, Harri saw a spark of excitement in the teenager's expression.

'Don't worry about him. Your mum will get you a cup of tea and we can have a chat afterwards.'

'Thanks, Harri,' said Mallory.

Harri felt a rush of pleasure at her speaking his name. He pushed on up the stairs until he reached the door. Jack Jones was lying on the ground, a covering of snow beginning to settle on him. Jesus, if he didn't rush, the guy would die of hypothermia. Harri pulled off his coat and laid it over the man, feeling for a pulse, which was strong.

He leant over the parapet and saw paramedics arriving. 'I need you up here quick,' he shouted down at them. The valley had the deathly softness that comes when the snow begins to fall and he was able to make himself heard. He saw two paramedics peel away and enter the cathedral with their bags.

Jack opened his eyes. 'What happened?'

Harri leant over him. 'Don't worry about that now. Let's get you to hospital and then we can have a chat, eh?'

Jack began to cough. 'This… this… It's all my fault. Duncan… I mean… he told me Heledd was asking questions about that night. She went to see him and his first thought was to protect me. Thought it would ruin me.'

'He killed her to shield your reputation? Heledd had a history of instability. No one would have believed her.'

'The writer of the note knew it was true, too. She'd carry more weight.'

'You guessed it was Eleri?'

'Not me, Duncan.' Jack coughed again.

'So, Heledd *did* mention the note to Duncan. He denied he knew what she was talking about.'

'Duncan was a good liar.'

The paramedics had reached the top of the stairs and Harri moved back to let them through, shivering with the cold. He left them to it and went to find Mallory, who was giving a statement to Siân, her arm still around Toby. It wasn't procedure and Mallory knew this. They would need to be interviewed separately. He waited until she'd finished and gently pulled her away.

'Let Toby make his statement now. You know the score. Siân will look after him.' Harri noticed again the pink blush on the boy's cheeks. He had enough experience of teenagers to recognise the signs of exhilaration.

Reluctantly, Mallory moved away and took in his thin shirt. 'Bloody hell, Harri. You'll catch your death. Where's your coat?'

'Covering Jack Jones.'

'I keep a spare in the locker. Come with me.'

In a room stuffed with bags and coats, she pulled out a blue waterproof and handed it to him. Harri pulled it on and felt his shivering subside. Mallory made to leave but he put out an arm.

'No, you don't. We need to chat.'

She looked like she was going to break free from his grip but he held on tight.

'All right.' She shrugged him off and crossed to the sink to put on the kettle. 'We might as well get warm but I do need to keep an eye out for Toby.'

'The lad's fine. I'm not, because I want to know why the hell Jack Jones was on a ledge on the cathedral.'

'You mean the roof.'

'Mallory.' Harri could feel his temper beginning to fray.

'OK. It's obvious, now I think about it. What I hadn't properly considered was the dynamics of couples.'

'Couples?'

'Exactly.' Mallory spooned two heaps of instant coffee into a mug. Harri, who couldn't stand the stuff, watched her without comment. 'I assumed there were two couples present in the house the night Huw disappeared. Bethan and Gruffydd, who subsequently parted in the aftermath of Huw's death, and Duncan and Eleri. We're not sure at what point they split up, but they remained friends – probably better friends than Bethan and Gruffydd, whose relationship was overshadowed by the fact that they both kept quiet about Huw's empty bed.'

'I know all this, Mallory.'

'What I'm now realising is that there was a third couple. Jack and Gemma. In her statements, Heledd continually says that something was off that night. Bethan also mentioned intrigue but she thought it was to do with her fiancé's attraction to Duncan. Heledd wasn't happy about going to Eleri's party and it was all bound up with the fact she didn't want to leave the house. Heledd was an instinctive person, we know this from reports after Huw's death. She could see something untoward was going on in her house but the dynamics of the friendship group were so complicated that she couldn't unpick what was happening under her nose.'

'Jack and Gemma were having an affair.'

'*Exactly.* The six people there that night made up three couples and I should have seen it before I encountered Jack on the parapet.'

'The sixth lie,' said Harri, 'Eleri's, was knowledge of Jack and Gemma's relationship.'

'And that lie provides an explanation to some of the others' untruths. For example, it was important for Gemma to hide the fact that she knew Heledd had been seeking help for depression without Jack's knowledge, as she wasn't sure what the news would do to their relationship. Perhaps Jack would feel sorry for his wife and put a stop to their fling. The affair also explains why Jack and Gemma didn't mention that Bethan wasn't with them but was actually following Gruffydd and Duncan. Calling attention to that would have emphasised that the two of them had been left alone.'

'So, the sixth lie wasn't just Eleri's but one told by everyone.'

Mallory looked affronted. 'It's Eleri's lie because she knew she was deliberately withholding the information in her statement.'

'And what happened to Huw that night?'

'He did what your original investigation concluded. He got out of bed and went to look for his mother. But I think, by then, there were only two people in the house, Gemma and Jack. I think Huw saw whatever they were doing from the doorway and left the house. If Eleri came to Y Bwthyn while Duncan, Gruffydd and Bethan were out of the house, she could have easily stumbled in on Jack and Gemma, and taken in exactly the same scene Huw saw.'

'Christ.' Harri pulled Mallory's coat tighter. It smelt of sea salt and earth. 'Your child is missing and you keep quiet about the fact that you were otherwise engaged that evening.'

'They probably didn't think it would matter. And for years, I don't suppose it did. Until Heledd learnt of the note and tried to unravel its meaning.'

'And I know why Gemma told Heledd of the note last July. It coincided with Jack remarrying. I remembered my sister saying the wedding had been during the hot summer months. Gemma had probably been hoping that Jack would eventually settle down with her and not use her for the occasional fling. But a country GP wasn't what Jack was looking for.' Harri exhaled.

'What I can't understand,' said Mallory, 'is why Duncan killed Heledd. It's an extreme way of shutting someone up.'

'It's about mothers and sons, Mallory. Only the truth would do for Heledd. Don't forget Duncan must have originally felt sorry for her. It's most likely why he hit Jack. Told him he was a stupid sod for carrying on with Gemma in his own house.'

'So, what changed?' asked Mallory.

'Nothing changed. Duncan was protective of Jack. Unnaturally so, and it was only a matter of time until Heledd confronted Jack with what she'd discovered. What do you think signing a false statement would do to the career of a successful corporate lawyer?'

Mallory threw away her coffee. 'I think I hate them all.'

As warmth returned to his body, Harri's senses began to sharpen. 'What happened up there? Was it you or Toby who hit Jack?'

'You heard my statement.'

'You said it loud enough to wake Bishop Henry Gower, and he's been dead eight hundred years. All right, I get the message. The thing is, we've cleared up what happened to Huw that night and confirmed our suspicions about Duncan's involvement in Heledd's death. But who killed Duncan Lyall?'

49

Mallory was ashamed to admit she felt less invested in finding Duncan's killer, although she was positive she had been the victim of the same assailant. Her heart had ached for a little boy walking to St Non's and, whatever happened next, at least she had unpicked the series of events leading to his death. Heledd was someone she had also come to empathise with, although she had thrown herself into danger by questioning Duncan. Mallory identified with Heledd's human frailty and perseverance, and she was glad she had concluded what Huw's mother had begun. She had unearthed the six lies. But it wasn't yet over. Finding Duncan's killer as soon as possible was critical. Both Bethan and Eleri felt threatened, and neither were inclined to be fanciful.

She continued to worry about the case in her flat, standing over Toby as he ladled tinned chicken soup into his mouth. Hovering while he was eating was probably the wrong thing to do, but soup was good for shock and she wanted to make sure he had something in his stomach. Harri hadn't wanted them to leave the cathedral while the other statements were being taken but she had insisted on taking the teenager back to the flat. The paramedic who'd taken Toby's blood pressure had winced at his thin arms and told Harri that home was the best place for him.

It had been a hollow victory. Now, away from danger, she agonised over what she'd started by covering up for Toby. They had been scuffling on the floor so her account would hold. Anyone watching from below would have simply seen the three of them fall to the ground. Only Gemma had been looking their way and she was now beyond help. Jack would be unlikely to know which of them had wielded the candlestick that had coshed him but Mallory still doubted the wisdom of her actions. Gruffydd had never moved on from the lie he had first told on the evening of Huw's death. Toby, however, Mallory thought, was made of sterner stuff. The way he'd launched himself at Jack had reminded her that he was the son of two police officers. Was it her imagination or did he look brighter? He managed half a bowl of soup before putting down his spoon.

'That's all I can manage, Mum.' Toby stood and brushed down his trousers. 'I'm going to change. Can I use your washing machine?'

'Sure. You—'

'I can work it out. Stop fussing.'

Mallory poured the rest of the soup down the sink and listened to Toby turn on the bath taps. A waft of Pomegranate Noir seeped under the door. Toby had used all her regular bubble bath and now was onto the expensive stuff. She resisted the temptation to go into his room and put his clothes into the machine herself. Her phone rang and Harri sounded frustrated.

'I've just double-checked Jack's alibi for the night Duncan died. It seemed like a good idea, considering he attacked you on the roof today. He was in court all day in Newcastle. We have witnesses who saw him have dinner in the hotel restaurant on Thursday night and go to bed around eleven p.m. He was then seen at breakfast at seven thirty. We've checked the timings.'

'That gives him eight and half hours. You can't get to St Davids and back in that time, can you?'

'Not a chance. It's a seven-hour drive one way. We've checked ANPR and his story checks out. He drove to Bristol Airport, left his car there and flew up. The vehicle was picked up late Friday night, by which time Duncan was dead.'

'So, where does that leave us?' Harri was silent. 'What is it?'

'You know, we've been concentrating so much on the group dynamics that we've kind of forgotten there are other people involved who cared about what happened to Huw Jones.'

'That widens the net considerably, though.' Mallory remembered Ffion upstairs texting her friend when she heard the news of Heledd's death.

'I mean those who were devastated by the death of Huw. Heledd, of course, but there were others too.'

'You mean… Oh no.'

'I've made the connection with the masked figure who attacked you. Stupid, really. It's been staring at me in the face all along. Do you want to come with me? You can ask your attacker what they've got against you. I'll be there in half an hour and I'll wait for you in the lay-by half a mile before the entrance to the mill.'

Mallory pulled on her warmest coat and took two codeine tablets she had left over from the days when the pain in her leg was unbearable. She hadn't liked to admit to Harri the squeak of fear she'd experienced at the thought of meeting her assailant. Toby was out of the bath, summoned by a phone call from his father. He chatted with Joe in the kitchen and emerged with the phone in his hand. He frowned when he saw her coat.

'Where are you going?'

'Out. Harri thinks he's worked out who attacked me.'

'Got another candlestick?' said Toby with a smirk.

Christ, thought Mallory. What have we started?

'Dad wants a word.'

Mallory took the phone from Toby. 'Hello?'

She steeled herself for confrontation but Joe's tone was conciliatory. 'Thanks, Mallory, for what you did today. Toby's told me what happened. He did whatever anyone would do if their loved ones were threatened.'

Mallory relaxed a fraction. 'You're not angry I altered the events in my statement? This case has been all about lies and I really hate the thought of adding my own into the mix.'

'You did the right thing.' They were both silent, probably thinking of colleagues in the force who had bent the truth.

'Anyway, look, I have to go.'

'I'm coming up tomorrow,' said Joe. 'I've booked a day's leave and I want to take Toby out somewhere.'

'I think that's a good idea. You two need to have a chat face to face. You've told Toby?'

'He suggested it. Look… there's a chance he might come back with me. Just a chance but I want you to know.'

'I'd like that. I want him back at school, whatever the problem is. We can look into his eating issues once he's settled back in.'

'OK, thank you, Mallory.' Joe's voice cracked and he coughed to disguise his display of emotion. 'I'll set off about six tomorrow so I'll hopefully get to you for midday.'

As Mallory drove out of St Davids, she could hear the dripping sound of the thaw around her. Small rivers were forming either side of the road and blocks of snow slid from cars as owners finally put their foot down after the freeze. Harri was waiting for her in the lay-by, as he'd promised, out of sight of the mill. She flashed her lights at him and followed his vehicle along the road, noticing that the dent in his car had been repaired.

They ignored the visitor car park, drawing up instead at the front door to the mill. Harri was first out, the exertions of the day etched onto his face. Siân followed him and gave Mallory a furious look. She'd either worked out or Harri had said something about the events of that morning. Mallory wondered if Joe had been a bit premature in congratulating her on their deceit. Maybe Siân would be the person to report that something didn't add up in the statements.

Felin Wen was quiet. A Monday evening was unlikely to be a busy day for Becca but, in the distance, Mallory could hear the knock of the machine weaving a blanket.

They walked past the reception desk, where a teenager was reading a magazine.

'Where's Becca?' asked Harri, showing her his warrant card.

'In the office. What's up?'

They made their way to the back of the building, where Becca was sitting at her desk. It held none of the detritus present at Mallory's previous visit.

'*Croeso*. Welcome to the mill. How can I help you?'

'Going somewhere, Becca?' asked Siân.

Becca made a face. 'Clearing the decks,' she said. 'I won't be able to keep this place going from inside, I know that. The best thing I can hope for is to sell it as a going concern.'

'Why kill him?' asked Harri. 'What good did it do?'

'Why kill Heledd? She never did anything wrong and she was the victim in all this. People like Duncan Lyall never get their comeuppance.'

'How much have you worked out?' asked Mallory.

'Enough. I knew straight away that Heledd was killed. She was sober. It didn't make sense she would suddenly drink herself into a coma and lie down in the field. She'd been getting her act together once she discovered the existence of the note.'

'You knew about the message?' asked Harri.

Becca pulled out a drawer and extracted a clear plastic bag, opaque with age and the ravages of the weather. 'Heledd gave it to me for safekeeping. She knew the contents by heart, as you can imagine. She wanted someone else to keep hold of it.'

'Do you know who wrote it?' asked Siân.

'One of the six. Not Duncan, obviously. A confessional isn't his style.'

'Why did you tell us that you thought Heledd had another man?' asked Harri. 'To throw us off the scent?'

'Of course. There had been no man in Heledd's life since Jack but she'd got herself together because she realised she had no culpability for the death of Huw. She knew a web of lies had been woven that evening and she wanted to bring them to light.'

'So you, what, just decided to kill Duncan?' Siân sounded furious, probably remembering the slaughter at the house.

'Why not? He murdered my sister to protect Jack's reputation. It could only have been Duncan. Could you actually imagine any of the others killing her?'

'But how did you know it was Duncan?' asked Harri.

'I didn't for sure until I killed him. Heledd sensed danger but she'd seen him already that evening so her guard would have been down. It made sense and that man would do anything to protect Jack. Duncan had no compunction about protecting his friend. He probably thought it a kind death, plying Heledd with alcohol and leaving her to freeze. He didn't have such an easy passing, I can assure you.'

Mallory felt sick and raised her hand to the wound still agonising to the touch. 'Why attack me?' she asked. 'What have I done to you?'

Becca shrugged. 'I'd have killed them all if you hadn't been getting so close. Don't you see? Duncan was to be the first.'

Mallory swallowed. Bethan had been right. Her sense of scrutiny had been spot on. 'Who was to be next?'

'No order. I just wanted time and you were the one most likely to stop me.'

Siân was staring at Becca aghast. 'Isn't there a big difference between killing your sister and telling a lie? You were seriously going to target the other friends?'

Becca shot the DC a look. 'What do you know about ruined lives?'

'How come you were expecting us?' asked Harri, looking round the room.

'I had a call from a contact at the cathedral. She told me what had happened and I thought it only a matter of time. I didn't actually expect you today. How do you know it was me who attacked you?'

Mallory looked across at Harri. 'I can't claim credit for that.'

'Mallory told her son that the figure was wearing a mask. He thought it sounded like a folk disguise and I thought of the Rebecca Riots. Of course, anyone can wear a mask but it's got a particular resonance for you, hasn't it?'

'Clever. Do you know what the rioters also used to do?'

'Go on, tell me.'

'They conducted mock trials before they attacked people. Did you know that?'

Mallory frowned. 'There wasn't any time—'

'Not with you but Duncan Lyall knew exactly the extent of his sins when I killed him. You know, I actually think he was relieved to die.'

Mallory felt nauseous at the rough justice meted out to Duncan. He'd brought about Heledd's death but he'd deserved a fair trial. Despite Becca's warped thinking, Heledd had not been avenged. Mallory watched as Becca shrugged on a coat.

'Shall we go?'

50

Toby was up early and in the shower the next morning. Steam seeped under the bathroom door, and she had to resist the temptation to bend down and sniff to see if the aroma was anything more sinister than shampoo and shower gel. Getting up early was a good sign and suggested he was excited to see his dad again. Whatever was going on in his life, it was a relief that home, either in London or here in Wales, wasn't the issue.

She went into the box room to give the place a tidy. She'd decided she would invite Joe back for a cup of coffee so he could see how Toby had been living these past few days. Other than buying the TV and PlayStation, she had done nothing to entice her son to stay. The room was tidier than she'd expected and she saw he'd packed his clothes into his rucksack. He was going home. Feeling guilty, she knelt down and looked under his bed but couldn't see any evidence of food wrappers.

'What are you doing, Mum?'

Toby stood with a towel wrapped around his waist. She saw his ribs pushing against the skin of his chest. 'Toby, we still need to talk about your eating.'

'Don't, Mum. I'm trying.'

'I've tried not to pry. If you're going back to your dad's, I just need to know everything is OK.'

'It's... I don't know... just OK.'

'But what's happened?'

'I don't want to talk about it. I can't go to school around here, though, can I? I won't know anyone. I'll go back and finish my final year and then I'm leaving.'

'There are plenty of colleges in London or here if you want.'

Toby shrugged, pulling on a clean T-shirt he'd left on the bed.

'Would it help if I was nearer? I could move back to London, you know.'

'And do what?'

His dismissal of her abilities made her fume but she kept her tone even. 'I don't know. Anything.'

Toby straightened and looked at her. 'I think Harri would like you to stay.'

'Harri's not my priority, you are. Would it help if I lived nearer?'

She saw his face infuse with colour. 'I'm not sure. I like coming to visit you so maybe stay here for a while. This place looks like it might be nice in the summer.'

'Surfing, boat trips, ice-cream. I'm actually looking forward to it myself.'

'Murders, criminals, hidden letters. That's the Wales you know.' He paused. 'Can I have some privacy? I need to put on my jeans.'

'Sorry.' Mallory went into the kitchen and took two croissants out of the freezer to heat up. She looked at her mobile. She'd expected Harri to be on the phone this morning to give an update on both Becca's and Jack's interviews but it looked like that wasn't a priority for him. She wouldn't tell him she'd given the hospital a call to check on Jack's condition. Concussion, nothing more. He'd live, which was a bloody relief for everyone.

Upstairs, she could hear Ffion moving around. She must, by now, know what had happened yesterday but the fact she hadn't come down to check on her suggested there was still resentment over Mallory's role in the investigation. Time for a move, thought Mallory. Maybe she'd try further inland. It might be romantic living near the sea but she didn't like the wind as it whipped over the headland. Perhaps a small house in a valley would be perfect. She would keep an eye out to see if Heledd's home came on the market. From there, she could commute into the cathedral, or perhaps it was time to move on from that job too. She was likely to bump into Gruffydd and Bethan regularly and that would be embarrassing for all of them.

She jumped at a tap on the window and saw Harri's face peering in. He still looked unwell and she hadn't got to the bottom of what was actually the matter with him. She could try to wheedle it out of him but she had enough on her plate sorting out Toby's medical issues. She didn't need a man teetering on the brink of ill health, and especially not one with as much baggage as Harri. Nevertheless, she repressed a smile of pleasure at his appearance and opened the door.

'I still haven't warmed up since yesterday.' Harri brandished a bag of freshly made cinnamon rolls that filled the kitchen with their aroma.

'Where did you get them?' asked Mallory, switching off the oven and putting the croissants back in the freezer.

'Bought them en route. Just wanted to check you were both OK.'

'We're fine. Toby is going home today.'

'That's good... I mean... it is good, isn't it?'

'It's brilliant news, although I'm not sure what brought about the change of heart.'

'You know,' Harri pulled out a chair, 'I had a good look at your boy yesterday and I think he needs a bit more freedom. Stop worrying about him and let him live a little.'

'It's more complicated than that.'

'Is it? If you say so.'

Mallory pulled the coffee pot off the shelf. 'I wondered if you'd call. I wanted to know how the interviews are going.'

'Becca has confessed to the killing of Duncan, which is no surprise, as she did so in our presence yesterday. Seems proud of it, although she was slightly more sheepish when questioned about the attack on you. How's your head, by the way?'

'Sore, but I'll be fine. What about Jack Jones?'

'Haven't interviewed him yet. He's under police guard in Haverfordwest but you'd know that anyway, as you called this morning to check up on him.'

Mallory turned and busied herself with the kettle. 'Busted. I just wanted to see how much damage I'd done with the candlestick.'

'Right.' Harri ripped the bag open and offered a roll to Mallory. 'Get stuck in. Here's to our working partnership.'

Mallory took the cake and sunk her teeth into the pastry. 'Partnership?'

Harri finished his roll in two bites. 'Who knows what other cases might come up.'

'Oh no…' Mallory brushed the crumbs from her jumper. 'No, no, no.'

Harri grinned at her. 'Sure.'

Acknowledgements

Thanks to my editor at Canelo, Siân Heap, for her excellent input into this book. As ever, the story is much better for her comments. Thanks also to the team at Canelo for their support including Iain Millar, Thanhmai Bui-Van and Kate Shepherd. Also to copyeditor Daniela Nava.

My agent Kirsty McLachlan at Morgan Green Creatives is always a great advocate of my writing and I appreciate her support. I also couldn't do without Tony Butler whose sharp eye always find things I've missed.

Thanks too to my fellow Canelo authors – Marion Todd, Jeanette Hewitt, Rachel Lynch and Sheila Bugler – for the advice and laughs, to other Crime Cymru members for help in promoting Welsh crime fiction and to my colleagues at the Crime Writers Association especially Maxim Jakubowski.

Vicky Dawson from Buxton International Festival and Siân Hoyle at Derby Book Festival are constant supporters as are Sara Bullimore and Gill Hart at Newark Book Festival. Thanks too to all the wonderful bookshops who stock my books. I always appreciate your support.

The Royal Literary Fund's Fellowship scheme has provided me with time and funds to write and I'll be forever grateful.

Thanks as ever to my family especially Dad who sends my books far and wide.

I began this book living in England and finished it after a move to Wales. Thanks above all to Andy Lawrence, alongside me on this new adventure.

☉ CANELOCRIME

Do you love crime fiction and are always on the lookout for brilliant authors?

Canelo Crime is home to some of the most exciting novels around. Thousands of readers are already enjoying our compulsive stories. Are you ready to find your new favourite writer?

Find out more and sign up to our newsletter at canelocrime.com